"I love to read a well-written and quirky cozy mystery. Manansaia has created just that with her debut novel, a tale full of eccentric characters, humorous situations, and an oh-so-tricky mystery."

—*The Washington Post*

"This book hits the exact right spot. . . . I've heard it described as a 'cozy mystery' and that's exactly what it is, a perfectly cozy puzzle to solve."

—Taylor Jenkins Reid, *New York Times* bestselling author of *Carrie Soto Is Back*

"This breeze-right-through-it mystery follows baker Lila Macapagal as she investigates the murder of her ex-boyfriend. . . . As satisfying as it is climactic, with just the right amount of drama." —*Bon Appétit*

"[An] enjoyable and endearing debut cozy . . . Manansala peppers the narrative with enough red herrings to keep readers from guessing the killer, but the strength of the novel is how family, food, and love intertwine in meaningful and complex ways."

—*The New York Times Book Review*

"Manansala, a Chicago Filipina, has reinvigorated tired tropes to create a multicultural, queer-friendly culinary mystery, making *Arsenic and Adobo* an envelope-pushing, world-expanding debut that goes down easy." —*Los Angeles Times*

"Mia P. Manansala has crafted a delicious mystery full of wit and wile that kept me laughing and guessing as I devoured every page. . . . I can't wait to read more in this fabulous new series!"

—Jenn McKinlay, *New York Times* bestselling author of
Sugar Plum Poisoned

"A much welcome entry into the culinary cozy genre. . . . It's guaranteed to be your next favorite cozy series."

—Kellye Garrett, Agatha Award–winning author of *Hollywood Ending*

"Mouthwatering dishes and a funny, smart amateur sleuth make *Arsenic and Adobo* by Mia P. Manansala my favorite new culinary cozy mystery series."

—Lynn Cahoon, *New York Times* bestselling author of
the Kitchen Witch Mysteries

"You will be rooting for Lila Macapagal to save the family restaurant. . . . The first in a lip-smacking series!"

—Naomi Hirahara, Edgar® Award–winning author of *An Eternal Lei*

PRAISE FOR
Homicide and Halo-Halo

"An enjoyable series worth reading." —DailyWaffle

"Another fantastic book in the Tita Rosie's Kitchen Mystery series! This cozy mystery was just as wonderful as the first book in the series!" —She Just Loves Books

"A delightful small-town mystery with fun characters and an easy to read story. It will also make you hungry and at the end of the book are a lot of recipes to make what you read about." —Red Carpet Crash

Murder

and

Mamon

Mia P. Manansala

BERKLEY PRIME CRIME
NEW YORK

BERKLEY PRIME CRIME
Published by Berkley
An imprint of Penguin Random House LLC
penguinrandomhouse.com

Library of Congress Cataloging-in-Publication Data

Names: Manansala, Mia P., author.
Title: Murder and mamon / Mia P. Manansala.
Description: First Edition. | New York : Berkley Prime Crime, 2023. |
Series: Tita Rosie's Kitchen Mysteries
Identifiers: LCCN 2023006172 (print) | LCCN 2023006173 (ebook) |
ISBN 9780593549162 (trade paperback) | ISBN 9780593549179 (ebook)
Subjects: LCGFT: Detective and mystery fiction. | Novels.
Classification: LCC PS3613.A5268 M87 2023 (print) |
LCC PS3613.A5268 (ebook) | DDC 813/.6—dc23/eng/20230309
LC record available at https://lccn.loc.gov/2023006172
LC ebook record available at https://lccn.loc.gov/2023006173

First Edition: October 2023

Printed in the United States of America
1st Printing

Book design by Kristin del Rosario

This is a work of fiction. Names, characters, places, and incidents either are the product of
the author's imagination or are used fictitiously, and any resemblance to actual persons,
living or dead, business establishments, events, or locales is entirely coincidental.

PUBLISHER'S NOTE: The recipes contained in this book are to be followed exactly
as written. The publisher is not responsible for your specific health or allergy needs that
may require medical supervision. The publisher is not responsible for any adverse
reactions to the recipes contained in this book.

To my brothers,
Nolan and Neil

Thank you for being the best street team
and hype men I could ask for.
Nolan, please continue to give me nursing advice
so I don't shame you with my inaccuracies.
Neil, I appreciate you being my connection to the youths
so I don't sound like the Steve Buscemi "fellow kids" gif.
Continue buying and not reading my books,
please and thank you. 🖤

Author's Note

Thank you so much for picking up *Murder and Mamon!* This book focuses on my favorite characters to write, the Calendar Crew! They've gotten themselves into big trouble, and Lila's investigation touches on some heavy, potentially troubling topics.

If you want to avoid possible spoilers, skip this section. If you'd like to know the content warnings for this book, see below.

CONTENT WARNING:

infidelity, physical violence, mentions of attempted suicide, bullying, slut shaming, gambling addiction, substance abuse, parental incarceration, parental death, parental chronic illness

---

Glossary and Pronunciation Guide

HONORIFICS/FAMILY
(THE "O" USUALLY HAS A SHORT, SOFT SOUND)

Anak (ah-nahk)—Offspring/son/daughter

Ate (ah-teh)—Older sister/female cousin/girl of the same generation as you

Kuya (koo-yah)—Older brother/male cousin/boy of the same generation as you

Lola (loh-lah)/Lolo (loh-loh)—Grandmother/Grandfather

Nanay (nah-nai)—Mother. Tita Rosie refers to Lola Flor as "Nay," a shortened version of the word

Ninang (nee-nahng)/Ninong (nee-nohng)—Godmother/Godfather

Tita (tee-tah)/Tito (tee-toh)—Aunt/Uncle

FOOD

Adobo (uh-doh-boh)—Considered the Philippines's national dish, it's any food cooked with soy sauce, vinegar, garlic, and black peppercorns (though there are many regional and personal variations)

Arroz caldo (ah-rohz cahl-doh)—A savory rice porridge made with chicken, ginger, and other aromatics

Champorado (chahm-puh-rah-doh)—Sweet chocolate rice porridge

Lumpia (loom-pyah)—Filipino spring rolls (many variations)

Malunggay (mah-loong-gahy)—An edible plant, also known as moringa, with many health benefits

Mamon (mah-mohn)—A Filipino chiffon cake, made in individual molds as opposed to a large, shared cake

Matamis na bao (mah-tah-mees nah bah-oh)—Coconut jam (also known as minatamis na bao)

Pandan (pahn-dahn)—Tropical plant whose fragrant leaves are commonly used as a flavoring in Southeast Asia. Often described as a grassy vanilla flavor with a hint of coconut.

Patis (pah-tees)—Fish sauce

Salabat (sah-lah-baht)—Filipino ginger tea

Ube (oo-beh)—Purple yam

OTHER

Bahala na (bah-hah-lah nah)—Both a phrase and a social-cultural value, it roughly translates to "It's in God's hands" or "Whatever will be, will be."

Bruha (broo-ha)—Witch (from the Spanish "bruja"); the name of the Brew-ha Cafe is a play on this word

Diba (dih-bah)—"Isn't it?"; "Right?"; short for "hindi ba" (also written as "di ba")

Diyos ko! (dee-yohs ko)—"Oh my God!"

Hoy! (hoy/hoi)—"Hey!"

Macapagal (Mah-cah-pah-gahl)—A Filipino surname

Malditang babae (Mahl-dee-tahng bah-bah-eh)—Has several meanings, such as "bad girl," "mean girl," "spoiled girl," and overall refers to a girl who has an attitude and is not well-behaved

Mano (mah-noh)—Literally Spanish for "hand," this is a gesture and greeting of respect (similar to hand-kissing) where one takes the hand of an elder and presses it to their forehead. This is also used as a way to ask for a blessing.

Oh my gulay—This is Taglish (Tagalog-English) slang, used when people don't want to say the "God" part of OMG. "Gulay" (goolie) literally means "vegetable," so this phrase shouldn't be translated.

Susmaryosep (soos-mah-ree-yo-sehp)—A portmanteau of Jesus, Mary, and Joseph. Used as an exclamation of surprise, disappointment, shock, etc.

Tama na (tah-mah-nah)—"That's enough"; "Stop"; "Right"/"Correct" (depends on context)

Tsinelas (chi-neh-lahs)—Slippers, flip-flops

Tsismis (chees-mees)—Gossip

Walang hiya (wah-lahng hee-yah)—Literally "without shame" or "shameless"

Murder and Mamon

Chapter One

You do realize we're a cafe, not a plant shop, right?"

I stared at the array of blooms and greenery filling the front of the Brew-ha Cafe, all lovingly grown and arranged by Elena Torres, the cafe's resident green witch. Her plants, dried herbs, and teas had always been an important part of our business, but they usually had their own corner, which she carefully tended.

Today, they spilled out over almost every surface in the shop: Our floating shelves held potted spring flowers, adding a riot of color that popped against our brick accent wall. Long tendrils of lush greenery trailed down our pastry cases. And the invigorating aroma of fresh herbs wafted around the cafe from their places at each table, the fragrance of basil, rosemary, mint, and lavender providing a wonderful antidote for those getting over the winter blahs. You'd think it'd be overwhelming combined with the cafe scents of coffee, tea, and pastries, but they somehow worked in harmony and created our own version of Brew-ha Cafe aromatherapy.

Elena just grinned at me. "We are a business that likes to make money, and I guarantee you that all the plant parents and aspiring plant parents who come here will snatch these up in no time. Besides, spring is so beautiful and fleeting, we should really take advantage of it. Our customers love our seasonal offerings."

Spring had most definitely sprung in my little hometown of Shady Palms, Illinois, and all the residents were preparing for the Big Spring Clean taking place in about two weeks, an annual monthlong event where local business owners offered discounts to entice customers out after a long winter. It was also the perfect time to clear out old stock and start advertising our new seasonal offerings.

My best friend and other business partner, Adeena Awan, was embracing spring's floral vibes by pushing her signature lavender chai latte as well as her new seasonal creations, including a lavender honey latte (the honey sourced from Elena's uncle's local apiary), lavender calamansi-ade, and a sampaguita matcha latte (I didn't really like floral flavors, but even I had to admit the matcha drink was stunning).

As for me, I was leaning into "spring means green" and had prepared pandan-pistachio shortbread and brownies with a pandan cheesecake swirl. I also came up with a red bean brownie recipe, which wasn't particularly spring-like, but hey, I was in a brownie mood. And for a quick no-bake option, I developed buko pandan mochi Rice Krispie treats, which would be sure to delight our younger customers (or anyone, really; I had to keep smacking Adeena's hands away from the tray when I was testing it because she kept snatching bits of it while it cooled). I finished stocking the pastry case and moved to prop open the cafe door—we weren't due to open for another fifteen minutes, but on a sunny day like today, the gentle breeze and fresh air were more than welcome in the shop.

I stood in front of the cafe for a moment, my face lifted to the sun. My preference for cold weather and dark color palettes aside, there was something about me that absolutely craved a good bit of sunshine. Maybe it was my Filipino heritage, and the love of sunlight ran deep in my islander blood. Or it could just be a vitamin D deficiency, I don't know. Either way, I appreciated this moment of zen before the morning rush began.

"Hey, Lila, get back in here! I made you another iced sampaguita matcha!" Adeena yelled.

Forget zen, caffeine was calling.

As I picked up my drink from the front counter, the money plant next to the register caught my eye and I remembered that I had plant-based business with Elena to take care of. I joined my partners at the table, a tray of my pastries and several dishes of honey waiting for us.

"What's with all the honey?" I asked as I split open a fresh-baked scone. A curl of steam escaped, and I hummed to myself as I dolloped a bit of clotted cream on top and added a drizzle of honey.

Elena studied my face as I took a huge bite. "The honey I've been sourcing from my tio's apiary has been selling really well here, so I thought it'd be fun to play with an infused honey recipe. Something exclusive to the Brew-ha Cafe. What we've got here is—"

Elena pointed at the dish of honey I'd just used, but before she could tell me what was in it, Adeena interrupted her. "Wait, don't tell her! We wanted to test her, remember? See if she can guess what you used to infuse each honey."

I had a pretty good, though untrained, palate and sense of smell, and Adeena was forever coming up with little tests to see if I could determine what was in certain food and drinks. I didn't mind—these tastings had fast become a ritual with us, a fun way to start the day and keep my senses sharp. Plus, I did enjoy showing off a bit.

I was pretty sure I knew what spices were in the honey I'd just sampled, but just in case, I took another healthy bite of the honey-topped scone and chewed slowly, letting the contrasting textures and flavors permeate my mouth. The crisp crust of the scone yielded to a soft, fluffy interior that melted in the mouth. The clotted cream added body and richness and perfectly complemented the sweetly spiced honey.

"Star anise, cinnamon, cardamom, cloves, black pepper, and just a touch of ginger," I pronounced. "Did you take inspiration from Adeena's chai spice mix?"

Adeena applauded and Elena laughed and said, "There's fennel, too, but that's exactly what I was basing it on. I wish I could get a better ginger flavor in there. Fresh ginger doesn't impart enough flavor unless it steeps for a while, and ground ginger gets close but just isn't the same. Which is the problem I'm having with my next infused honey. I'm working on a salabat honey for you, but it's going to take some time to get that ginger right."

"Yay, looking forward to it. I'm guessing the chai honey represents Adeena and you're working on the salabat for me, so one of the dishes here is your signature honey?" I asked.

She pointed at the dish in front of her and I broke off a piece of scone to sample this new flavor. One bite and my tongue flared with a powerful, exciting heat. I couldn't decide if I wanted to gulp down an iced latte to cool my mouth or guzzle down the rest of the honey straight—it was a sweet, delicious pain.

"Oh my gulay, is this red chile?" I asked, trying to play it cool as if my nose wasn't running and I didn't have tears threatening to spill over. The heat finally got to me, and I gulped down my sampaguita matcha, letting the milk in the tea latte sit on my tongue to stop the burning.

Adeena and Elena cracked up at my reaction, the latter handing me a napkin to dab at my runny nose and watery eyes.

"I'm so sorry, but Adeena insisted that I not tell you, to better test your powers. And that's the spicy variation, for people like me and

Adeena. I also have a mild variety for people who only want a hint of heat," Elena said, a contrite smile on her face.

Adeena, that jerk, just laughed harder. "She'll be fine. You should've seen her the first time she ate at my house. She started crying after her first few bites, but she wouldn't stop eating. My parents were so weirded out, watching this kid shoveling biryani in her mouth with tears running down her face."

My face was already flushed from the spiciness of the honey, and I turned an even deeper shade of red as Adeena relayed that embarrassing childhood story. "I'd never had spicy food before that! Tita Rosie's food is usually on the milder side since Lola Flor's stomach can't tolerate too much spice. I wasn't expecting my food to hurt me."

"So then why did you keep eating it even after it made you cry?"

I dabbed at my watery eyes, careful to only touch them with the napkin in case there was chile residue on my fingers. "It would be rude to not eat the food your family served me. Plus it was super delicious, so the pain was worth it."

There were two other infused honeys on the tray, floral ones if my trusty nose was correct, but I'd have to wait and taste them later—the chile pepper had overwhelmed my taste buds and I would need some time before I could properly taste anything with a more delicate flavor. Once I'd gotten my runny nose under control, I brought up the topic I'd forgotten to ask Elena about earlier.

"Is the money tree for the Calendar Crew ready yet? I want to give it to them before their grand opening."

My godmothers, Ninang April, Ninang Mae, and Ninang June (or the Calendar Crew, as I privately referred to them), had recently gone into business together, opening a laundromat next door to the dry-cleaning service Ninang June had taken over from her deceased husband. Their grand opening was timed to start the same day as the Big Spring Clean, which was rather genius on their part since Shady

Palms residents likely had tons of heavy winter bedding and clothing that needed professional cleaning. To congratulate them on their new business, I'd commissioned Elena to grow the biggest, most eye-catching money tree possible. These lovely trees with their ornate braided trunks were symbols of good fortune, and I wanted to show my appreciation to the aunties who'd provided so much help (and stress and judgment, but that's neither here nor there) this past year.

Elena handed me her phone to show me a picture of the plant. "I know you said you wanted the biggest tree possible, but these things can reach eight feet tall, and that seemed a bit much. This one is closer to six feet and really lovely."

After I gave her (and the money tree) my nod of approval, she swiped to the next picture. "I also have a potted orchid I was thinking of giving them. At first, I was going to gift them these gorgeously scented jasmine flowers since you said it was the flower of the Philippines, but I figured the aunties would want something brighter and more eye-catching."

I laughed. "Your instincts were spot-on. Orchids give off a more luxurious feel and the aunties are all about appearances. Thanks for handling this for me, Elena."

As I gave her back her phone, the chimes above the door signaled our first customers of the day. When I saw who they were, I shot out of my chair. "Oh, good morning, ninangs! What brings you here so early?"

All three of my godmothers stood near the register, completely ignoring me as they continued their conversation, talking over each other in rapid-fire Tagalog.

"Honestly, April, this is too much—"

"She's family!"

"I know, but it's so last minute—"

"We need more help anyway—"

"Exactly, and we don't have the time—"

"We'll figure it out—"

"But does she even know what she's—"

"Of course she knows what she's doing—"

"Yes yes, she's very smart, you keep on saying that, but—"

The three women volleyed these half-finished statements back and forth so quickly, I was getting whiplash trying to keep up with their conversation.

I waved my hand to get their attention. "Um, can I get you all anything? We've just released our seasonal offerings, and—"

"Lila!" Ninang April interrupted me. "Just the person I wanted to see. You're close to her age, you'll be the perfect guide."

Ninang Mae and Ninang June, both wearing grim expressions, brightened up as they studied me. "You might be right, April," Ninang Mae said. "We don't have time for this distraction, so it's better for the young people to welcome her."

"Welcome who?" I still had no idea who or what they were talking about, but now that their plan involved me, a sense of dread pooled in my stomach.

"My niece just arrived from the Philippines, and she'll be staying with me for a while. She recently graduated from college, so she's only a few years younger than you. I thought we could have a welcome dinner for her at your restaurant, and you and your friends can play tour guide," Ninang April said, smiling first at me, then at Adeena and Elena.

Behind her back, Ninang Mae and Ninang June shook their heads vigorously at me but stopped as soon as Ninang April turned to look at them. That definitely didn't bode well for me, but I couldn't think of a way to turn down Ninang April without upsetting her and incurring her wrath.

"Why don't we see if Tita Rosie and Lola Flor are available for that welcome dinner first and we can go from there?" I suggested.

My aunt and grandmother ran Tita Rosie's Kitchen, the small Filipino restaurant next to my shop. Considering my aunt was the kindest, most welcoming person ever—and her nurturing nature meant she was determined to feed the world—I knew this was just me delaying the inevitable. Of course Tita Rosie would host the dinner. But I needed time to talk it over with my crew and figure out what the heck was going on and why my godmothers were so divided over this.

"You're right, I need to go over the menu with them anyway. Divina is rather picky, I have to make sure the food meets her standards," Ninang April said, almost to herself, as she turned away and headed toward the door. Ninang Mae and Ninang June just shook their heads and followed her out.

"Yo, what was that all about?" Adeena asked as she cleared the table we'd been sitting at.

Elena took the tray of dirty dishes from her girlfriend and started back toward the kitchen. "Sorry to say this, Lila, but this is your family we're talking about, so you know what this all means."

I groaned, as the truth of her words sank in. There was no doubting it. A lifetime of dealing with my aunties and all their drama told me one thing:

Ninang April's niece was going to be trouble.

Chapter Two

When I pictured what a relative of Ninang April's would look like—the strictest, harshest, least appearance-obsessed of my trio of godmothers—Divina de los Santos absolutely was not it.

Divina had been too jet-lagged for a welcome dinner the night before, so the ninangs had convinced me and the Brew-ha crew to head to Tita Rosie's Kitchen for a quick breakfast and introduction the next day.

As we all greeted each other politely, I studied this newcomer. I wouldn't call her beautiful, exactly, but there was something about her that drew you in anyway. She held court in the middle of my family's restaurant and she gave off the aura of . . . I wasn't even sure how to describe it. Poise, maybe?

She was a few inches taller than me, putting her at around five foot five, which was tall for a Filipina. I peeked down to see if those extra inches were due to heels, but nope. She was rocking rust-colored d'orsay flats, so gorgeous (and clearly expensive) it was hard for me to tear my eyes away. Her hair, makeup, and outfit were immaculate, a level of perfection that I couldn't handle at seven in the morning. Her biological clock was thirteen hours ahead of mine, so maybe that was why? Doubtful though. And to pull the look together was the most gorgeous scarf I'd ever seen: sheer, gauzy, and covered with woven peonies and butterflies. I had to fight the urge to reach out and touch it. I appreciated a great fit as much as the next person, but Shady Palms had dulled my fashionista tendencies and I found myself putting less and less effort into my appearance. Looking at Divina made me think I had to step my game up.

"Lila, this is my niece, Divina. She just graduated from the top art school in the Philippines and wanted to experience life in the U.S. before settling down," Ninang April said. "Divina, this is Lila Macapagal. Her aunt and grandmother run this restaurant and Lila and her friends own the cafe next door."

"Welcome to Shady Palms, Divina," I said, shaking her hand, and my friends echoed my words and actions. A little formal considering we were all in our twenties, but better I seem overly polite than have the aunties on my back about not having any manners.

"Lovely to meet you all," Divina said, a smile lighting up her face. "Tita April has told me so much about everyone here. Sometimes I think she must be exaggerating some of her stories, but she insists they're all true."

"Ninang April, what have you been telling her?" There's no way she'd told her about all the murders that happened last year, right? Not if she wanted her niece to feel safe and comfortable here. But as always, I underestimated her.

Divina laughed. "She said you're secretly a detective! And that she's helped you solve a bunch of cases."

"That's . . . not quite right."

"But it's not wrong either, diba?" Ninang April shot back.

I had no answer to that, so Divina continued. "Well, it sounds really cool. Way more interesting than I thought it would be in this town. I hope I can help you with a case while I'm here."

I hoped I never had to get involved with another case again, but I bit my tongue to stop my sharp retort. Ninang April had made my amateur sleuthing seem like a fun hobby, not the devastating and life-threatening experiences I'd been forced into. I couldn't be mad at Divina for her aunt's thoughtlessness.

"How long are you staying in Shady Palms?" Adeena asked, probably sensing my mood shift and looking to change the subject. "And are you visiting anywhere else in the States?"

Divina flicked her hand. "Oh, who knows? I'm supposed to be here helping at Tita April's new business while planning my next career move. But maybe I'll stay longer, get my master's in Chicago. Wouldn't that be great, Tita?"

Ninang April did not return her niece's grin. "We'll see."

There was a sense of finality in that short statement, and we stood around awkwardly until my aunt and grandmother came out from the kitchen with our massive breakfast.

As much as I loved my aunt's food, Adeena, Elena, and I had to return to the cafe, so we only had time for quick bowls of porridge, Adeena and Elena enjoying the sweet, chocolaty champorado while I had arroz caldo.

"Sorry to eat and run, Tita Rosie, but we've got to open up the shop," I said after scraping the last bit of ginger-laced, chicken-y goodness from my bowl.

"Hoy, what about Divina? I thought you were going to show her around?" Ninang Mae asked.

"We close at six today, so would you want to grab dinner later? We can introduce you to some of our friends," I said.

"But what is she supposed to do until then?" Ninang Mae pressed.

"Mae, she can come with us to the laundromat. Maybe help with the paperwork. Why are you being so tactless? I mean, more so than usual," Ninang April said.

"I don't want to get in the way if you don't want me there," Divina said, keeping her eyes down at the table.

"Oh, no, of course not," Ninang Mae said. "It's, just, you know . . . you're a guest here. We don't want you to get bored on your very first day in town."

"Why don't you call Marcus? He's around the same age and he works nights, so he should be free," I said.

Marcus was Ninang Mae's younger son, and he worked as a security guard at my cousin's winery. Ninang Mae was constantly trying to hook us up even though I wasn't interested and had a boyfriend, but she was nothing if not persistent. I thought she'd be thrilled to have a new woman to push her son on, but she narrowed her eyes at me.

"Like you said, he works nights, so he's sleeping right now."

"You told us he gets up around noon, so he can take her out for lunch," Ninang April said.

Ninang Mae begrudgingly agreed and texted her son that he had a lunch date.

Elena, probably sensing her peacemaker skills were needed to smooth over the moment, said, "Divina, until Marcus is free, do you want to hang out at the cafe? Adeena can fix you up a nice drink and we've got free Wi-Fi, so you can just hang out on your phone or laptop, if you've got one."

"Oh, that would be perfect. I really need some caffeine right now, and I've been meaning to update my online portfolio."

She started to pack up her things, but I stopped her. "No rush, you're still eating your breakfast. We're right next door, so just come over when you're done. Tita Rosie and Lola Flor's food is too good to leave a half-full plate behind."

She agreed, and my partners and I returned to the cafe.

"What was with Auntie Mae getting super weird about having Divina around?" Adeena asked as she moved to her position behind the counter.

."I know she tends to just blurt out what's on her mind, but it did seem rather strange," Elena said as she grabbed a spray bottle to mist the plants in the window.

My baked goods and snacks were already neatly stacked in the glass cases, so I just poured a glass of water and sat down to watch them work. "I have no clue. The biggest red flag was that she didn't jump at the opportunity to hook her up with Marcus."

"Seriously. She's even tried setting me up on a date with him, and she knows I'm not into men," Adeena said.

Elena laughed. "That poor guy. He's really quite cute. I bet he'd have more luck if his mom wasn't so invested in his love life."

Ninang Mae had managed to scare away just about every girlfriend Marcus had ever had. He needed to be more like his older brother, Joseph. Ninang Mae had also tried to hook me up with him, but we'd managed to dodge her. The only reason he was able to get married was because he'd avoided introducing his then-girlfriend to the family until after he'd proposed to her. Ninang Mae had referenced that fact three times during her wedding speech, which for her was holding back.

"She and Ninang June both seemed kind of upset yesterday. I don't think they want Divina to work with them at the laundromat, but I have no idea why. I mean, I get that her art degree isn't much help, but I'm sure she can learn on the job."

The three of us were quiet for a moment, and I figured the others had moved on from the topic until Adeena said, "Not to be that person, but . . . do you think Divina is lying about why she's here? Like, maybe she's actually super wild and her parents kicked her out or something. Or she could be pregnant."

I'd been crunching on the last of my ice and choked when Adeena said that. "Oh my gulay, that would so make sense. Like, of course Ninang Mae would be super prissy and not want her around her son."

"Careful, you two," Elena warned. "You don't even know her, and there could be many reasons your godmother is acting that way. Let's not judge her before we even have a real conversation with her."

Adeena and I grumbled, but we knew she was right. I was too busy to be speculating about my godmothers' drama anyway.

"You two all set? I need to take Longganisa for her morning walk."

My adorable dachshund accompanied me to work every day and was content to spend most of the day napping in my office, but I tried to be a good dog parent and take her out for multiple walks throughout the day. The Brew-ha Cafe was dog-friendly, and Nisa proved to be one of our most successful promo attempts. Whenever people saw her walking around in her adorable Brew-ha Cafe–themed outfits, custom-made by my friend's daughter, they'd stop and ask to pet her. The perfect opportunity to hand over my business card and invite them to the cafe.

Today, Nisa was outfitted in a lemon-yellow Brew-ha Cafe dress and a little flower crown to welcome spring. As I looked her over, I realized even my dog was starting to outdress me and I made a note to go on a shopping trip soon. Maybe I'd take Divina with me to welcome her to town and take advantage of her artistic eye and obvious taste. Decision made, I grabbed a stack of flyers advertising our Big Spring Clean offerings and headed out. The walk proved particularly fruitful when we came across a group of power walking moms with toddlers in tow. They were all too happy to cut their exercise short for the promise of premium caffeine and snacks for the kids.

Twenty minutes later, Nisa and I had worked our circuit and returned to the cafe. Divina was seated at the counter, a steaming mug of coffee and piece of mamon next to her as she worked on her laptop.

She smiled and closed her computer when she saw me coming toward her.

"Hey, Ate Lila! Lola Flor gave me a bag of mamon to share with you all. I guess Tita April told her they were my favorite. Who's this fashionista?"

She bent over to pet Nisa, who reveled in the attention, while I helped myself to the delicious chiffon cakes from my grandmother.

"This is Longganisa. My friend's daughter is an aspiring artist and makes all of Nisa's clothing. She also designed some of the swag we sell here." An idea came to me. "Wait, Ninang April said you graduated from a top art school, right? Would it be OK to introduce you two? She's in her first year of high school and her heart is set on studying art, but her parents are a little worried about her future."

Divina bent her head, keeping her gaze focused on Nisa. "I don't know that I have anything important to say."

"Just your experience, what you learned, what it's like to be a professional artist—"

"I really don't think I'm qualified. It's not like I have a job yet, so . . ."

I decided not to push the subject, but I was starting to get an inkling that there was a lot Divina was leaving unsaid. If I needed to, I could just have Yuki bring Naoko by and pretend it was a surprise visit. But no point in alienating my guest so soon.

Obviously wanting to change the subject, Divina reached into her purse and held out a bag of loose-leaf tea. "By the way, I wanted to give this to you as a souvenir. Tita April told me about you way before I got here and I knew we'd be meeting today, so I figured I should have something ready for you. She said your cafe has an herbal tea section, so I thought you'd like this."

Elena, our resident herbalist, stepped up to accept the gift. "Ooh, what's this? I love learning about new teas."

"Malunggay. It's considered a superfood and is full of antioxi-
dants. I love it because it's good for skin and hair," Divina said,
smoothing her hand down her shiny black locks, and I made a note to
start drinking that tea if my hair would be as glossy and healthy-
looking as hers. "There's also a powdered version that people like to
use for lattes and as a decaf alternative for matcha. The flavors can be
similar, depending on how it's prepared."

"Thanks so much! I can't wait to try it," Elena said. "Any suggestions on how to prepare it?"

"Most people just drink it as a plain tea, but I like to use it in
smoothies and stuff. I know some people that make a blended tea out
of it with dried fruit, and you could also . . ."

As the two of them discussed brewing suggestions and other
preparation methods, Adeena made her way over to me.

"Hey, Lila! Catering order just came in," she said, sliding the order
form over the counter. "There's a chamber of commerce meeting in a
couple of days that might turn ugly, so Beth is hoping your bakes will
put people in a good mood."

Beth Thompson was the head of the most successful company in
town, and I both feared and admired her. Beth and I weren't particularly close, but she and her sister-in-law Valerie (technically former
sister-in-law, but it's a long story) were great about hiring us to cater
their various meetings and events.

I whistled. "It's a breakfast meeting, so she wants me to go all out.
Even said she'd pay extra if I included a savory option since she knows
that's not on our typical menu. Luckily, I know exactly what I want to
make."

I'd binge-watched yet another season of *The Great British Baking
Show*, which had left me buzzing with ideas. I'd never had a sausage
roll before, but how could you go wrong with yummy sausage meat
wrapped in puff pastry? I think it was technically a lunch or picnic

dish, but sausage made me think two things: breakfast and longganisa (not my dog; the Filipino sausage, obvs). Tita Rosie handmade her own longganisa, so I could grab some from her and then go on a grocery store run to pick up some puff pastry (not a cheat if you get a good brand).

My halo-halo chia seed parfait and ube scones with coconut jam were specifically requested, as well as some sort of cake. Instead of my usual calamansi chia seed muffins, I could try a calamansi lavender loaf, to advertise our spring menu. Though if it's for breakfast, maybe coffee cake would be more appropriate. Coffee cakes usually had streusel and cinnamon, so a salabat streusel would be quick and easy to whip up.

I was so into thinking up ideas for Beth's order that I didn't realize Jae had walked in until Divina let out a gasp next to me. I looked up at the sharp noise and grinned when I saw my boyfriend leaning against the counter next to me.

"Jae!" I set down the form I'd been scribbling ideas on to give him a big hug. At just over six feet tall, he towered over me, and I had to go up on my tiptoes to embrace him.

Divina cleared her throat loudly behind me, and I wondered if it was too much PDA for her, but all she said was, "Aren't you going to introduce me to your friend?"

"Oh sorry! Divina, this is my boyfriend, Jae. Jae, this is Ninang April's niece, Divina. She just arrived from the Philippines and will be staying in Shady Palms for a while."

Jae moved his arm from around me to shake her hand. "Welcome to Shady Palms. Is this your first time here?"

Divina grasped his hand with both of hers and tilted her head up to smile at him. "Yes. It's my first time in the U.S., so I'm looking forward to having people show me around. Tita April said everyone here is so nice."

Warning bells started going off in my head, but I quieted them. Last year, my jealousy had almost ruined our relationship before it even started, and I didn't want to keep making the same mistakes. Besides, I couldn't really blame her. Jae was supremely hot, and he had that effect on just about everyone.

"Since we're all busy with work, Marcus is supposed to take her out for lunch and hang out with her until the cafe closes so that Adeena, Elena, and I can show her around."

"A girls' night out, huh? Sounds like fun. I'm guessing you're going to Sushi-ya?"

Sushi-ya was the restaurant owned by my friend Yuki Sato and her husband, Akio. Their daughter, Naoko, was the one who made Longganisa's clothes.

"Why would we be going there?"

"Didn't they hire you to revamp their dessert menu? I thought you were supposed to deliver the samples tonight."

I whipped my bujo out of my purse to check my schedule, and sure enough, I was set to present four different Japanese-inspired desserts, of which they would choose two to permanently add to their menu. The Brew-ha Cafe's reputation had reached the point where local restaurants wanted to hire us to take care of the dessert portions of their menu. Our good name had spread so far in just a year, I had to turn down a lot of work since so many opportunities had come in.

I turned to Divina. "Are you OK with Japanese food for dinner tonight?"

She shrugged. "Sure. Will you be joining us, Jae?"

"It's my late day at the clinic, so I'll probably just head home and crash after work. I came over to see if you were free for breakfast at Tita Rosie's, but you probably already ate, huh?"

Jae had directed the question at me, but it was Divina who replied.

"Mind if I join you? Lola Flor's mamon was so delicious, I've been craving more."

Jae's eyes flicked over to me, and I smiled to reassure him. He smiled back before responding to Divina. "Uh, sure. My brother's already waiting there, so we should head over."

"Oh, you're meeting Detective Park? Or, I mean . . . Jonathan?" Jae's older brother had been the town's only detective until recently. He was now retired and dating my aunt, so not only did I keep stumbling whenever I referred to him, I had to deal with all the awkward teasing about Jae and me practically being related.

Dating in a small town was weird.

"Yeah, so I'd better go before he gets all hangry on me." He gave me a quick kiss and reassuring look as Divina followed him out of the cafe.

As soon as the door chimed closed behind them, Adeena and Elena made their way over to me.

I held up a hand. "Don't even start."

Adeena had never listened to me a day in her life and wasn't about to start now. "OK, I knew that girl was going to be trouble, but this is absolutely delicious."

Elena, bless her, was the sympathetic type. "Are you going to be OK?"

"After all the drama we've had to deal with in the past? This doesn't even register." I forced a smile. "She's new, he's hot, I totally get it. But he's not biting, and she'll get bored and move on. Everything will be fine."

As I moved to the kitchen to get started on Beth's order and put the finishing touches on Yuki's proposed dessert menu, I repeated that last statement to myself.

"Everything will be fine."

Chapter Three

I s there anything you don't eat, Divina?"

Yuki Sato, my friend and fellow restauranteur, had just seated me, Adeena, Elena, and Divina plus our friends Sana Williams and Izzy Ramos-Garcia, who had also joined us to welcome Divina to town.

"I don't really eat dairy, but other than that, I'm fine." Divina looked around the restaurant, taking in Sushi-ya's simple elegance. "This place looks pretty good."

"Let Akio know we're having a welcome dinner and we trust him to do Shady Palms proud," I said. Yuki's husband was the chef, and one of my greatest pleasures was ordering omakase to let him decide what to prepare for my meal. In the year-plus I'd been eating here, I'd never known him to miss.

Yuki smiled at us. "Oh, that's going to make his night. I'll put in the order and come join you. Naoko and the other servers can handle the rest of the tables."

We made small talk until Yuki rejoined us, at which point Izzy set her insulated tote bag on the table and pulled out several bottles of chilled white wine. "I know this place isn't usually BYOB, but Yuki gave me the OK since this is a special occasion."

"Izzy and my cousin Ronnie run the Shady Palms Winery. They make most of the regular varieties, but they specialize in Filipino fruit wines," I explained to Divina, who was examining the bottle. "I forgot to ask if you were a drinker, so if you're not into alcohol, don't feel like you have to drink with us."

"I'd be happy to try a glass. Both alcohol and dairy are bad for my skin, so I avoid them, but it's not like I can't have them. And I was just studying the bottle because the label is really cute. Whoever designed it did a great job."

Izzy beamed at Divina. "Right? Lila introduced me to her friend Terrence, and he handled the winery's logo, wine labels, website design, everything. Best graphic designer I've ever worked with."

A spark of interest lit up Divina's face. "Could you introduce me too, Ate Lila? My degree is in visual arts, which includes graphic design. I'm supposed to be using this time to figure out which direction I want to go in, so I'd love to talk to someone who does it for a living."

"Oh, is that why you've come to Shady Palms? Lila told us you graduated recently, so I'm assuming this is your chance to recharge and strategize?" Sana asked. "If you need help, feel free to reach out. I own the Mind & Body Wellness Studio and do life coaching for women of color entrepreneurs. If you're thinking of striking out on your own, I could give you some pointers."

"That's so generous of you," Divina said, accepting Sana's business card.

"Sana's the best," I said. "Her advice has been invaluable in helping the Brew-ha Cafe grow, and she actually makes exercise kind of fun."

"Her yoga classes are fantastic," Adeena said, reaching out to snag a bit of the seaweed salad that a server dropped off at our table.

"I'm partial to the Latin dance classes myself," Elena said, helping herself to the fried oysters.

"What you really mean to say is that both the Zumba classes and Zumba instructor are absolute fire, right?" my cousin Bernadette said as she slid into the last empty seat. She picked up her chopsticks and waved at Divina as she nabbed a piece of takoyaki. "Hey there, I'm Bernadette Arroyo."

"Count on you to show up as soon as the food arrives," I said, shaking my head as I loaded up my plate with a bit of everything.

"Hey, unlike the rest of you, I don't get to set my own hours. I'm a nurse at the Shady Palms Hospital," she explained to Divina. "Though I guess the scrubs probably made that obvious."

Divina smirked. "A nurse! So, you gave in to the peer pressure, huh? My parents also wanted me to go into nursing, but I refused to give up on my dreams."

That was easy for her to say. According to the other aunties, Ninang April's family was loaded, so going to a prestigious art school was no big deal for someone like Divina. But like most families in Shady Palms (including mine), Bernadette's family toed the line between working class and middle class. Growing up, Bernadette's dream was to be a dancer, but her parents had drilled into her that dancing was an impractical career. Without her parents' support, she didn't have the money to study dance, so she chose the next best thing for herself: nursing.

"Not everyone can afford to chase after their dreams, you know. We don't all have your privilege. And besides, nursing is a noble profession and Ate Bernie is fantastic at what she does. The Shady Palms Hospital is lucky to have her," I said.

Bernadette's eyes widened in surprise, and I busied myself with my chopsticks to avoid her gaze. I was all for following your dreams and finding your passion, but I didn't care for Divina's condescending tone. Next thing you know, she'd be calling Bernadette a sellout.

"I guess I shouldn't talk. My passion is for textiles, and even though there's been a huge resurgence in traditional weaving, my parents thought it wasn't practical enough. So I specialize in textile design instead." Divina shrugged. "We all make compromises. I'm sure your parents are proud of you, at least."

"She's Ninang June's daughter," I said. "And yes, she's extremely proud of Bernadette. Never shuts up about her."

"Only because she likes rubbing it in the other aunties' faces," Bernadette muttered, flushing slightly. "Not like she'd ever say anything nice to me."

Ninang June and my mother had been best friends and rivals, and they used to pit me and Bernadette against each other when we were younger. Even after my mother passed away, Bernadette and I had felt the need to compete against each other in everything. It wasn't until recently we realized how toxic our relationship was and took the first baby steps toward an actual friendship. Amazing the clarity you get from solving murders together.

Naoko and another server arrived to set down bowls of Sushi-ya's special chirashi-don—a bowl of sushi rice topped with various kinds of sashimi as well as slices of tamago, crisp cucumber, and pickled ginger. All chatter ceased as we dug into our main course, silence being one of the surest signs of a good meal. It wasn't until Naoko returned to refill our water glasses that a plan came to me.

"Hey Naoko, you're meeting with Terrence soon to brainstorm more design ideas, right? Is it OK if Divina joins you? She's an artist too and wanted to pick his brain about the business side of things."

"Ooh, you're an artist? What medium do you work with?" Naoko swung around to face Divina, her eyes sparkling with excitement behind her giant red plastic frames.

"Oh, um, a little bit of everything, I guess. I prefer textiles, but most of my classes focused on graphic and textile design," Divina said, not meeting Naoko's eyes. For some reason, whenever she talked about her artwork, she showed a surprising lack of confidence, and I wondered how much of her poise was natural and how much was armor meant to hide her insecurities.

"I've been wanting to learn more about textile design!" Naoko said. "I design the Brew-ha Cafe merchandise and Longganisa's clothes and would love to learn more techniques. Plus I know you can use that for interior design, which could be fun. Did you make that scarf as well?" she asked, gesturing to the gorgeous scarf Divina wore like a shawl over her dress.

Divina smiled, lightly caressing the fabric before taking it off and carefully folding it into her purse. "Yes, this scarf was the first thing I made that got me recognition. Won a pretty prestigious prize at my uni. It's very special to me, which means I should've taken it off before I started eating. Thanks for the reminder."

"Well, it's gorgeous," Naoko said, and we all agreed.

Lightbulb moment. "Could the two of you collab on a special design for the Brew-ha Cafe? We'd pay you, of course."

Naoko shrieked and looked at Divina, all eager beaver–like, and of course Divina couldn't turn her down. "I'd be happy to collaborate with you. It sounds like just the kind of project I need to get my mind off working at the laundromat."

"What's it like working with all the aunties?" Bernadette asked as we were finishing our main courses.

Divina grimaced. "Well, I haven't really started since the laundromat isn't open yet, but I can already tell I'm not going to like it. They were all upset when they realized I didn't know how to do laundry or mop floors or anything like that."

"You don't know how to do laundry?" I asked, shocked that Divina, a grown adult, didn't know how to do one of the simplest chores. Because Tita Rosie and Lola Flor were often busy with the restaurant, I'd been in charge of the family's laundry since I was a child. Then again, taking in Divina's expensive-looking outfit, maybe everything she owned was dry clean only?

"That was the househelp's job. They did all the cooking and cleaning for my family." Divina shrugged. "There was no point in wasting time learning skills I don't need."

"Househelp? Wow! You must be rich," Naoko said, her eyes shining.

"It's common for people to have househelp in the Philippines. I guess it's different here. A lot of things seem to be different here." Divina looked down at her manicured hands. "I didn't go to college just to end up doing this kind of labor. I really don't get what my family's trying to prove."

Just like when she was commenting on Bernadette's nursing job, there was a hint of arrogance in her tone that I didn't care for. But I'd be lying if I said I wasn't sympathetic to a young woman who had very different dreams for her future and was trying to figure out how to navigate the life she was stuck in now. And of course, the nosy side of me that loved tsismis was intrigued by her and the circumstances that brought her here.

I was hoping she'd explain what she meant about her family, maybe open up to us a bit, but she just took a sip of green tea and smiled at us. "What did you bring for dessert, Ate Lila? You said you were working on something special."

"Oh, right! I think you'll really like this." I reached into my tote bag and pulled out one of our huge carryout boxes. "Matcha mamon!

Mamon isn't too different from Japanese castella, and I figured adding matcha would give it a little extra flavor and make it perfect for a Japanese restaurant. I also made matcha white chocolate chip cookies and strawberry-matcha mochi donuts, plus a basic parfait idea that you can adapt seasonally. Tell me what you all think."

My friends all reached out to snag a chiffon cake, and I watched their reactions carefully. I had basically just added matcha powder to Lola Flor's mamon recipe and wasn't sure how well they'd turned out. I thought they were good, but I hadn't changed the sugar levels, so maybe there wasn't enough sugar to counter the bitterness of the green tea?

My fears were realized when Adeena said, "They're good, but I think they could be sweeter. And maybe a stronger matcha flavor? It's a little light for my taste."

But Elena rolled her eyes. "You always say you want it sweeter and stronger. I actually appreciate that slight bitterness. There's something elegant about it."

Yuki agreed. "It suits our style to have something a little more delicate and subtle for dessert. I think these are perfect."

Considering "subtle" wasn't a word that existed in Adeena's vocabulary, I trusted Elena's and Yuki's opinions, but could use someone else's point of view. I looked at Divina, who'd just helped herself to a second piece. "What do you think?"

"Green tea mamon is nothing new in the Philippines, but yours is pretty great."

I smiled at her. "You said mamon was your favorite, so I wanted to try putting my own spin on it for you."

Divina stopped eating and looked at me. "For me? You made these for me?"

"Well, technically for Yuki, but I wanted to make you feel welcome. I can't do much, but I can bake, so . . ." I shrugged. "I'm glad you like it."

She looked down at the mamon in her hand. "You're so nice. All of you are so nice. I didn't expect that."

Bernadette laughed. "What did you expect?"

"Not this. Thanks, everyone." Divina smiled at us, a real smile this time, but there was something sad about her eyes. "Maybe things will be different here."

"What do you mean?"

"Nothing." She took another bite of mamon before changing the subject. "Anyway, what's the deal with Tita Mae? When Marcus took me out for lunch, she was texting him nonstop. He spent more time messaging his mom than talking to me."

"Yeah, that sounds about right," Bernadette and I said in unison, while everyone else laughed.

"None of the aunties know how to mind their business, so if you're going to work with them, you'd better get used to it fast." At her worried look, I added, "They can be annoying, but it's mostly harmless gossip. Don't worry about it."

"I hope Tita April is careful. If I know my aunt, what you all call gossip is most likely just her speaking the truth. And if there's one thing I've learned, it's that people don't actually want to hear the truth." Divina's voice was as soft and bitter as the green tea leaves lingering at the bottom of our cups.

She was quick to change the subject after that, but for the rest of the night, I couldn't help but wonder: What truths did Divina speak, and were they part of the reason she was forced to come to Shady Palms?

Chapter Four

You're a lifesaver, Lila. Sorry for the last-minute order, but I'd fool-ishly left the catering up to my assistant. When I saw she only had a fruit platter and coffee on order, I knew I had to step in."

Beth Thompson surveyed the spread on the community center ta-ble, noting down the various breakfast items in her champagne-colored planner. She was outfitted in a well-tailored peach pantsuit, the beautiful cut highlighting her lithe figure and the pastel color popping against her lovely dark skin. Her nails matched the suit per-fectly, and I idly wondered if she changed her manicure daily to match her outfits. I wouldn't put it past her.

"No worries. I've been wanting to experiment with savory pastries for a while now, so this was the perfect opportunity. And you know I appreciate all the business you send my way, so definitely not com-plaining," I said as I finished setting up the carafes of coffee and tea. "What's with the early morning meeting anyway? I know I've missed the last few meetings, but I didn't think there was anything urgent coming up."

She rolled her eyes. "The Big Spring Clean starts soon and people are still arguing over the schedule, who gets to host which event, et cetera. And by people, I mostly mean your godmothers and Ultima."

Now it was my turn to roll my eyes. Ultima Bolisay was a member of our church and had been butting heads with the aunties since time immemorial. Her family owned and operated the only laundromat chain in town and hadn't liked that Ninang June's husband ran a dry cleaner since it "stole her customers," even though laundromats and dry cleaners were not the same thing. And when the aunties announced they were opening their own laundromat, therefore cutting into Ultima's monopoly? According to Tita Rosie, Father Santiago and the church outreach group almost had to break up a fistfight in the church vestibule.

"Let me guess: Ultima is complaining that the Calendar Crew is getting special treatment again?"

Beth just sighed and filled a mug with black coffee. "I wish I could've dumped this on Valerie, but she's run the last two meetings. Tell me why I can handle a boardroom full of entitled old white men with no problem, but the minute your aunties get involved, I break into a cold sweat?"

"Yeah, they definitely have that effect on people." I filled my own mug and set a longganisa roll on my plate. "We better fortify ourselves before everyone gets here. I bet they start fighting the minute they all see each other."

Beth eyed the sweets-laden table. "No offense, Lila, but there's not enough sugar and caffeine in the world to prepare us for what's about to happen."

The chamber of commerce meeting was, to put it lightly, a hot mess. You'd think an organization dedicated to helping and connecting fellow business owners would be a little more, I don't know, professional? Yet in the last few months since I'd attended a meeting, it seemed like cliques and clear divisions of interest had arisen. In some ways it made sense—after all, I was way closer to the other restauranteurs of the group since we had more common interests than, say, the guy who ran a roofing business. But I at least tried to be friendly with everyone and support the local businesses as much as possible. Now suddenly it was like being in middle school again, with people you were forbidden to talk to without incurring the wrath of the group.

And right now, the Calendar Crew were part of the unpopular crowd.

"Technically, most people don't agree with Ultima since healthy competition leads to a healthy economy for Shady Palms. But the tide turned against the aunties recently after they let it slip that Glen Davis has been stepping out on his wife. You know, the hardware store guy? Now there's talk of divorce, and a lot of people are upset with your aunties for getting involved in grown folks' business," Beth had informed me when we were setting up.

I always knew their nosiness would get them in trouble someday. Who knew it'd bite them in the butt like this though?

The Calendar Crew and Ultima had started arguing as soon as the meeting had come to order, and it was getting uglier and uglier as Ultima's attacks became more and more personal and the aunties did nothing to course correct the conversation.

One of the reasons I hadn't been to many meetings lately was because things had been getting heated like this more often and my conflict avoidance tendency made these meetings way too stressful. If they were free, Adeena or Elena would go instead, but we'd been so busy lately that keeping up with the meetings was not a priority. My instinct was to say goodbye to Beth and head to the safety of my cafe, but I knew my ninangs would be hurt if I didn't back them up.

Luckily, or I guess unluckily considering the situation, I didn't have to make a choice because I received a call from Marcus before I was forced to jump in.

"Lila! Are you with my mom?"

"Yeah, we're at the chamber of commerce, but—"

"She's not answering her phone and neither is Tita April. I need you to bring them over to the laundromat. The police are already on their way."

I gripped my phone. "The police? What happened?"

Marcus, likely sensing my panic after all the problems we'd had the past year, said, "Don't worry, nobody's hurt. But you need to get here right away. Someone's smashed up the laundromat."

W̶e̶ rushed over to the laundromat to find the words **MIND YOUR BUSINESS** spray-painted across the storefront and Divina and Marcus waiting beside the graffiti.

"The SPPD should be here soon. I know you want to go inside, but it's better not to mess with anything until the cops get here. You'll need their pictures and report for the insurance claims," Marcus said to the Calendar Crew.

"But—"

"There's nothing you can do in there, Tita," Divina said to Ninang April. "I'm sorry."

"They're right," I said to my godmothers, who kept fighting to go inside. "Let's not disturb the crime scene. When the cops come, we can assess the damage and we'll help you clean after. Want me to call Amir?"

Amir Awan was Adeena's big brother and a fantastic lawyer. He'd helped me and my family out of some tough jams and had advised us more times than I could count. His clear, analytical mind was exactly what we needed with emotions running high, plus he could guide the ninangs on next steps. The Calendar Crew agreed it was a good idea, so I put in a call to Amir, as well as my aunt.

Luckily, Amir was free and nearby so he arrived at the same time as the SPPD. He talked to the officer in charge for a moment before herding the aunties to the side.

"Once they're done taking photos, they want you to go inside to check if there's anything missing. I'll also note down the extent of the damage, so don't worry about any of that. Just let me know if you notice anything important."

An officer soon waved us inside, and our large group made our way into the laundromat. Last year, Tita Rosie's Kitchen had been vandalized, and I remembered the helplessness and outrage I'd felt seeing our kitchen, our family's sacred space, destroyed. The ninangs had been there for us in the aftermath, so I wanted to be strong for them.

But I couldn't help but gasp when I took in the damage—several of the washing machines had their glass doors smashed in and shards of glass littered the floor. Whoever did that either got tired or bored partway through and abandoned the hammer they'd used on the floor, instead switching to several cans of spray paint to tarnish the remaining machines and dryers. On the wall by the cash register, the same words that appeared on the front window, **MIND YOUR BUSINESS**, were spray-painted in large red letters.

A shiver ran through my body as I stared at the message until the warmth of Amir's hand on my shoulder calmed me down. He had his phone in his other hand, taking a photo of the damaged wall.

"It'll be OK, Lila. I'll handle it. The police will catch who did this and I'll make sure the aunties are taken care of. With a little bit of el-bow grease, they might even be able to open as planned, without delays."

"There is no 'might.' We absolutely will open as planned," Ninang April said as she joined the two of us in front of the graffitied wall. Her eyes narrowed as she read the message. "We sunk our savings into this, and to miss all the business that the opening week for the Spring Clean could bring us? Absolutely not."

"Do you have any idea who would do something like this? That message implies that this destruction was personal." An officer pulled out a notebook to take our statements as we all gathered in front of the graffiti.

"It's obvious who did this," Ninang Mae said, her face flushed red with anger. "Ultima Bolisay! She's been threatening us ever since we announced this business venture. This is her way of sabotaging us, making sure we can't take part in the Big Spring Clean."

"Why would she go this far?"

"She considers us competition. She's been trying to get the cham-ber of commerce to stop backing us, but it hasn't worked, so now she's resorted to petty vandalism," Ninang June said, her eyes narrowed and lips pursed as she stared at the damaged wall.

"Um, I hate to say this, but . . . Ultima was at the meeting with all of us just now. How could she have done this?" I asked.

Ninang April nodded in approval. "Good question. Marcus, you were the one who reported it, right? When was that?"

"We were on our way to Tita Rosie's for breakfast when Divina re-alized her scarf was missing. She thought she'd left it in the office at the laundromat the other day, so we stopped by to check and saw the graffiti on the windows. We didn't go in, just called the police and then tried contacting you and my mom. Neither of you answered, so I finally called Ate Lila to see if she could get ahold of you all." Marcus glanced at his call list. "It's been a little over half an hour since that first call."

The officer taking our statement said, "The spray paint isn't fully dry yet, but that doesn't tell us much. From what I can tell, this was an acrylic spray paint, and those can take anywhere from eight to twenty-four hours to dry."

The officer must have noticed that I looked surprised at his knowledge (it was the SPPD—any show of competence impressed me) because he added, "We got a lot of bored kids in this town. Graffiti is one of our main problems."

He turned his attention back to the trio. "When was the last time you were on the premises? That might help us narrow down the time frame."

"Yesterday afternoon, around four p.m.," Ninang April answered promptly. "We were showing my niece around the business since she's going to be working with us."

"Have you noticed anyone suspicious around the shop? Any other people we could be looking into?"

Where to even start? My godmothers had upset so many people with their nosiness at one time or another, I wouldn't be surprised if half the town had a grudge against them.

"Well, Officer, I do hate to gossip, but there's maybe one more person who could've done this and wasn't at the meeting this morning," Ninang Mae said.

I quickly disguised my laugh as a cough when she shot a dirty look my way. She continued, saying, "Glen Davis is separated from his wife right now, and he claims we're the reason they're getting a divorce. Even though the *real* reason is that he was cheating on his wife with a woman almost half his age and—"

"Yes, he was extremely angry with us when the news got out.

Warned us to stop messing with people's lives if we knew what was good for us," Ninang June said, cutting off Ninang Mae before she could build up too much steam.

"We'll look into these two individuals and also see if there are cameras in the area that can help us identify the vandal or vandals. The businesses next to your store seem to be closed on Sundays, so it's unlikely they saw anything, but maybe you can talk to them to see if they noticed anything suspicious the other day. We're done taking photos here, so if you can follow me to the station, we'll file that report."

"All right, so I guess I'll see you at home—" Marcus started to say before his mom cut him off.

"What are you talking about? You're coming with us! I might need your help with the paperwork."

"Oh, uh, well, I guess . . . I mean, I promised to run errands with Divina, and we still haven't had breakfast, but I can —"

Ninang Mae clutched her chest. "No, go have fun. Never mind me. I'll just call Joseph to come to the police station. He's a good boy, he'll take care of me."

She made a big show of turning away from him and pulling out her phone. Marcus raised his eyes to the ceiling and shook his head before sighing.

"Hey Divina, you mind coming to the station with us? It shouldn't take long, and then we can get back to our plans."

Divina eyed Ninang Mae, who still had her back turned to them. "Why don't I wait for you at the cafe? I need coffee and we can head next door whenever you're ready."

"Lila, is that OK with you?" Marcus's eyes begged me to help him out. Poor guy. I decided to throw him a bone.

"Yeah, of course. Divina, you can help me taste test the new menu we're releasing for the Big Spring Clean."

"Mind if I join you? I want to stick around just in case the aunties need help again, but I could use a coffee break," Amir said, glancing at his watch.

"Lila, let your family know what happened here. We'll need help cleaning and your Tita Rosie will know who to contact. Divina, I expect you to help as well, so don't stay out gallivanting."

After giving us that order, Ninang April beckoned to her business partners, and they headed out with Marcus.

I sighed and turned to Divina and Amir. "Let's get going. Something tells me this is going to be a very long day. Better assemble the squad."

Chapter Five

"More shady stuff has happened around your family? Shock of all shocks, Lila."

Adeena set drinks in front of me, Divina, and Amir. "At least no one was hurt this time. Wait till Elena's done in the back before giving us the full story though. Right now, I need your opinion on this new drink. Elena thinks there's too much lavender on the current menu, especially with my seasonal additions. She wanted to add a drink that uses the malunggay tea Divina gifted us, but she hasn't perfected the blend yet so I'm testing out this pistachio-rose latte as a replacement. I think it fits with our spring menu, but I wanna hear what you all think before officially adding it."

"This is so pretty," Divina said, whipping out her phone to take pictures of the light green concoction topped with whipped cream, crushed pistachios, and dried rose petals before trying the drink. "I've never had pistachios or rose before, but it's a really nice flavor and it photographs well. I'd order this again."

Amir nodded in agreement. "The creamy nuttiness of the pistachio is well-balanced with the subtle floral notes. It tastes like home to me."

"That's a heck of a compliment," I said, smiling at him. "And I agree, this should replace one of your lavender drinks. I bet it's great iced as well."

"You think all coffee is better iced," Elena said, coming out of the kitchen with a fresh batch of dog biscuits and kitty treats. After filling the jars at the counter, she opened my office door to let Longganisa out and presented her with a fresh dog biscuit.

"Why is she dressed as a frog?" Amir asked as Longganisa waddled over to say hi.

I snatched her up before she got too close. "Nisa, you know he's allergic. Stay over here, OK? And she's dressed like a frog because frogs are adorable, obvs."

"If you open the door to let fresh air in, I should be OK. My new allergy shots have been really effective."

"Look at you, Amir Bhai. Sana tells you she wants a cat and suddenly you're not afraid of needles anymore?" Adeena said, teasing her brother over his sudden desire to get allergy shots despite refusing them for years. "Love really changes people, doesn't it?"

"Who's Sana?" Divina asked, reaching for a slice of the salabat streusel cake I set on the table.

"His girlfriend. You met her last night at dinner, remember?" I said, helping myself to a slice as well.

"Oh, the business coach, right? She was so kind to me. Beautiful, too," she added almost wistfully as she eyed Amir.

"She's the best, isn't she?" Amir grinned, not catching Divina's look or tone. His phone chirped, and he skimmed the message before standing up. "Sorry, but can I get a to-go cup? They need me back at the office."

He headed out after Adeena transferred his drink to one of our re-usable takeout cups, his attention focused on his phone and still un-aware of Divina's eyes on him. She caught me watching her and grinned.

"All the good-looking guys in this town are taken! I was hoping to have some fun while I was here, but it seems like more trouble than it's worth. And I promised my aunt I'd stay out of trouble. Guess this is a sign that I should behave after all." Her face lit up as if she were amused, but her eyes held a more complicated emotion. Her phone vibrated and she glanced at the message and sighed. "It's time to meet Marcus. See you later."

Elena, who'd been quietly taking care of her plants during the whole exchange, waited until Divina left before speaking up. "I know I said we shouldn't gossip without even knowing her, but watch your-self, Lila. That's a woman who's used to playing games, and I think she considers you fair competition."

I groaned. "I think you're right. Anyway, are the two of you free later? The aunties need our help."

D amn, Lila, it's like your godmothers called out 'Aunties Assem-ble!' and every auntie in a twenty-mile radius answered their call."

Adeena, as usual, was exaggerating. There were only a dozen or so members of the Calendar Crew's church outreach group milling about, though with the high levels of auntie energy they were giving off, it really did feel like the room was packed. Arguments over the correct way to remove spray paint, whether or not the floors had been swept clean enough, and even whose dumplings were the superior dumplings could be heard scattered throughout the large main area of the laundromat.

Adeena passed me the gloves she'd picked up after dropping Elena at her mom's restaurant. Elena had wanted to help with cleaning too, but a server had called off and Elena needed to fill in for them. Instead, she had her mom donate a bunch of green chile tamales and some cleaning supplies to the cause.

"The aunties have been trying to remove the spray paint without damaging the machines or wall for the past hour and it's barely budged. They were able to clean the windows and sweep up all the glass though," I said, leading Adeena over to the damaged wall.

"Good thing I went through that graffiti art phase in high school. My parents let me do whatever I wanted to my room as long as I cleaned up when I was done."

She got to work mixing a paste of baking soda and hot water and smeared it on the graffitied wall by the cash register. After waiting about fifteen minutes, she got to work scrubbing the surface, and the spray paint peeled right off, leaving the wall underneath it unharmed.

"So you actually know how to do something besides make expensive coffee, ha? Very nice." Ninang April looked approvingly at Adeena. "Make more of that cleaner for the washing machines and dryers and give it to the aunties. Then you can wash your hands and get something to eat."

"Something to eat?" Adeena looked around the room. "You mean from the vending machines over there?"

Ninang June made a noise with her lips. "Do you really think we'd make you buy a candy bar from a machine after helping us? There's food in the back room. Save me some of those tamales though, they smell wonderful."

After making the cleaning paste, Adeena and I made our way to the back. I usually didn't interact with the other aunties in town besides mine and Adeena's family, especially since I didn't attend church regularly. I'd forgotten how deep they rolled when someone sent a distress signal. Almost every member of the church outreach group my aunt, grandmother, and godmothers belonged to were in that room or the main area of the laundromat, a motley crew of mostly middle-aged and older Filipino, Mexican, and Polish women who all attended Mass at St. Genevieve.

A chorus of "Sit down, sit down! Eat, eat!" greeted us. One of them took the bag of tamales out of Adeena's hands and set them out on a platter, another shoved plates in our hands, and a third one started shoveling food onto them without asking what we wanted.

"We can serve ourselves! Thanks, Aunties," Adeena said, carefully maneuvering away from a woman trying to put a barbecue skewer on her plate. "Ooh, pierogi!"

"Yes, there's potato and cheese, sauerkraut, and mushroom and onions," an auntie said, smiling proudly as Adeena piled the Polish dumplings on her plate.

Tita Rosie made her way over to us. "Lola Flor made dessert too, Adeena." She gestured across the room to my grandmother, who was talking to a Filipino woman around my age. I'd seen her around town before but had never really talked to her. Pretty sure she'd moved here shortly before I left for college. "I know how much you love sweets. There's also someone I want to introduce you to, anak. And you need to say hi to your Tita Lynn, she just got back yesterday."

I perked up. "I didn't realize she was back already. I thought she'd planned on staying for another few months."

Tita Lynn Mari Belgea was my aunt's best friend, and I loved her dearly. Just as sweet and caring as Tita Rosie, but not as naive, and with a good head on her shoulders. I hadn't seen her in at least a year because she'd been in the Philippines taking care of her sick mother since before I'd returned to Shady Palms. But when Tita Rosie gave me a sad look, I realized why Tita Lynn had returned early and that maybe we wouldn't be throwing that welcome back party we'd had planned for her after all.

We followed my aunt over to Lola Flor, Tita Lynn, and that other woman. I quickly did mano to Tita Lynn before giving her a big hug.

"I'm so sorry, Tita Lynn. But I'm happy to see you."

Tita Lynn smiled sadly and placed her hand on my cheek. "It was her time. And I'm glad to be back home, and that you're here again. It's been too long, Lila."

"We'll have you over for dinner as soon as you feel up to it," Tita Rosie promised. Then she gestured to the woman I didn't know, who'd been standing awkwardly to the side during this exchange. "Teresa, this is my niece that I told you about. And her best friend, Adeena. They run the cafe next to our restaurant along with Adeena's girlfriend. Where is Elena, by the way?"

"She had to help out at El Gato Negro," Adeena said, then waved at Teresa. "Hi, I'm Adeena Awan, the barista at the Brew-ha Cafe."

"And I'm Lila Macapagal," I said, reaching out to shake her hand. "I do the baking."

Teresa laughed. "Wow, full name introduction and handshake? You're so formal!"

Lola Flor swatted at her. "Ay, you young people. We raised her to be respectful, how else is she supposed to introduce herself?"

"I'm sorry, Lola, of course you're right." Teresa grinned at us. "So nice to finally meet you. I'm Teresa Uy. I manage the #1 Ultima Cleaning and Laundry over on Grove Street."

"Wait, you work for Ultima? Does she know you're here?" I asked.

She rolled her eyes. "Just because I work for her doesn't mean I'm part of her little feud. I know Tita April, Tita Mae, and Tita June from church, and they've always been nice to me."

I hadn't always been the paranoid type, but considering that someone had tried to destroy my ninangs' store earlier, I figured I could be forgiven for not trusting her.

She must've sensed that because she said, "I swear I'm not, like, a spy or anything. Tita Ultima's daughter may be my best friend, but that's way too much. And she wouldn't ask that of me anyway."

The Calendar Crew and Divina joined us before I could reply.

"Teresa is a good girl, don't worry, Lila," Ninang June said.

"Yes, she's a very good girl. Never misses church, helps every week with the outreach group, and isn't afraid of hard work. Unlike some people here . . ." Ninang Mae said, muttering that last part under her breath. But, of course, just loud enough to make sure we heard her.

Ninang April threw a dirty look her way. "Anyway, this is my niece, Divina. She's staying with me for a while and helping out at the laundromat once we open. Divina, Teresa is also Bicolano. You're around the same age, maybe you went to school together?"

Divina's eyes swept over Teresa, taking in her makeup-less face, practical clothing, and sensible shoes, as well as her straight black hair pulled back into a neat ponytail. "It's a large region, so I doubt it. Even if we did, we probably didn't run in the same crowd. Nice to meet you, though."

"Plus, I left in middle school, so even if we had met, I doubt we'd remember each other," Teresa added. "It was a long time ago. We probably changed a lot in that time."

Divina made a noncommittal noise and moved to grab a plate from the table. Ninang Mae said, "You didn't help with the cleaning at all, but you show up in time to eat?"

Divina kept her eyes on the food she was piling on her plate. "I was helping your son with his errands. Remember? That long list you gave him to do?"

"Yes, but I gave it to him. He didn't need your help, we did."

"But you had so much help already, it's not like there was anything for me to do," Divina said, gesturing around the room. "I don't know how to do any of this. And you're the one always saying I'm in the way."

"So now it's my fault that you weren't here?" Ninang Mae turned to Ninang April. "I didn't realize your sister raised her child to talk back to her elders."

"Why don't we let the young people get to know each other better?" Tita Rosie suggested. "We still have lots of food left, so make sure to take home a plate."

My aunt gently led Ninang Mae away, but she kept looking back at us as if she wanted to say more, and my grandmother jerked her head to signal to Ninang April and Ninang June that they should follow them. Tita Lynn smiled at us all, saying how lovely it was to see everyone, and left with the others. Adeena, Divina, Teresa, and I stood around awkwardly, watching the Calendar Crew as they whispered furiously amongst themselves.

"You know, Auntie Mae has never had a filter, but I feel like she's been extra bad lately," Adeena said as she piled a plate with sweets. "What's her deal?"

"It's me," Divina said, a small smile on her lips. "I'm not a 'nice' girl, so she doesn't like having me around. And she definitely doesn't like me spending time with her son. I'm surprised she isn't pushing Marcus on you since you're such a 'good girl,'" she added to Teresa, who was looking more and more uncomfortable.

"Um, Tita Mae's already tried to get me to go on a date with Marcus, but we're just friends. I don't think he's interested in anything more than that. Not that I'm interested either," Teresa said, blushing furiously. "Excuse me, I just remembered I needed to ask Tita Rosie something."

We watched her scurry away to the safety of my aunt's side.

"That poor girl. She's so obvious. But enough about her," Adeena said, her eyes alight with interest. "What would make these aunties think you're not a good girl?"

Divina tilted her head and studied Adeena for a moment. "Next time we have a girls' night out, I'll tell you all about it."

"I'll hold you to that," Adeena said with a grin. "When and where are we doing this?"

The three of us spent the next hour or so chatting and laughing and eating while we planned a get-together that would never happen.

Chapter Six

The next couple of weeks passed in a whirlwind of planning, baking, and cleaning. Even Longganisa was doing her part, freshly groomed and turned out in her new spring clothing line to draw in more customers for the cafe.

All attempts at planning a girls' night out went out the window since it seemed the Calendar Crew were keeping Divina busy getting the laundromat ready for their grand opening. I'd seen her a few times when they stopped by the restaurant for dinner, but we hadn't had a chance to hang out since that day cleaning up the laundromat. At first, I thought Divina was using the laundromat as an excuse to avoid me. But then I started getting whiny texts from Marcus about how his mom was keeping Divina so busy, he could barely see her.

Poor guy. It seemed like he was really getting serious about her even though it had only been a couple weeks. Oh well, I figured once the kickoff happened, things would calm down enough for us all to have a fun night out. The Brew-has and I were all busy getting ready as well, and Jae had taken to joining me and Longganisa on some of our midday and early evening walks since I was too busy to spend time with him otherwise.

Shortly before the laundromat was set to open, we got a lucky break. Divina, Marcus, and I had finally convinced the aunties that Divina deserved a proper day out since she hadn't had the chance to go anywhere or do anything fun since she'd arrived. Tita Rosie guilted them into saying yes, but only on the condition that we run a bunch of errands and pick up some things for them while in the city. Considering I had to promise Adeena and Elena the same thing for covering for me at the shop, we were happy to agree. I also had to promise them to try and get the tea from Divina about what brought her here, or at least convince her to finally do our planned girls' night, but with Marcus tagging along, I doubted I'd get the chance.

The three of us piled into my ancient SUV and made the roughly two-hour drive to Chicago, where we promised Divina plenty of food, shopping, and people-watching. I'd originally asked if she wanted to hit up the Fashion Outlet in Rosemont since I figured it was more her speed, but she vetoed that.

"The Philippines is nothing but malls, plus that place isn't even in the city. I want to walk the streets and actually see Chicago. Somewhere cool but not too touristy."

"I know just the place," I said, and drove to Wicker Park.

I'd spent a lot of time in this area back when I was in college. Before most of my friends sided with my ex-fiancé after the breakup (to be fair, they were his friends first; that's what happens when you move to a new place and start dating someone from the area almost immediately), we'd come out here to eat (a bowl of Kizuki Ramen followed by Jeni's ice cream across the street were my go-tos), attend gallery shows, shop in the fun boutiques, and just hang out. If we were feeling wild, we'd hit up Insomnia Cookies on our way to a four a.m. bar. Shady Palms may be my hometown, but oh how I loved this city.

"Wait, this is a boutique and jewelry store *and* art gallery?" Divina practically shrieked when we walked into Heaven Gallery. "I can't believe you left Chicago for Shady Palms. This is so cool!"

Divina's eyes shone as she took in the small jewelry cases that awaited you when you reached the top of the stairs, with racks of clothing on one side and artwork on the other.

"It's primarily an art gallery, but it's also a vintage shop. One of my friends used to do shows here all the time," I said. "It's small, but they've got a great mission. I wish we had places like this in Shady Palms. I mean, I don't really 'get' a lot of this stuff, but we actually have quite a few artists in our community."

"Really? You need to introduce me sometime," Divina said. "Are there any studios in town? I miss creating."

"Adeena, Elena, and Elena's mom are all artists," I said. "Elena's mom throws pottery, so if you're into ceramics, I'd be happy to introduce you. I don't know if you paid attention to the tableware at Tita Rosie's Kitchen, but she created all the dishes we use there, as well as some of the mugs and things at the cafe. And there's burgeoning artists like Naoko. We really could use an arts center."

"Maybe you could work together with some people in town and start one, Divina!" Marcus looked at her all puppy-dog-eyed, so excited I could practically see him wagging his tail. "You've been wanting to find work outside the laundromat. How cool would this be?"

Throughout the entire (may I reiterate, two-hour-plus) car ride here, Marcus had kept up a steady stream of conversation with Divina, totally leaving me out. It wasn't Divina's fault. She kept trying to steer some questions my way, but Marcus would just volley them back to her. It's like, now that his mom couldn't get in his way, all the things he'd wanted to say and ask her came tumbling out. Anytime I questioned how he and Ninang Mae were related, all I had to do was listen to his incessant chatter, and then it was like, "Oh yeah, definitely mother and son."

I expected her to brush him off yet again, but she actually brightened at the suggestion. "That would be really cool! I wanted to do something similar in my old neighborhood, actually. My friends thought it was a waste of time and that I should focus on creating a name for myself instead."

Her expression faded and I figured this was the perfect time to learn more about her and the circumstances that brought her here. "Why would it be a waste of time? I admit that I know nothing about art or the art world, but everyone has different goals, right? Success doesn't only mean becoming a name."

Divina looked at me like, *oh you sweet summer child*. Which, fair, but also she was at least three years younger than me. "That's the thing. I do want to become a name. I want huge gallery showings and tastemakers letting the world know that I'm the one to watch. I want to stop playing it safe with my art and have my textiles revolutionize the industry. I want to be so successful that I never have to rely on my family name or supposed friends ever again. But I also want to use my art to help people. I want it all."

As she spoke, I finally understood how and why Marcus was falling for her so fast. Was there anything more appealing than a person who was passionate about their interests? I didn't think so. Jae could spend hours waxing poetic about dentistry or basketball or board games, all things I had zero interest in, and somehow it just made him hotter. And watching Divina light up, seeing how animated she got as she talked about her art and her dreams, even I was charmed. Though I couldn't ignore a certain phrase she let slip.

"I'm sorry, but 'supposed friends'? I'm sensing a story there."

"Nothing that interesting, I'm afraid," she said, as she studied a placard next to a tuft of multicolored organza that somehow managed to look simultaneously like a sea creature and an open wound. But in a cool way. "How about you? The aunties told me all about you leaving Chicago after breaking off your engagement. Do you still keep in touch with your college friends?"

I grimaced. "The friend who introduced me to this place, yes. She moved to Wisconsin to teach at a liberal arts college and missed all the ugliness of the breakup. But everyone else chose Sam."

"Even though he was cheating on you?"

I didn't ask how she knew that dirty detail—of course the aunties told her.

"Yep. The worst part was they knew about the cheating way before I did. But most of them had been friends with him first. Plus, he was rich and his family was influential in the restaurant world." I shrugged. "I hate it, but I know why they did it. They were just looking out for themselves."

"Everyone just cares about saving their own skin, huh?" Divina looked thoughtful. "Kinda sad that this is the thing we both have in common. You're lucky though. Your friends in Shady Palms are genuine. I can't see them ever betraying you like that."

Remembering that dark time in my life and all that I'd given up, my heart felt like it was being squeezed tighter and tighter. But after she said that, I looked at Marcus, who had been wandering the small gallery room, intently studying each piece as if it would help him better understand Divina. I remembered all the ways he'd backed me up over the last year, ready to risk his job and safety to help me out. Same for Bernadette, who had been my family and rival for so many years before finally becoming my friend. I thought about Adeena, who knew me at my worst and was still the most ride-or-die person I'd ever met. And Amir, with all his guidance and legal support and (now platonic) love. And Elena. And Terrence. And Sana. And Yuki. And Jae, of course. And and and . . .

And I knew Divina was right. Maybe it was a cliché that I'd left my big city dreams and settled back into small town life, but I also knew that it wasn't about the place. It was the people. And the place I now proudly called home surrounded me with lots of good ones.

"They could all be your friends too, Divina. If you let them. Shady Palms could be your home too," Marcus said, putting into words all that I'd been thinking.

Divina playfully bumped Marcus with her elbow. "Maybe it could be. I think I'd like that."

She looked around the room one last time and took a deep breath, her body relaxing, and gave us a smile so innocent and unguarded she almost looked like a different person. "Now let's go get something to eat. I'm starving."

Time passed quickly but peacefully and finally it was the morning of the Big Spring Clean kickoff. Adeena, Elena, and I were all in overdrive getting everything ready—the ovens were loaded with the day's specials while Elena fussed with her plants and Adeena scrawled our new spring offerings on the giant chalkboards behind the counter and in front of the cafe. It wasn't until I saw Elena misting the money tree near the counter that I remembered the gift I needed to deliver to the Calendar Crew.

I glanced at the clock. The Brew-ha Cafe wouldn't open for another hour and the grand opening for the laundromat wasn't for another two hours, though they would likely arrive there soon to get things ready. I'd already promised Tita Rosie I'd help her drop off breakfast for the ninangs and Divina, so it would also be the perfect time to give them their gift. Maybe I could fit in Longganisa's walk and do more advertising while I was at it.

I let my partners know my plans and Elena loaded the Calendar Crew's gift in my car while I dressed Longganisa in her sunflower costume and grabbed the flyers we'd prepared for the event.

"Elena, the quick breads will be done in half an hour, so can you take them out and set them on the cooling racks when they're ready? I should be back in time for opening."

"Got it. I'll also finish boxing up their order, just in case. I can always drop it off for you since I plan on swinging by the winery once they open." The Calendar Crew had put in an order for dozens of cookies and muffins to celebrate their launch, but they were scheduled to be delivered right at opening to ensure freshness.

Elena went to the kitchen to grab the timer I set, and Adeena handed me my signature drink, the Brew-ha #1, an iced pandan cold brew coffee with coconut water and coconut milk.

"You're both lifesavers. Be back soon."

Tita Rosie was ready next door, and we quickly loaded the trays in the car. I texted the aunties to let them know we were on our way to the laundromat. If they weren't there yet, I could still use the opportunity to walk Nisa and hand out flyers till they arrived.

Ninang April's reply arrived just as I buckled myself in.

Bring Divina with you. We will be there soon.

I raised an eyebrow, but chose not to reply. If Ninang April thought Divina was with me, it meant Divina had lied so she could go off and do things she didn't want her aunt to know about. High school Lila knew that trick very well. I didn't want to be the reason she got caught though, so I sent Divina a quick message on WhatsApp to warn her. Hopefully she'd give me a good excuse to tell the aunties, but if not . . . she was a grown woman. Besides, it's not like she'd asked me to be her alibi. She couldn't get mad at me for not being prepared.

Another thing I wasn't prepared for? Seeing a bunch of cop cars in front of the laundromat.

"Susmaryosep!" Tita Rosie exclaimed. "What now?"

I parked and we both raced over to my godmothers, who were talking to the same cop from last time. It wasn't hard to see why—the same message from the previous week, **MIND YOUR BUSINESS**, was spray-painted across the front window again.

"Lila! Just in time. Can you call Amir for us?"

"Officer, when are you going to catch this vandal? This is going to ruin our opening day!"

"Marcus, wake up. We need you at the laundromat now. No, I can't wait!"

While the aunties let that all out and Tita Rosie tried to calm them down, I called Amir to let him know what had happened. He said he'd be here soon, but to go ahead inside to start documenting the damage. I passed along his message, and Ninang June unlocked the front door to let us in.

The lights flickered on, the fluorescent bulbs illuminating the pristine space. Maybe the vandal only had time to graffiti the windows? Considering the door was locked, they probably hadn't gotten inside since nothing seemed to be broken. We all split up to investigate different areas. On my side of the laundromat, everything seemed to be in order. The machines were glistening and from what I could tell, the graffiti was only on the front window. At least the damage was minimal and wouldn't interfere with the Calendar Crew's opening day.

That hopeful thought was crushed when Longganisa, who'd been sniffing around the space, started barking near the back folding area. Ninang April, who'd been going up and down the aisles to check for damage, went over to my dog to see what the fuss was.

Her screams mingled with Longganisa's frantic barking, drawing everyone's attention.

Ninang June had gone into the side office with a police officer to check if anyone had broken in there, and Ninang Mae was near the front talking to another officer, but we ran to where Ninang April had fallen to the floor, whispering as she stared at something in front of her. It wasn't until I rounded the last row of machines that blocked her from view that I could hear what she was saying.

She was praying.

And in front of her was that same message, **MIND YOUR BUSI- NESS**, spray-painted right next to Divina's lifeless body.

Chapter Seven

April, I am so sorry. Please let us know if you need anything. The church is here to help you through this senseless tragedy."

We had just finished the nightmare of having to answer the SPPD's questions about who would want Divina dead and why (answer: no freakin' clue since she'd only been in town for two weeks and exclusively spent time with family and family friends) when Ninang April requested that we take her to the church to talk to Father Santiago. She was in no position to drive, and we were in no position to leave her alone, so after I let Adeena and Elena know what had happened and Tita Rosie called Lola Flor and Detective Park to let them know what was going on, we followed the Calendar Crew to St. Genevieve's.

Church may not have been my favorite place, but Father Santiago was one of my favorite people. He radiated warmth and wisdom, and was one of those rare people who really, truly listened. Unlike the rest of us, Ninang April had no other family in Shady Palms. She'd never married, never had kids, and her family was mostly in Canada and the Philippines, so she didn't have the same safety net as the rest of us.

But she had the Calendar Crew and Father Santiago and my family as well. I hoped it would be enough.

We sat with her in the church basement for hours, just keeping her company as members of the church came and went, offering condolences and casseroles in equal measure.

When Ninang April finally said she was tired and wanted to go home, it was Father Santiago who said what I'd avoided bringing up.

"April, I don't think you should be staying in that house alone. You need—"

"I'll be fine."

"I'm not so sure about that. Whoever did this left a message behind, remember? A message that was likely aimed at the three of you."

"What are you trying to say, Father?" Ninang April avoided his eyes, as if she knew what we were going to say and wanted to prolong that painful moment.

Father Santiago glanced at me and his eyes prompted me to say what I'd been thinking ever since we stumbled across Divina's body. "We don't know if Divina was the intended victim, or if she was just in the wrong place at the wrong time." I paused to look each of my godmothers in the face so they could see how serious I was. "Until the police catch Divina's killer, we have to assume that your lives are in danger as well."

"Susmaryosep! Who could possibly want us dead?" Ninang Mae sputtered.

"Honestly, it was probably just bad luck. Divina must've stumbled upon the vandal and they accidentally killed her when trying to flee," Ninang June reasoned.

The two of them went back and forth like this, with Ninang April keeping quiet. Father Santiago also noticed because he asked, "What do you think, April? Do you think there's a possibility that there's someone after you?"

"I don't want to think that. I don't like the idea of our friends and neighbors wanting us dead. And I especially hate the idea of Divina being gone because of some grudge against us." Ninang April took a deep breath, and I could practically see that heavy inhalation stoking the fire in her eyes. "But someone killed my niece. And until we find the person who did it, we are not taking any chances. I refuse to remove any possibilities because I'd rather stick my head in the sand and pretend they're not there."

Ninang Mae puffed up. "We are not pretending anything! I'm just saying, what possible reason could people—"

"We caused Glen Davis's divorce," Ninang April cut in.

"He caused his own divorce. His wife had a right to know what he was doing."

"We got that one kid fired from his job."

"Well, he shouldn't have been stealing from the church collection plate. If you can't trust him with the church's money, you think you could trust him with your business's?"

"We told everyone about that old news anchor's botched nose job. She ended up quitting in humiliation and her plastic surgeon lost his job."

"Anyone with eyes knows she was getting plastic surgery, and poorly at that. We saved a lot of people's money warning them away from that quack. And that woman is much happier now that she's not a news anchor, so—"

"What about—"

"Ay, honestly, April, what's wrong with you? People should be thanking us for what we've done for the community. We haven't done anything wrong," Ninang Mae said, her head held high.

"And maybe that attitude is the problem."

"What does that mean? You always think you know everything but—"

"Tama na!" This surprising outburst came from Ninang June. "Just stop. This is not the time to be fighting."

She threw a hard look at Ninang Mae, who at least had the good grace to look ashamed. Ninang June continued, "April, you know my home is your home. Bernadette works a late shift tonight, so why don't we have her meet us at your place and she can help you pack?"

Ninang April nodded and I could actually feel my jaw unclench from the sudden drop in tension in the room.

"You all haven't eaten yet, right? Why don't you stop by the restaurant for lunch?" Tita Rosie had stayed quiet in the background the whole time (so silent I actually forgot she was there, to be honest) but now that the conflict was over, she rushed in to help the main way she knew how.

"I am pretty hungry—" Ninang Mae started before Ninang April cut her off.

"Maybe later. We have a lot to do and I don't want to be around other people right now."

"Oh, of course. I understand. Lila can drop off some food for you later," Tita Rosie said.

The Calendar Crew left soon after that, leaving me and Tita Rosie with Father Santiago.

"Would you like to join us, Father?" my aunt asked.

"I appreciate the offer, but I've got work to do. Besides, I'd probably just get in the way of your investigation talk."

"What makes you think we're going to investigate?" I asked.

Father Santiago smiled and shook his head. "You say that as if I don't know you by now. Those women are your family. And you've never been one to back down when your family was in need. Besides, I'm not telling you to investigate. In fact, I very much want you to *not* do that. Just look out for your Ninang April, will you? And be careful."

When he put it that way, who was I to say no?

Chapter Eight

I knew that girl was trouble."

Lola Flor had closed the restaurant early and I let the Brew-has know I wouldn't be back that day. Instead, Tita Rosie and I had called the Park brothers to invite them to our house for lunch so we could discuss what had happened.

"Nay, that's a terrible thing to say," Tita Rosie said as she brought dish after dish to the table. As usual, she'd channeled her emotions into cooking, and her anxiety meant she'd prepared enough food for three times the number of people instead of just two (it's a good thing we all liked leftovers since the Park brothers would have enough to make their lunches for the rest of the week). It seemed like she was going for the comfort aspect since the menu leaned heavily on soups and carbs, rather than the protein-focused dishes she usually prepared for the meat loving Park brothers. Shrimp sinigang, nilaga, and lomi were among the soup offerings, along with two pancit dishes, fried rice, and a huge steaming bowl of lugaw with tokwa't baboy on the side. I was particularly happy to see the last offering since there are few things more comforting than savory rice porridge topped with the salty, spicy tofu and pork side dish.

We'd just finished setting the table when Longganisa's barking alerted me that our guests had arrived. Jae had quickly become her second-favorite person (I was her number one favorite, obvs), so as soon as I opened the door, she launched herself at him. Jae dropped down on a knee so he could give her all the belly rubs and attention she desired (and deserved). The two of them were so darn adorable, my heart could barely take it and I tried to not be jealous that my dog got first dibs on Jae's cuddles and kisses. Oh well, not like we could be that cutesy in front of my aunt and grandmother anyway.

After giving Jae a quick hug, I greeted his brother. Jonathan Park was fifteen years older than his little brother and the age gap meant that the Park family often treated Jae like a child despite him being in his thirties. Jonathan had been a detective until a few months ago and still carried himself with that no-nonsense rigidity that made it hard for me to treat him more casually. However, we had become allies over the past year, and he absolutely adored Tita Rosie, who was roughly a decade older than him and deserved a hot age gap romance more than anyone. For her sake, I wanted to get used to treating him more like family.

The brothers greeted my aunt and grandmother and quickly washed their hands before sitting down to eat. The dishes were all passed around to idle chitchat, and it wasn't until everyone's bowls and plates were full that the real discussion started.

"Jonathan, have you heard anything about Divina's case?" Tita Rosie asked while she waited for everyone else to start eating. He might not be a detective anymore, but he still had close ties to the department and could get information we weren't privy to.

Jonathan nodded, his expression grim. "Detective Nowak is on the case. Right now, he's trying to determine if it was accidental man-slaughter or murder."

"What does that matter?" I asked, squeezing a bit of calamansi over my bowl of lugaw. "I mean, isn't that something for the court to decide?"

"Yes, but he wants to narrow down the potential suspects and gauge the threat level for your godmothers. From the evidence at the scene, it looks like she died from a blow to the head after hitting the corner of the folding table."

"If she died after hitting her head on the table, she was probably pushed, right? How can he prove that someone pushed Divina intend-ing to kill her versus, like, a shove in the heat of the moment that went horribly wrong?"

I helped myself to more lomi, needing the healing powers of Asian noodle soup. Once it was in my bowl, though, I couldn't bring myself to eat it. Not while picturing Divina's last moments. I sipped on a cup of ginger tea instead, to try and settle my stomach and mind.

"Are they even sure someone else was involved? Maybe she slipped or had some medical condition and fainted, and she just hap-pened to hit her head when falling down," Jae said.

"Great question," Jonathan said, smiling approvingly at his little brother. "But unless she managed to fling herself at the table, the amount of force needed to cause that kind of blow to the head points at her being pushed."

"Another thing to keep in mind is that the front door was locked when you all arrived. And after an inspection, the police determined that the back entrance was also locked. So how did the killer get in? Was Ms. de los Santos the target? If so, that means she likely knew the killer and let them in. Or is someone trying to send a message to your godmothers?"

"There's also a chance she didn't know her killer. I mean, she was only in town for a couple weeks and didn't really talk to anyone out-side of our circle. But she was young and pretty. Maybe some creep fixated on her and followed her to the laundromat. Forced his way in somehow," I said, thinking out loud with a shiver. "Or she thought the person was a customer and let them in. Anything is possible. Were there any fingerprints at the scene?"

"You're thinking more and more like a detective, Lila." Jonathan fished out a large chunk of beef from the nilaga pot. "Fingerprints, or should I say the lack of them, are yet another reason we're sure there was another person there. The only prints on the front door were from your godmother June, who opened it to let you all in. Divina's weren't there, and there's evidence of someone wiping the door and area around Divina's body. Her keys seem to be missing, too, though there's a possibility they're somewhere in her room. Her purse was still at the scene."

I pulled my abandoned bowl of lomi back toward me. My stomach had finally settled and I knew I needed the nourishment and comfort the soup would provide.

After Jonathan and I had made it through most of our bowls of soup, he continued. "As for your other theories, it's too early to rule any of those possibilities out, but Detective Nowak is doing what he can to narrow the focus of his investigation."

"With you gone, the SPPD is down to just one detective again," Tita Rosie said as she heaped more rice on his plate. "Can Detective Nowak handle it alone? He's still new."

Jonathan contemplated the growing mound of rice on his plate, ei-ther frightened by the amount or weighing how honest to be. "I per-sonally trained him. He's a good detective. But I do worry about the lack of resources he has to work with."

"Then you should help him," Lola Flor said. She tended to stay quiet during these conversations, only speaking up when she wanted to deliver an order. "You know what the rest of the department is like. You were the best they ever had, not counting that time you thought my granddaughter was a murderer and drug dealer. Without you guiding them, who knows what will happen."

Jonathan flushed, but otherwise ignored the allusion to the first case I ever got involved in. "There's not much I can do now that I'm no longer affiliated with them."

"My granddaughter was never affiliated with them and yet she managed to do more than Sheriff Lamb could ever hope to accomplish. I would rather you get involved than have her stick her nose into this."

I was both touched and annoyed that she was worried about me jumping into another murder case. First Father Santiago and now her? "Lola Flor, what makes you so sure I'd get involved again? It's not like I wanted to investigate those last few times."

"So you're going to do what that message said and mind your business? You're going to ignore the fact that a young girl was killed and your ninangs might be in danger and let the police do their jobs for once?" Lola Flor made a noise with her lips. "I don't believe you."

"There's no proof that your godmothers are targets, so there's no reason to get involved." Jae put his hand over mine, stopping me before I could respond to my grandmother. "Please, Lila. Your grandmother is right to worry about you. You've managed to escape the last few times, but there's no guarantee that you'll be safe this time. And I need you to be safe."

He stared into my eyes, as if to make me understand what he was really trying to say. And I did understand. Of course I did. But I wasn't sure if I could say the things I knew he wanted me to say.

Jonathan nodded at his brother. "He's right, Lila. I'll keep an eye on your godmothers and help Detective Nowak in any way I can. You've pulled off some pretty amazing things in the past, but there's no reason to get involved this time. Let the professionals handle it."

I looked over at Tita Rosie, who also seemed to be struggling with this. On the one hand, she wanted to help people. She believed if there was something we could do to improve someone's situation, we should do it. That's why she wholeheartedly supported my previous investigative efforts. But those had all been situations where our family had been suspects and the true killer needed to be caught to clear our names. That wasn't the case here. Yet I couldn't ignore the possibility that the killer would come after my godmothers, who weren't blood, but were family all the same. What should I do?

Finally, Tita Rosie seemed to come to a decision. "Jonathan, you've mentioned before that you have friends that work in security. Could you arrange it so that someone could watch over them? At least when they're at the laundromat or at home? Marcus works nights, so Mae is usually alone at home. April is staying with June, but Bernadette's schedule means they'll be alone many nights, too."

Jonathan smiled at her. "I've got a lot of time on my hands now that I'm no longer on the force. I'll need to find a new job sooner or later, but right now I'd rather help you and your family. I've also got some friends who owe me a favor, so we can work something out."

Jae sighed in relief. "Thanks, Hyung. I'll feel a lot better knowing that someone's looking out for the aunties and that that someone won't be Lila."

I shot him a look. I was happy that my godmothers would be watched over by people who could actually protect them, but there was something incredibly patronizing about having everyone tell me to stay out of it. Even if they were kinda sorta right.

I guess I wasn't so good about minding my own business after all.

Chapter Nine

Later that night, Tita Rosie, Lola Flor, and I stopped by Ninang June's with dinner for everyone. We figured that if they wanted company, we'd stay and eat with them, and if not, we'd be on our way, knowing they had my family's food for comfort.

Bernadette met us at the door. "Thanks for coming over. We've all been too busy to think about food and they definitely need it. Ninang April's in the room she's borrowing from us. She shut herself in there to call Divina's parents as soon as she arrived, and she hasn't come out since."

She glanced around to make sure nobody else was around before leaning toward us. "I heard she got into a fight with Ninang Mae earlier. They've both cooled down, but we thought it best to leave Ninang April alone until she's ready."

We followed her to the dining room and put our trays down. My aunt and grandmother went to the kitchen to find my godmothers, but I stayed behind to set the table with Bernadette.

"Did your mom and Ninang Mae fill you in on everything?" I asked.

"Yep. They feel so awful about everything." Bernadette glanced at Ninang April's closed door and leaned forward. "They didn't really like Divina, you know? But they never wanted anything like this to happen. I'm really worried about them."

"Why?"

"I just, I get the feeling that they're going to overcompensate for the situation out of guilt. Knowing them, they're planning something reckless to catch Divina's killer."

That . . . sounded exactly like them.

"Detective Park promised my aunt he'd provide security at the house and laundromat for the ninangs. Even if they are planning something ridiculous, I doubt it'd go far with people watching them."

"I hope you're right." Bernadette looked thoughtful for a moment, then laughed. "So you're still calling him 'Detective'? It's a hard habit to break, huh?"

"I honestly can't stop thinking of him as anything but a detective. Even if he quit, he still looks, acts, and talks like one. And it feels weird just calling him Jonathan since he's way older than me."

Bernadette grinned. "Why not call him 'Tito Jonathan'? That'd be more correct than calling him 'Detective' anyway."

I threw a lumpia at her. "Don't even start."

Bernadette, her reflexes way quicker than mine, caught the lumpia easily. "Hey, no wasting food!"

As she nibbled on the fried spring roll, Ninang April finally came out of her room. "Where is everyone?"

Hearing her voice, everyone in the kitchen came out and crowded around Ninang April.

"April! Are you OK?"

"Here, drink something. You look faint."

"Are you hungry? I brought your favorites."

My aunt and godmothers hovered protectively around Ninang April, fussing over this and that until my grandmother got annoyed.

"Hoy! She is not a child. She doesn't need you treating her like one. Let her breathe!"

Ninang April smiled gratefully at my grandmother, who nodded at her. "I'm fine. Really. Let's just eat, OK? I don't want to talk about it right now."

Out of respect for her, we kept the conversation light but not forced, instead focusing on our food to avoid any unnecessary chatter. It wasn't until Lola Flor brought out the desserts that the mood shifted. Ninang April had reached for a piece of mamon, but her hand faltered before it reached the chiffon cake, instead dropping to the table as she let out a dry sob.

Ninang Mae and Ninang June awkwardly patted her on the back as she cried, saying empty words of comfort to calm her down.

"Ay April, you need to eat more. Keep up your strength."

"Divina is with God now. She's OK."

"Yes, and you'll be OK, too. Everything will turn out fine, I just know it."

"There was nothing you could've done. Bahala na—"

"Bahala na?" Ninang April threw back her shoulders and shook off my godmothers' hands. "That's how I'm supposed to look at this tragedy? That this was just God's will?"

Ninang Mae and Ninang June glanced at each other, not sure how to react.

"My little sister and her husband trusted me. They trusted me with their daughter. And now she's dead." Ninang April sniffed angrily and wiped at her eyes. "I had to tell them that their only child is gone because of me. So don't act like you understand. And don't you dare act like everything's going to be OK. You're not the one who has to live with this."

She whirled around and fled back to her temporary room, slamming the door shut behind her. In the silence that followed, we could hear her heaving sobs and it was as if her pain leaked through the door and spread throughout the house and into my heart. She was right. We could never understand. But was it right that she blamed herself for this? Even if the killer had been targeting the aunties due to their gossip, the killer was still the one at fault.

Ninang Mae, her eyes trained on the door Ninang April had gone through, said, "Diyos ko! Is there really nothing we can do?"

Lola Flor said, "Keep the laundromat closed this week, out of respect to Divina and April. We'll handle the cleaning while you help her with the arrangements. After that, you need to get back to business. You didn't sink your savings into this only to lose it all now. April understands this. Give her time, but a routine may be what she needs to get through this. She won't appreciate all your hovering and hand-wringing."

As usual, my grandmother's solution was to put your head down and work through it. For people like her and Ninang April, that's how they coped with everything—no time for tears or regrets, there's work to be done. Which I guess was fine sometimes; we all had different ways of processing trauma. But it couldn't be the only way. Sooner or later, they had to deal with the real issue.

Maybe finding out the truth behind Divina's death would hurt Ninang April. But maybe it would be the one thing to bring her peace.

Chapter Ten

I would like to remind everyone that we're having an informal memorial after Mass today for the dear departed Divina de los Santos. Though she was only part of the congregation for a short time, her aunt April Lucero has been a devoted member for many years. If you can, please light a candle and remember their family in your prayers."

Father Santiago finished the Mass after the announcements, and most of the congregation headed to the basement, where refreshments awaited them. Tita Rosie, Lola Flor, and I hung back to light candles for Divina and my parents and drop money in the donation box before joining everyone.

My aunt, grandmother, and various members of their church outreach group had provided food and drinks for Divina's memorial. A large framed portrait of Divina from her college graduation stood on a table in the middle of the room where people could pay respects to both her and Ninang April, who stood next to the photo.

People milled about the room, eating and chatting and laughing as if this were any other church social event and not a remembrance of a young life lost. Divina was new in town and most of these people had never met her, I reminded myself before I could get worked up. These people were all here out of respect to Ninang April, but they were not personally affected by this loss. This level of casualness was to be expected. At least people were being civil. Even Ultima Bolisay was here, though she just dropped a condolence card in front of Divina's portrait without saying a word to Ninang April.

Ninang Mae came next to me, making a *tch* noise when she saw Ultima. "Doesn't even have the decency to speak to your ninang April. Typical."

"It was good of her to even come and pay her respects. Don't—"

"What do you mean, 'don't'? She's not here out of the goodness of her heart. She's here because it would look bad otherwise. Only cares about appearances, that one," Ninang June said as she, Marcus, and Bernadette joined us.

Both Marcus and Bernadette tried to shush their moms. "Even if that's true, there's no need to point that out . . ."

"This is not the time or place for that. Ninang April needs our support, not a fight at her niece's memorial."

The aunties had the good grace to flush and left us to get meryenda for Ninang April, leaving me, Bernadette, and Marcus to shake our heads at them.

"You ever feel like the parent when they get like that?" Bernadette asked Marcus.

"All the time. My mom likes to tell me that I'm just a kid and can't make decisions without her, but it's like, who's the immature one here?" Marcus rolled his eyes and tried to sound exasperated, but as his gaze strayed toward Divina's portrait, his voice came out achingly sad.

Oh. Oh, poor Marcus . . .

I put my hand on his arm. "Hey, I'm so sorry. I know you two were getting close. If you ever need to talk . . ."

He rubbed the back of his hand across his moist eyes. "I'm fine. It's just, it's so hard to believe she's gone. It was so sudden. There was still so much she wanted to do, and we were the same age, and . . . it really makes you think, you know? What could've been?"

Bernadette met my eyes and we both moved to comfort Marcus, linking our arms through his on either side and leaning into him. The three of us stood together silently, enjoying each other's company as we watched the quiet chaos around us.

That bit of calm didn't last long, though—Ultima and my god-mothers were a toxic mix and it seemed like the temporary truce the memorial brought about was already broken.

"How dare you accuse me of that! I am here as a loving member of the church, and you want to slander my name in front of the congregation?" Ultima screamed at my godmothers as a young woman who I recognized as her daughter held her back. That girl we met at the laundromat cleanup was there too, Teresa. She did say she was best friends with Ultima's daughter.

"Nay, stop it, this isn't the place. Just let it go," Ultima's daughter begged. I racked my brain to see what I remembered about her but came up blank. She was a few years younger than me and we had gone to the same Catholic grade school together (I think she was in Marcus's class), but I'd gone on to the town's public high school and she'd remained in the Catholic school system, so there was no real reason for our social circles to intersect, especially with her being on the other side of town.

"Let it go? First they try to interfere with my business, now they want to spread lies that I had something to do with that malditang babae's death? That whole family is shameless. You hear me?" Ultima called out to Ninang April. "Walang hiya!"

Several people gasped and Bernadette swore under her breath, then immediately crossed herself, probably to make up for cussing in church. I couldn't blame her though. Not only had she referred to Divina as a "bad girl" (to put it politely) but "shameless" was one of the top-tier Filipino insults, a term that was only used when gossiping behind someone's back or when starting a fight. Count on Ultima to go for one of the nuclear options, and at a church memorial, no less.

"Marcus, go get Father Santiago. We need to stop this now," I said. The priest's calming presence was the only way to stop this scene before it went too far.

Marcus ran off, returning with Father Santiago in time to see me, Bernadette, and Tita Rosie holding back the Calendar Crew, with Ultima's daughter and her friend holding back the screaming Ultima.

"What's going on? Is this how you behave in a house of worship?" Father Santiago stepped in between the warring factions, a look of disappointment on his kind face. "A young life was lost. People are in mourning. And this is how you want to behave? You all know better than that."

The older women all hung their heads, the censure and distress in Father Santiago's voice enough to bring them back to themselves, and they all apologized profusely.

Father Santiago accepted their apologies but didn't let them off the hook. "I understand that this is a difficult time and tensions are high right now. But you need to set a better example for the young people. It's getting late, so we should all clean up now."

My family and the Bolisays got to work packing up the food, wiping down the tables, and stacking the chairs while the rest of the congregation left with plates full of leftovers. When Ninang April moved to take Divina's portrait, Father Santiago stopped her.

"If you want, you can leave that here for a while. There might be people who'd like to pay their respects that couldn't make it today."

Ninang April smiled at him, tears of gratitude threatening to spill out of her eyes. "Thank you, Father."

Once we finished cleaning, the Bolisays left without saying goodbye, but the daughter and friend had the decency to shoot apologetic looks at Ninang April before following Ultima. My aunt invited everyone over to the restaurant since they needed to open for lunch service soon, but my godmothers begged off, all of them claiming they wanted a nap. They were probably just ashamed of what had happened and didn't want to risk running into anyone from church at the restaurant.

"I have to get back to the cafe," I said. "Ate Bernie, Marcus, you want to come with? You haven't been over since we added our new menu items."

They both agreed, eager to get away from their moms and indulge in some premium Brew-ha Cafe goodness. When I pulled in to the lot in front of the shop, I spied a familiar car and ran into the cafe.

"Jae! You're back!"

He'd been away at a dental conference in Chicago the last few days and wasn't supposed to return until later tonight. I threw myself into my boyfriend's arms and he gave me a tight squeeze and kissed my forehead before pulling away to study me.

"I rearranged some of my appointments and skipped out on the last panels so I could surprise you. I tried to make it back in time to attend the memorial, but there was a breakfast program I couldn't miss. I'm sorry I couldn't be there with you." He glanced toward Bernadette and Marcus, who were grinning at the two of us, and blushed. "Hey, sorry about the PDA. You all just coming back from the memorial?"

I nodded. "The Calendar Crew wanted to rest at home, and we wanted to avoid the crowd that's probably gossiping at Tita Rosie's Kitchen."

"How much drama was there? Any fistfights or life-changing revelations?" Adeena asked after helping the last customer at the counter.

"A bit of a screaming match between the aunties and their laundromat rival, but nothing too exciting."

"That was more than enough, trust me," Marcus muttered as he scanned the pastry cases. "Give me both types of brownies and a mocha. Extra strong and extra sweet."

"Sugar therapy, huh? I got you." Adeena started on his order. "How about the rest of you?"

"I'll prep a dessert platter to share so you all can try everything," I said to my guests, moving behind the counter to fill a tray with sweets. "For drinks, I recommend the sampaguita matcha latte, but the whole seasonal menu is good as long as you like floral flavors."

"I'll take the matcha," Bernadette said, joining Marcus at the table. "I'm trying to reduce my caffeine intake, so don't let me have more than one."

"Oh, if you're looking for a decaf beverage, we're experimenting with this malunggay-strawberry latte," Elena said. "I loved that tea Divina gave us and convinced Adeena to order more, in loose leaf and powder form. We don't have enough decaf drinks on the menu anyway."

Bernadette agreed that sounded perfect, and Elena asked Adeena to make one for her as well.

"And I'll have my usual. Thanks, Adeena." Jae pulled out a seat for me as I approached with our sweets.

I smiled at him, then explained the various desserts on the platter. "I put extra brownies for Marcus since I figured you need them. I didn't realize you were such a chocoholic."

He shrugged. "I'm not, usually. But I'll get these cravings sometimes and nothing else will do."

"Is it stress?" Elena asked, setting our drink orders in front of us.

"Sorry to pry, but that's usually when I crave chocolate. My mom would make a huge vat of hot chocolate or champurrado whenever I had exams and it was the only thing that kept me going."

"Damn, hot chocolate sounds really good right now," Marcus said, breaking a red bean brownie in half and shoving a piece in his mouth.

"I'll put in a special order for you. We switched it out for our seasonal menu, but we should have all the ingredients. My treat." Elena winked at him before patting his shoulder and making her way behind the counter.

"Elena's good people," Marcus said. The tension in his body slowly left him, his shoulders drooping down and face relaxing into a genuine smile. The sadness in his eyes remained, though.

"Of course she's good people, I chose her," Adeena said, dropping into a seat next to him and snagging the last brownie.

"You mean she's good people because she willingly puts up with you," I said. "You're a saint, Elena."

Elena set a cup of Mexican hot chocolate in front of Marcus and another in front of her girlfriend before sitting next to her. "This is true. But it's OK, people like to remind her of that, so I don't have to say anything myself."

"You two are so cute it makes me sick," Bernadette said, rolling her eyes. She took a sip of her malunggay-strawberry latte. "Though if you keep providing stuff like this, I guess it's forgivable."

"We really are adorable, aren't we?" Adeena did a cutesy pose. "If Shady Palms had a cutest couple contest, we'd absolutely crush it."

"I bet Lila and I would give you a bit of competition," Jae said, slinging an arm around my shoulders. He grinned at me. "What do you think?"

Jae, *no.* Do not awaken the beast.

Adeena was the most competitive person I'd ever met in my life— even Bernadette, my lifelong rival and one of the toughest people I knew, was afraid of playing against Adeena. Game nights were banned in our friend group because Adeena took it way too seriously. She'd made people cry on multiple occasions. Just the sight of a pack of Uno cards was enough to make me start hyperventilating.

"Is that a challenge, Jae? Because Mayor Gunderson is always looking for new events to add to the town programming. I'd be happy to let him know there's two couples eager to compete already."

Elena must've noticed the gleam in Adeena's eyes because she quickly changed the subject. "So how are the aunties doing? They must still be shaken up. And what's going to happen with the laundromat?"

Bernadette snagged a cookie from the platter. "Ninang April is staying at our house until they solve the case. The guy in charge seems to think my mom and her friends are the real target and that Divina was just in the wrong place at the wrong time."

"Detective Nowak actually said that? Detective Park told me that was just one of the angles the SPPD would be investigating," I said.

I glanced at Jae, who shrugged. "He never talked to me about his cases, and that still holds true now that he's retired. All I know is that he's helping with security detail for your godmothers."

"As far as I know, they've decided the vandalism and murder are connected. They told my mom she should also move in with the others since I'm working most nights and won't be around to protect her," Marcus said, stirring his hot chocolate. "Divina was only in town for a couple weeks, so they figure there's no reason to think the killer was after her, especially with that message they found next to her."

The image of Divina lying so still next to those vivid red letters flashed in my mind, and my hand unconsciously clenched around the scone I'd just helped myself to. I didn't even realize I'd done it till I felt Jae's fingers around my own, carefully coaxing my fist open and brushing the crumbs away before enclosing my hand in both of his. The warmth was like an anchor, grounding me to reality before I spiraled into nightmarish memories. It also brought me a moment of clarity, and I knew why I'd been feeling so restless.

"If the police are focusing on the Calendar Crew, that means they're ignoring Divina. As the victim, don't you think she deserves their full attention?" I asked.

Jae's hands tightened around mine in response, but he didn't let go. I knew he wouldn't. No matter how much he disapproved of me putting myself in danger with my investigations, he would never abandon me. Maybe it was unfair of me, but I was counting on that loyalty to get me through.

As if to prove me right, Jae took a deep breath and said, "You know how much I worry when you do stuff like this. But I also know how deeply you care about the people involved and the lengths you'd go to help them. That's one of the reasons I . . ." He trailed off. "Anyway, I'll ask Hyung to help you. If you just have questions about Divina, it shouldn't be too dangerous. Still, be careful."

"Do you really think the killer was after Divina?" Marcus had been steadily making his way through all the chocolate offerings on the dessert platter, but he finally raised his eyes to mine to ask that question.

"I'm not sure," I admitted. "The police's theory makes sense, I'm not going to lie. But I still think they're dismissing her too quickly. She at least deserves the dignity of a full investigation."

"You're right, she does." Marcus nodded slowly, and I could practically see the wheels turning in his head. "All right, I'm in. Let me know what you need me to do. I'll help however I can."

Surprising, but not unexpected.

"Be prepared to find out stuff about Divina and maybe even your mom that you'd rather not know." At his nod, I reached in my purse and pulled out my bujo. "Tell me everything you know about Divina and why she was here in Shady Palms."

Chapter Eleven

S he knew I was into her, but she was very up front with me," Marcus said, a sad smile twisting his lips. "Part of the reason she came to Shady Palms is because her last relationship ended badly and she needed to get away. So she wasn't looking for love or anything like that. All she cared about was getting her career on track."

I found that hard to believe, considering the way she looked at Jae and Amir and some of the comments she'd made. But I didn't need to make Marcus feel worse than he already did.

"Was it her decision to come here? I always got the impression that her parents sent her away," I said. "And the way Ninang Mae and Ninang June acted around her, I assumed there was a scandal involved."

"There was definitely a scandal, but my mom doesn't have all the details or she would've told me." Bernadette glanced at Marcus. "All she'd say was that Ninang April came from a very respected, wealthy family, but her niece had disgraced them all and she was being sent to

Ninang April as punishment. I guess Divina's parents figured Ninang April could get her to act right, considering how strict she is."

"You said part of the reason she came here was because of a bad breakup. Do you think that breakup was part of the scandal?" Jae asked Marcus.

"I have no idea. She didn't give me any details and I honestly didn't wanna hear about her ex after she basically rejected me." Marcus sighed. "She liked to act as if nothing bothered her and she had it all together, but I don't know. It was obvious her ex messed her up pretty bad. I wouldn't be surprised if there was some scandal around their relationship."

"Divina did say that she wasn't a nice girl," Adeena said as she cleaned up the empty glasses. "And she came from money. I bet she dated an 'unsuitable' guy as, like, an act of rebellion against her parents. Remember, Lila? When we did the cleanup. She said she was going to tell us about it, but we never got a chance to hang out after that."

"I know. I tried to get her to talk during that shopping trip to Chicago, but other than a brief mention of fake friends, she avoided my questions about her life in the Philippines. And then after that, she seemed busier than ever. She said both of your moms kept her running around so much, she didn't have the energy for a girls' night," I said to Marcus and Bernadette. "Any idea what that was about?"

"Probably just errands for the laundromat," Marcus said. "She hated cleaning and paperwork and learning about the business. Complained about it all the time. That's what my mom said, anyway. But she had an international driver's license, so the aunties probably thought sending her out to shop or whatever was a better use of her time. I'm sure Divina thought so, too. I love them but I can't imagine being stuck with them for eight hours a day, every day."

"I work in the ED and even I couldn't handle that kind of stress," Bernadette said.

"Could you ask your moms what Divina did while she was out? If we could get an idea of how she spent her time here, that might give us some leads. I assumed she was at the laundromat all day, but if she was out and about, she might've gotten to know other people in town."

They both agreed, and there was a brief lull in the conversation as we all finished the last of the snack platter and our drinks.

Bernadette set her mug down and glanced at her watch. "Lila, could you box up some pastries for me to bring home? Actually, make it two boxes. I've been doing a lot of last-minute shift switches the past couple weeks, so I want to drop off some goodies in the break room as thanks to the other nurses."

"Sure. You want an assortment?" At her nod, I said, "I'll add on a box of coffee for free. You all work so hard and have been such a big help in the past. Just make sure to leave some business cards behind, too. We could always use more catering contracts."

While Adeena and I prepared Bernadette's order, Elena was helping Marcus with his purchase. "I've got some calming tea and bath salts that I think would be good for you and your mom. And she loves our hand cream, so I'll give you some samples of the new fragrances I'm working on."

After Bernadette and Marcus completed their purchases and left, Jae stood up and brought the tray of dirty dishes to the counter. "I think it's about time I head out, too. I'm going over to my parents' house for dinner tonight and have some errands to run before that. Can I get two dozen cookies to go? Mom and Hyung both love your cookies and I promised to bring dessert."

"I'll bake them fresh and drop them at your place on my way home. Does your brother have a favorite flavor? I want to thank him for his help watching over the Calendar Crew, so I can make some extra for him. It doesn't have to be on the current menu, either. I need to do a grocery run soon anyway, so if we don't already have the supplies, I can pick them up after you leave."

His eyes lit up. "In that case, his favorite cookies are the peach mango crumble cookies you made at Christmas."

I raised an eyebrow. "Really? His favorite cookies just so happen to be *your* favorite cookies as well?"

"All your cookies are my favorite cookies. And uh, I'm sure we have similar tastes, being brothers and all."

Jae looked at me, his eyes all puppy-dog-like, and I laughed. "I'll choose to believe that. I'll prepare one dozen assorted for your parents and two dozen peach mango crumble for you and your brother."

Jae fist pumped at his victory. "Yes! And you don't have to stop by, I'll come here at closing time to pick them up."

He gave me a quick kiss and left. Soon after, business at the cafe picked up and I was too busy replenishing our stock to go over what I'd learned with Adeena and Elena. I didn't even have time to walk Longganisa, leaving that to Katie, our teenage apprentice. Before I knew it, it was closing time and Jae had returned for his order.

"It all looks great! Sure you don't want to come over? I think we're breaking out the tabletop grill for samgyeopsal tonight."

My stomach growled at the thought of grilled pork belly and banchan, but I already had plans. "You know any other day I'd love to, but Sundays are sangria nights at Sana's."

"How could I forget? You deserve a night to unwind. Have fun, and text me when you get home, OK?"

Once he left, Adeena, Elena, and I got to work closing the cafe for the day. I hadn't hung out with the girls since that welcome dinner at Yuki's restaurant, and even though it was only a couple weeks ago, it felt like an entire lifetime had passed.

The weariness must've shown on my face because Adeena slung an arm around my shoulders and said, "No murder talk tonight unless it's of the fictional variety. Tonight is for drinking, gossip, trashy movies on Lifetime, and more drinking. That's it."

Count on Adeena to know just what I needed. "You're right. Just a chill night drinking with the girls and watching Eric Roberts stalk one of his teenage patients for the millionth time. And maybe just a tiiiny bit of murder talk."

Adeena rolled her eyes but didn't push it, and I decided to count that as a win. Considering the difficult case I had waiting for me after this night of rest, I needed one.

Chapter Twelve

D idn't expect you to lean into the whole spring aesthetic, Sana. I mean, it's not like you need seasonal offerings for a fitness studio, right?" Adeena eyed her glass suspiciously. "This looks like it's going to be good for me. I don't trust it."

Adeena, Elena, Bernadette, Yuki, Izzy, and I had all gathered at Sana's apartment above her fitness studio for our Sangria Sunday hangout. Sana had a few tried-and-true sangria recipes she kept in rotation, but this was the first time she'd served us this particular concoction.

Sana smiled indulgently. "An old client brought me a bottle of Vinho Verde, so I thought I'd try making a green sangria. Perfect for spring, isn't it?"

The pitcher was full of honeydew, green apple, green grapes, lime, basil, and mint. It was light and refreshing, with just the right hint of herbal sweetness. I was in love.

Adeena, the sugar fiend, was less convinced. "I really liked the Moscato version you made last time."

Elena nudged her girlfriend. "Don't be rude. This sangria is delicious and unique. Not everything has to be drowning in sugar."

"I guess the lighter sweetness makes it a better match for the desserts we brought . . ." Adeena grumbled as she set out the cookies, brownies, and longganisa rolls that were our contribution.

"How are your godmothers doing?" Yuki asked as she set her platter of gyoza and vegetable tempura on the table.

"Not great," Bernadette said, reaching around me to snag a longganisa roll. "Tomorrow's the laundromat's belated grand opening. They're worried they're either gonna have no customers because everyone knows a murder took place there, or a bunch of ghouls hanging around trying to interview them or take pictures. Again, because of the murder."

I grimaced. "Yeah, I can see that. But it's a laundromat, right? Those are basically self-service, so it's not like they'll need to deal with customers unless there's a problem."

"Marcus told us they're offering a range of services. Wash and fold, drop-off and pickup, delivery . . . his mom roped him into helping with delivery, so we had to negotiate his hours." Izzy pulled a bottle of lightly chilled Shady Palms Pinot Noir from her tote and added it to the bounty on the table before pouring herself a glass of sangria. "Marcus has been stretched pretty thin lately. Ronnie tried talking to him about it, but Marcus insisted he was fine."

That didn't surprise me. Marcus had had a grudge against Ronnie since he was a little kid after being the victim of one too many of my cousin's pranks. He'd gladly take Ronnie's money, but it's not like he trusted him or anything.

"He'd gotten pretty close to Divina in the short time she was here," I explained. "On top of that, he's worried about his mom. Both her safety and the business. If the laundromat fails, it's not like he makes enough money as a security guard to support the two of them."

Izzy frowned. "His brother's an accountant though, isn't he? He seems stable enough to help them out if they need it."

"Joseph is expecting his first kid soon and his wife plans on being a stay-at-home mom the first few years. Ninang Mae won't think anything of it, but I know Marcus would never be OK with putting that much of a burden on his brother just 'cause he's the oldest." Bernadette refilled her glass. "Luckily, we'll still be OK even if the laundromat fails since my job is stable and my mom has the dry-cleaning service my dad started."

"What about Auntie April? She's all alone here, isn't she?" Adeena asked.

Bernadette shrugged. "She comes from a wealthy family, but my mom said she worked hard to be independent from them. I don't know if they'd be able to help her financially if this fails. I mean, it's usually the other way around, right? Us sending money over there?"

Sana came over to us carrying a dish of freshly baked brie in puff pastry in her oven-mitted hands. "Hey everyone, sorry, this took longer than I thought. It needs a minute to set, so can one of you help me carry the accompaniments?"

Elena followed Sana to the kitchen while the rest of us did our best not to dive into the cheesy goodness before it was ready. Lactose intolerance be damned, there was always room for cheese.

Sana and Elena returned with fresh fruit, little jars of jam, crackers, and other goodies.

"I brought some infused honey too, which should go great with the brie," Elena said. "Spicy red chile, chai spice, and also a plain honey. Let me know what you all think."

"Be careful; when she says spicy, she means spicy," I warned everyone.

Sana's Sangria Sunday began in earnest then, with everyone filling their plates and glasses over and over again as we caught up on each other's lives. This weekly tradition began earlier this year when we realized we kept saying we wanted to hang out together but would never make concrete plans. Sana solved that problem by posting a pic in the group chat of a giant pitcher of sangria followed by a text saying that anyone who was free was welcome to come over to her place with snacks. Somehow, we all managed to make it over almost immediately. I loved having a set date to hang out with my friends because we didn't have to worry about scheduling issues—if you were free, you went to Sana's. If not, you were expected to treat everyone to something extra special the next time. Simple as that.

"Oh, by the way, I think Amir and I have finally decided on a cat to adopt," Sana said, wiping her hands on a napkin and pulling out her phone. "I originally wanted an older cat since I know he's never had a pet before, but he insisted on getting a kitten. He wants the experience of training and raising a cat."

"That sounds like Amir Bhai," Adeena said, rolling her eyes. "I bet you he's read a million books and thinks training and discipline will be fun."

Elena tilted her head. "Isn't the kitten going to be living with you? That means the responsibility of raising the kitten's mostly going to fall onto you."

"Oh, I guess I have another announcement for you all." Sana cleared her throat and grinned at everyone. "Amir's moving in with me!"

Adeena choked on the honey-soaked chunk of brie she'd just shoved in her mouth. "He's what?! He hasn't said anything to me about that!"

"He's just waiting to wrap up the case he's currently on. He plans on talking to your parents about it soon and will hopefully be able to move in next month." Sana's smile faded. "You're not upset, are you?"

"Yes, but not at you! That traitor. He accused me of moving too fast when I told him Elena and I wanted to get our own place, and we've been together way longer!"

"Only by a few months—"

"Are you kidding me? Months are like years in lesbian time! We should already have an apartment full of furniture I built myself and, like, five cats. Now my cishet brother is beating me on both the moving in with a partner and the cat front. How dare."

Elena laughed and grabbed her girlfriend's hand. "It's fine. Amir and Sana both have jobs that make enough money that they can support themselves. The Brew-ha Cafe hasn't even been open for a year yet, so until we become more stable, it doesn't make sense for us to move out of our parents' houses."

"Ugh, I know, it's just—"

"Soon, mi amor. The cafe is going strong and the brewery is growing steadily. My mom's ceramics side hustle is also doing well, so she won't need my help as much. It's just a matter of time."

Ugh, did they really have to be so disgustingly cute? I looked around the table. Yuki was married, so of course she lived with her husband. Things had been rocky between the two of them when I'd first met them, but they'd managed to work through their issues and their family had become even stronger. Izzy and my cousin had lived together for years as besties before finally making the transition to couple last Christmas. And now Sana and Amir were moving in together. I hadn't even slept over at Jae's place yet, instead dragging myself away ridiculously late at night because I refused to lie to my aunt and grandmother about where I was spending the night (I was a grown adult, after all), but I also couldn't bring myself to disregard their rules entirely.

I sat there thinking about how little progress I'd made to get out of this technically-an-adult-but-not-really space I'd been occupying for years when Bernadette's phone started blowing up with text after text.

She groaned. "I might have to head out soon. Ever since the thing with Divina, my mom's been extra overprotective and nosy."

"How's the investigation going?" Izzy asked, helping herself to a longganisa roll and more brie.

I glanced at Adeena, who sighed. "Fine, you're allowed to talk murder if someone asks you about it."

I held back a smile as I responded to Izzy. "Not great. Divina had little contact with anyone outside our circle, so it's nothing but dead ends on her part. And the security camera in the plaza where the laundromat is has been broken for a while, so there's no footage of that night or from the vandalism either."

Bernadette added, "Jonathan's security contacts were able to fix it for free, so that's great for future problems, but not for the current investigation."

"So, um, I've heard a bit of gossip during some of my classes," Sana said. "Seems like people are pretty evenly divided between 'those nosy aunties are finally getting theirs' and 'that girl was an evil temptress.' I wanted to speak up, but then thought better of it in case someone said something useful."

"Thanks for that. I wonder what they meant by evil temptress. Marcus said Divina had just had a bad breakup and wasn't looking for love."

Yuki, Izzy, and Sana all exchanged glances.

"Um, you know I'm not exactly the person to speak about infidelity," Yuki said, shifting uncomfortably, "but I've heard people mention Divina cozying up to at least one married man. And I've seen her flirting with Jae and Amir when I've stopped by the cafe or come here for classes. I'm not saying it means anything, but . . . maybe it does?"

I knew how hard it was for Yuki to say all that. For one, she avoided drama as much as possible, due to some poor decisions she'd made in the past. Decisions that had led to her becoming a suspect in the murder of my ex-boyfriend, a man she'd been having an affair with.

Our friendship had gotten off to a very weird start. Though I guess the same could be said for Sana. And Izzy. And Elena too. Any good friend who wasn't Adeena or Terrence, honestly, and I'd known them since high school. Making friends as an adult was hard.

"I appreciate you telling me this. I'll need to ask Jae if she ever let anything about her past slip. I'm not mad at him," I said, cutting everyone off before they lectured me. "I know he didn't reciprocate it. But I know so little about her, I need whatever scraps of info I can find."

Divina was the key; she had to be. And I knew what my next move was.

Chapter Thirteen

There was just too much I didn't know about Divina. Considering her only connection here was her super strict, religious aunt, something told me that Ninang April knew just as much about the real Divina as I did. So once I got home from Sana's, I did what most people my age would consider Research 101: I scoured Divina's social media.

Her Instagram account was as carefully curated as her appearance, and it gave me insight to her luxurious life back in the Philippines—lavish meals, vacations in resorts across Asia, elegant parties at luxe art galleries . . .

The pictures made Divina's life look amazing, but I didn't envy her (OK, maybe just a tiny bit) since I knew they didn't tell the whole story. She'd done something bad enough for her parents to cut her off and send her to a tiny town on the other side of the world. But what?

I scanned the photos to see if anyone showed up enough to qualify as best friend, boyfriend, girlfriend . . . anyone who could give me insight into Divina's real self. Nobody really jumped out since all of her pictures were group shots of her and the same three women, all students from the same art university Divina attended, according to the captions and hashtags. Not a single solo shot or photo of just her and one other person, which struck me as odd.

I switched over to Facebook to see if I could get a better idea of the people in her life and that's where I finally struck gold: a woman named Clara wrote a long, emotional memorial post on Divina's wall, claiming that Divina was "the most beautiful, passionate, and talented person and the best friend anyone could ever have."

She could've just been a random Facebook friend trying to make herself seem closer to Divina than she really was, but she'd included two photos: one a super cute group picture of four young girls who looked around middle school age, the two in the middle clearly a young Divina and Clara, their arms around each other's shoulders, and a more recent pic that had just the two of them, posing for Divina's first gallery showing according to the caption.

I clicked over to Clara's profile and saw more evidence of her and Divina's long friendship, so I did something even I knew was invasive and borderline creepy: I messaged her asking if she'd be willing to talk to me about Divina. I even sent a friend request, in case she didn't notice the message request since we weren't mutuals. Considering how random the request was, it was unlikely she'd respond anytime soon (if ever), but I caught myself checking my phone constantly. Go figure, the first time Facebook was relevant to me in lord knows how long, it was to help with a murder investigation. Somehow it felt very on brand for me.

It wasn't until closing time the next day that I was rewarded with a response. Apparently Clara wanted to know more about how her best friend died, so she was willing to chat with me. We set up a WhatsApp video chat for seven a.m. my time the next day. Once we'd confirmed our call time, I let out a weird whoop and fist pump.

"Jae is definitely rubbing off on you," Adeena said. She'd just finished closing out the register and cleaning up her area. "What's up? Either Rihanna brought back your favorite lipstick line or there was a break in the case."

I let out a sigh in remembrance of my beloved Fenty Mattemoiselle before saying, "You know not to bring up those lipsticks—it hurts too much. Anyway, I just scheduled a chat with Divina's best friend tomorrow morning at seven. I'm hoping she can tell me why Divina was sent here."

"Make sure you do a video chat so Elena and I can listen in."

"What?"

"What?" Adeena repeated. "If it's at seven, you'll already be here getting the baking done before we open, right? It makes sense to have me and Elena eavesdrop so you don't have to report the conversation later. It's not like you weren't going to tell us everything anyway. And it helps to have more ears listening in to make sure you don't miss anything."

Good point.

I appreciated their presence the next morning since a lack of sleep meant I wasn't exactly firing on all cylinders. My days always started super early due to my baking, so it wasn't the early hour that threw me off. It was me wondering what questions to ask without being insensitive and how honest I should be if she asked about the case.

I needn't have worried. Clara was only too eager to talk about Divina, how they grew up together, and how devastated she was now that she was gone. Clara did not have nearly the presence or refinement that Divina did, and it became clear why when she delved into their childhood.

"I'm the daughter of one of the live-in househelpers. I guess technically I'm househelp too, but Divina didn't treat me that way. And her parents were good enough to pay for my schooling, so we were always together. Until uni, of course." She sighed. "She was so talented. She could've really gone far. If only her parents . . . if they hadn't, maybe she . . ."

Her eyes filled with tears, and she kept starting and stopping her sentences. I hated taking advantage of her like this, but now seemed like the perfect time to pry.

"Sorry if I'm being insensitive, but . . . I noticed that Divina doesn't have any pictures of you on her social media and it didn't look like she ever commented on any of your posts. Did you—"

"It's not her fault. She just needed to look a certain way in public, so we only ever hung out at home." Clara quickly defended her friend. "It didn't used to be like that. Her family was always comfortable, but they didn't become a big deal till we were in middle school. That's when everything changed."

Divina was new money? For some reason I assumed she'd been born into wealth. Though I guess if her family had money but no status until she was in middle school, it'd make sense that she'd not only befriend the househelp's kid, but also hide said friendship once she entered a new social circle. I wondered if she had thought of Clara as a real friend. Maybe she saw Clara as the only person she could be herself around after she had certain expectations placed on her shoulders. Or maybe Divina had changed irreparably and Clara was fooling herself.

I glanced at the clock and saw that I needed to start wrapping up this call. Time to ask the burning question. "Clara, why did Divina come to Shady Palms?"

She wiped at her eyes. "She never told you?"

"I got the impression it was her parents' decision, not hers. But I never got the full story. We were actually planning a special girls' night out where she'd spill all about it, but it never happened."

"Divina was a good girl, OK? I don't want you thinking otherwise. Just because her friends did bad things doesn't mean she did too," Clara said defensively.

"I'm not looking to judge her. I just want to get a better idea of who she was. Maybe it will help with the investigation here. Divina deserves justice."

A spark came to Clara's eyes. "You're right, she does. Well, the thing is, when she started uni, she became part of a really elite group. Divina's family has money, but these girls were the daughters of politicians, entertainers, the CEOs of major corporations . . . those kinds of people. Because of their families, they also had major connections in the art world. Divina was really ambitious. She knew being friends with them would guarantee her a career in the arts. But those girls were not very nice."

The way she said it made it clear "not very nice" was an understatement.

"These girls weren't just part of high society, they were really talented too. That's why they welcomed Divina to the inner circle. They recognized her potential." Clara beamed as she spoke, her pride in having other people acknowledge Divina's talent shining through the phone screen. "They were always surrounded by people, but there were four girls in the main group, so everyone referred to them as the Elite Four. Anyone else who wanted to be part of their clique had to jump through so many hoops to get recognized. Kind of like hazing, I think it's called? Really it was just bullying."

"What did they do?"

"From what Divina said, stealing was the most common order. Makeup or perfume that the girls wanted. Exam answers. Jewelry from their family. I think one time they ordered a guy to steal and destroy the car of one of their ex-boyfriends."

"What was the point of having them do that?"

Clara shrugged. "I have no idea how those people think. Power, maybe? They were really good when it came to mind games and knocking down their competition. If they really didn't like a fellow student, they'd have one of the newbies sabotage their artwork or make up rumors to get them in trouble. Stuff like that."

"What does this have to do with Divina being sent away?"

"Well, one day the bullying went too far. I'm not sure of the details, but one of the girls who wanted to join the group tried to commit suicide. Luckily, she was saved, but when her family asked her why she tried to kill herself, she told them everything the Elite Four had done to her. It became a big scandal because of the people involved, and Divina's name got dragged into it even though she hadn't done any of those things." Clara's face crumpled and I could tell she was fighting back tears. "Everybody turned on her. Her boyfriend broke up with her so his name wouldn't be associated with hers anymore. He made her delete all the photos of them together online and refused to be seen around her. She was blacklisted in the art community here. Her parents sent her away hoping things would die down and she could start over eventually."

"Did Divina tell you what those girls were doing?"

"Once in a while, she'd complain about them going too far with their demands and that she wished they weren't so mean. But she never named any names. I only found out once the news broke and several people came forward."

"Did Divina participate in any of the bullying?"

"Of course not! She wasn't like that. She swore she had nothing to do with it."

Of course she'd say that, but if Clara wanted to remember Divina as a saint, that was her right. "Did she ever say anything about trying to stop them?"

Clara stayed silent for a moment. I took that as an admission of guilt, but then my phone pinged and I saw that she sent me an Instagram link to a profile called xoxoSAIP. The "xoxo" part of the name gave me big *Gossip Girl* vibes, and I wondered if it was a parody account.

"What's this?" I asked.

"Do you promise that you'll find justice for Divina?"

"What? I mean, I'll do my best."

"And do you promise not to drag my name into this?"

"Of course. There's no reason to bring your name into my investigation here."

She sighed in relief. "So, I might have been helping Divina with a secret project. Something that would show people who those girls really were. But I think they found out Divina was the one behind it. That's another reason they blamed her for everything. As punishment."

"And this Instagram is it?" I asked skeptically as I clicked the link. But as I scanned the pictures and captions, I realized why Divina was basically run out of the country. "Oh my gulay, are you serious? You actually *Gossip Girl*ed them?"

Clara winced. "That's exactly what we did."

The "SAIP" in the profile name apparently stood for School of the Art Institute of the Philippines, which, after a quick Google search, I found out was the most prestigious art school in the country and had a history of producing some of the most influential artists in Asia. So when Clara said it was the elite of the elite in the art world, she wasn't exaggerating.

Each photo featured a person (usually just a single person, but sometimes a group) whose face was blurred out but was referred to by their initials in the caption. And the caption would always be something salacious like, "Guess who got caught with drugs AGAIN but had their influential father hush everything up?"

Or "A.R. just aced her Art History exam! I mean, she's sleeping with the professor, but I'm sure that has nothing to do with it. Congrats, A.R.!"

Or "J.M.'s winning art piece looks JUST like her classmate's painting that mysteriously went missing last week. I'm sure it's just a coincidence tho."

And it went on and on like this, with pictures dating back over a year or so.

"Um, Lila?"

I'd been so into the IG that I'd forgotten I was still on a call with Clara. "Oh, sorry! I was just looking for clues in the posts."

"I need to go soon, but you can always message me if you have any questions about the profile or Divina or anything. I want to help."

"Thanks, Clara. You've been a huge help." I was about to hang up when I realized something. "Wait. You don't think this account has anything to do with her death, do you? I mean, all the people here are still in the Philippines, right?"

Clara looked troubled. "I'm not sure. I'm not part of that crowd, remember? I mean, it sounds pretty ridiculous for someone to follow her to another country to kill her. They could've done something while she was here, and it's not like their reputations suffered the way hers did. But from what Divina told me, those girls have tried to ruin people for way less. And they have lots of money and connections. Maybe they know someone over there who did it for them?"

A long shot. An extremely long shot. But not one I could rule out entirely.

We chatted a bit more, then I thanked Clara for her help and apologized if I upset her by contacting her like this.

"Don't worry about it. In fact, I'm glad you did. It's good to know that Divina has someone on her side who cares. I mean, I'm sure her parents care. But I also bet they're just as worried about how this will all reflect on their family name. So please, do what you can for her. And keep me updated, OK?"

I promised her we would and then ended the video call.

"Well, that explains a lot," Adeena said. "Though I don't see how any of that is relevant to what happened here. I mean, you were just humoring her when you said Divina's death could be tied to that IG account, right?" She laughed. "I can't believe she *Gossip Girl*ed them. That's so awesome. Also, I can't believe that group calls themselves the Elite Four. That is absolutely hilarious."

"Why is that hilarious? Seems more pretentious to me."

"Because the Elite Four is a Pokémon thing. They're the top four trainers in their region. How do you not—"

"That's funny, I didn't think of Pokémon, I thought of *Boys Over Flowers*. Like the F4," Elena said.

"Me too!" I may not know much about cartoons and anime, but J-dramas and K-dramas? Elena was speaking my language.

"Pretentious name aside, we may understand the circumstances that brought Divina to Shady Palms, but it's not likely any of that could've led to her murder," Elena said. "Unless . . ."

"No dramatic pauses, you're not Adeena," I said. "Unless what?"

Elena looked uncomfortable. "I'm not saying this to be judgmental, just stating a possibility. But Divina was part of this Mean Girl group. And somebody almost died because of it."

"But she was trying to expose them," I argued.

"But who actually knew that? The account's anonymous, remember? Clara said the group found out, but we don't know when that happened and who actually knows her identity," Elena said. "Yes, she was trying to expose them, but she was also part of the group. Which means she had to go along with what they were doing."

"So what are you trying to say? That the girl who tried to commit suicide or one of the group's other victims followed Divina here to exact their revenge? She wasn't even the main bully. Allegedly. Why come all the way here to kill someone who was just a bystander? Or are we to believe Clara, who thinks that Elite Four group hired an assassin to take her out?" I laughed. "That's all a little far-fetched, don't you think?"

Elena shrugged. "I didn't say it wasn't. But this is Shady Palms. Weirder things have happened."

Chapter Fourteen

A men."
 Lola Flor finished saying grace and gestured for everyone to eat. We were having a dinner at our house with the Calendar Crew, the first we'd had since Divina passed. The trio usually ate with us several times a week, but with the stress of their new business, the pain of Divina's passing, and the threat that continued to linger over them, they'd turned down invitation after invitation until Lola Flor had had enough.

The morning after their grand opening, she and Tita Rosie stopped by the laundromat with breakfast and orders. "We're preparing dinner tonight to celebrate your new business. Be at our house by six. Don't be late."

They knew better than to say no to my grandmother, so the three of them arrived right on time. Tita Rosie had taken care to prepare their favorite dishes, so we got to enjoy pork and chicken adobo with hard-boiled eggs, seafood ginataan, Bicol Express (Ninang April's favorite, a spicy, coconut milk–based stew from her region), and other delicacies that my aunt hadn't cooked in a while. Even Lola Flor had gone all out and prepared silvanas, the frozen cashew meringue and buttercream sandwich cookies. They were a deliciously decadent and time-consuming dessert, and Ninang April's absolute favorite.

We all filled our plates again and again as stilted conversation drifted around us. Usually you couldn't get the aunties to be quiet, but a weird pall lay over the table, like every attempt at a normal conversation was choked off by the sadness and unease blanketing the three women.

Again, Lola Flor had to take the lead when another tepid conversation started and died almost immediately. "How are things at the laundromat? Any problems?"

"So far business is steady. Not the rush we'd hoped for with the Big Spring Clean, but enough that we should be OK as long as this keeps up," Ninang Mae said, ladling more adobo on her plate.

"Any problem customers?"

Ninang Mae's hand stilled in the middle of scooping out the last salty, tangy soy sauce and vinegar–soaked egg before she collected herself enough to say, "Just the usual people you have to deal with in any business. Nothing special."

Lola Flor nudged Tita Rosie, who reluctantly said, "Really? That's not what Jonathan said."

"What did he say?" Ninang Mae set her utensils down with a clatter. "I don't appreciate your boyfriend spying on us, Rosie."

Tita Rosie had been tentative with her earlier statement, but now her head whipped around to glare at her old friend. "Spying? He's been providing security for you all, day and night. And for free, I might add."

I had never seen Tita Rosie so angry. Annoyed? Rarely, but it happened. Upset? Plenty of times. That's what happened when you had a son like my troublemaking cousin Ronnie. Or a niece that frequently got pulled into murder investigations, I guess. But angry? Never. I didn't even think she could feel such a negative emotion, but here she was, face blazing red and fists trembling (she'd actually clenched her fists!) as if holding herself back.

"I hope you don't think we're ungrateful," Ninang June said, jumping in to de-escalate the situation. "I, for one, appreciate being able to focus on my work without having to worry about the threats. I think Mae is just surprised because we didn't know that he'd be reporting to you, that's all. Right, Mae?"

Ninang June nudged her, and Ninang Mae grunted her agreement. "Right. I just don't like the idea of someone talking about us behind our backs. That's all."

I snorted into my plate of Bicol Express and covered it up with a cough when Ninang Mae shot me a dirty look. "Bit into a pepper. It was spicier than I expected. Sorry about that."

Really though, it was hard not to laugh when the Calendar Crew, a group whose lives revolved around talking about people behind their backs, were suddenly all huffy when people were doing it to them. Did they realize the irony? Judging by the stony expressions on their faces, probably not.

As I finished my plate and reached for a silvana, something Ninang June let slip came to me. "Wait a minute. Did you say something about threats? Has there been more vandalism?"

My godmothers held a conversation with their eyes before Ninang April turned to me. "Someone sent us an anonymous letter yesterday. Your detective friend found it in our office when he did a quick sweep after closing. He said it had been slipped under the door."

She pulled her phone out and selected a photo before handing it over to me. I double tapped the photo of a single sheet of white computer paper to enlarge the typed message to a readable size.

Congratulations on your new business!
If you want it to stay open, you better keep
your mouths shut
and mind your business from now on.

"'Keep your mouths shut' . . . about what?" I looked at my god-mothers. "Any idea what this note's referring to?"

They shook their heads.

"I'm guessing Detective Park took the actual letter to the police as evidence?"

They nodded.

"And?"

"Nothing. Just like they have nothing to tell us about the vandal-ism or about Divina's murder. I know these things take time, but it's not like the SPPD is particularly busy," Ninang April said bitterly.

"No suspects, no witnesses, no evidence, and no new updates. So says Detective Nowak. If it weren't for Jonathan and his security friends, we'd be going out of our minds right now, wondering if we're next," Ninang June said.

And that made me think: Was I going about this the wrong way? I assumed the police were in the wrong for not focusing on Divina, de-spite her being the victim. But based on this letter, the ninangs were obviously being targeted. Was I mistaken? Or were Divina's death and the threats against my godmothers two separate issues? That felt like too much of a coincidence, but it's not like murder was totally logical. Plus I already said I wouldn't rule anything out too early. Maybe it was time for me to share what I'd learned about Divina and see if there was a connection I was missing.

Worried that Ninang April would be pissed I went behind her back to learn about her family's scandal, I took a huge bite of a silvana, savoring the contrasting crunchy, chewy, and creamy textures, letting the sweet richness of the buttercream melt in my mouth to give me courage.

"Ninang April, I have something to confess. I was getting frustrated with how the police didn't seem to be paying any attention to Divina, so I did a little digging to see if maybe she was the intended victim or just a victim of circumstance." I paused to gauge her reaction. When it didn't look like she was going to raise a tsinela at me, I continued. "I talked to her best friend on Facebook and she told me why Divina had to come here."

I relayed everything Clara told me. "I get that a girl almost died, but Divina wasn't directly involved. I don't see why her parents took such drastic measures."

"The other girls in her friend group are from powerful families. Much more powerful than mine," Ninang April said. "When the scandal hit the news, the other families had PR teams spin it so that Divina took the brunt of the blame. She had a job lined up, but the company rescinded the offer. She found herself blacklisted from the more reputable companies, too. She begged her friends to help her out, but there was talk of pressing charges for the mental and physical damages that other student suffered, so her friends decided Divina worked best as a scapegoat. Her parents sent her to stay with me to protect her from those backstabbers and take the time to regroup."

Ninang April took a shuddering breath. "They went through all that to keep her safe, only for this to happen."

We all sat in silence after that statement, even Lola Flor looking like she didn't know what to say after such tragic irony.

I nibbled at my silvana, wondering where to steer the conversation next. Ninang Mae reached out to refill her mug with decaf coffee, and the sudden movement reminded me of something I'd been meaning to ask her.

"Ninang Mae, I heard you sent Divina out on a lot of errands in the lead-up to your opening. What did you have her do?"

"It wasn't just me! June had her do things, too," Ninang Mae said, childishly throwing Ninang June under the bus to divert attention away from herself.

"I wasn't accusing you of anything," I said, though her reaction let me know she'd done something worthy of an accusation. "I'm just trying to get a better idea of her life in Shady Palms. I'd assumed that she spent all her time at the laundromat or Ninang April's house since she told me she was too busy to hang out before the opening. But if she was out doing errands most of the time, it makes me wonder if she'd gotten to know anyone else in town. Someone who could give us some insight into what happened to her."

Ninang Mae and Ninang June exchanged an uneasy look. Ninang April caught the guilty expressions on her best friends' and partners' faces.

"What? What is it? You said she was just picking up supplies and dropping off flyers on those trips."

"Well, yes, she was doing those things. But . . ." Ninang Mae trailed off. Out of all the aunties, she was the one quickest to blurt out whatever she was thinking. For her to be so hesitant meant she must've done something so bad, even she felt guilty about it.

"Mae, it's time. We were being selfish keeping this to ourselves," Ninang June said. She looked at me. "There's something we haven't told you all yet. Glen Davis came over to the laundromat about a week before we opened. It seems like the divorce is destroying him, at least financially. He still blames us for the rumor about his affair leaking, so he said that he was going to join forces with Ultima to make sure our business failed."

"OK? What does it have to do with Divina?" I asked.

Here Ninang June dropped her eyes. "Mae and I both noticed that Divina caught his eye. Glen tried to keep up a tough image while yelling at us, but his gaze kept straying over to her. So Mae and I thought..."

"We asked Divina to convince Glen to leave our business alone," Ninang Mae blurted out.

"You what?!" Ninang April and Lola Flor both erupted. Tita Rosie and I were both frozen in our seats, her with her hand in midair as she reached for the coffee pitcher, me with a silvana halfway to my mouth.

"She didn't want to do it at first. Said that she came here to stay out of trouble, and that everything about the situation sounded like nothing but. So we explained that it wasn't like we wanted her to date him or anything. Just . . . talk to him, soften him up a bit. Just until he changed his mind about us, that's all. We didn't think—"

"Yes, clearly you didn't think or you wouldn't have thought it would be OK to sell my niece like that!"

"We didn't sell her! April, please believe us. We would never ask that of anyone, least of all family." Both Ninang Mae and Ninang June looked horrified. "All they did was talk. We told her to stop immediately if it got too uncomfortable."

"And did it reach that point?" I asked. I knew the two of them felt guilty enough, but not only was I on Ninang April's side for this, I could also sense there was something they were still holding back.

Ninang June avoided the question. "That's not all. Glen wasn't the only person we sent Divina to befriend. She also spent time with Ultima's daughter, Nabila, to see if she could convince her mom to stop coming after us."

"You sent her to spy on the woman who's considered us an enemy from the very beginning? You don't know what she's capable of! What if Nabila realized Divina was just using her? Or worse, what if Ultima saw through her? We don't know how low she'd stoop to beat us!"

Ninang April's voice went higher and higher as she yelled at the other two, her face so red I started to worry about her blood pressure. I wished Elena were here to play peacemaker; I wasn't really cut out for that role, but I stepped in to direct the conversation in a more productive way.

"Did you tell the police this?" I asked.

Ninang June bit her lip. "It didn't seem relevant at the time. But we will now. I'll go see Detective Nowak first thing tomorrow."

She squared her shoulders and looked Ninang April in the eye. "April, I'm so sorry we did this behind your back. Divina hated working at the laundromat, but she didn't want to let you down or be a nuisance. So she asked me and Mae if there was something else she could do that would actually help. It seemed like a good idea at the time, but now I see how we betrayed your trust."

Ninang June nudged Ninang Mae, who quickly said, "I'm so sorry, April. Please let us know how we can make this right."

"Don't put the burden of forgiveness on April's shoulders," Lola Flor cut in. "You're the ones who wronged her. You be the ones who figure out how to fix this."

Ninang April smiled gratefully at Lola Flor before standing up. "Lila, can you take me back to the house? I can't stand to look at them right now."

Tita Rosie and Lola Flor nodded at me, so I got up, too. "Sure, Ninang April. Let me just grab Longganisa really quick since she needs to go out soon."

While I got Longganisa ready, Tita Rosie packed some of the leftovers for Ninang April. I dawdled, hoping Ninang Mae and Ninang June would say something to defuse the situation, but they kept their eyes down, their faces flushed red with shame. Well, at least they admitted what they'd done. That honesty was the first step in repairing their relationship.

The drive to Ninang June's house was quiet, the only sound in the car Longganisa's gentle panting as she looked out the window.

When I pulled into Ninang June's driveway, Ninang April finally spoke. "Wait, Lila. We need to talk."

I turned off the car and turned to her. "I'm sorry for going behind your back to talk to Divina's friend like that. I honestly just wanted to help. But I can see how doing that was an invasion of privacy, for both Divina and your family."

"Don't apologize. In fact, I wanted to thank you for taking the initiative. You've done more for me and Divina than the SPPD and my supposed best friends." Ninang April shook her head. "I know this is terrible of me. I shouldn't ask you to put yourself in danger like this after all you've been through. But you're the only one I can count on now."

Anyone could see where she was going with this, but I just said, "What do you need me to do?"

"Can you look into Divina's murder? And ask Jonathan for help? Divina means nothing to the SPPD. I already knew that, but after hearing what Mae and June did . . . I feel like nobody cares about my niece. Nobody is bothering to see her as a person. But I know you're not like that. And neither is Jonathan." Ninang April's eyes bored into me, begging me to help her. "We need to find Divina's killer. If we don't, her soul won't ever find peace. Her parents and I will never know peace. Please."

Sure, I'd been asking questions about Divina and kinda dipping my toe into the investigation already. But I hadn't been planning on taking the full plunge—I'd just wanted to understand Divina better so I could pass along the info to the proper authorities. If I agreed, Jae was going to be so upset with me. He'd already asked me not to get involved, and could I really disregard his concern and drag his brother into this mess?

I couldn't. I shouldn't. But honestly, what else could I say with my godmother looking at me like I was her only hope?

"Of course I will. I'll talk to Detective Park tomorrow. And I promise to do all I can to find justice for Divina. You can count on us."

Ninang April thanked me and left the car. As I watched her enter the house and turn on the lights, I grabbed my phone and composed a message to Jae. Something told me I'd have a lot of groveling to do.

Chapter Fifteen

"Did you actually think these cookies would be enough to make up for what you just said?"

Jae clutched a half-eaten silvana in his hand as he stared at me in disbelief. I'd waited until he'd taken a few bites before informing him that I planned on investigating Divina's murder despite promising him that I wouldn't. Oh, and that I'd hoped his brother would help me, despite not being a detective anymore.

"Not make up for it, exactly, but maybe soften the blow?" I said. "I also brought Longganisa along, if that helps."

I held up my dachshund, this time dressed in a bumblebee costume, hoping the adorableness and butter and sugar would temper his reaction, but that was probably too much to hope for. Jae was a very understanding and not at all demanding boyfriend, but I guess "be cool with his girlfriend's weird murder-solving hobby/calling" was too much to ask for. Jae took Longganisa and settled her on his lap, but he still glared at me in a way that let me know we were not OK.

"I'm sorry. I know you're just looking out for me. I can't even pretend I don't know why you're so upset, and how ridiculous it is to find myself in this situation again. But Jae, if you were there . . . if you knew what's been going on—"

"Then tell me." Jae set down his silvana and took my hand. "I don't like you investigating, but I also don't want you thinking I don't care about something so important to you. Just help me understand why it has to be you."

So I explained everything I'd learned so far: the secret behind why Divina was in Shady Palms, the way Ninang Mae and Ninang June had used her, how the police had made zero progress so far and that the Calendar Crew had been receiving threats . . . All the things, big and small, that had piled up until my frustration and worry pushed me to take action.

He only interrupted me once, when I mentioned Divina and the Elite Four, to say, "The Elite Four? Like in Pokémon?" I gave him a look and he apologized and motioned for me to continue.

By the time I was done laying everything out, Jae had a look of resignation on his face. "She gets me every time, doesn't she, Longganisa?" he said, rubbing her belly. "All right, Lila. I get it. I hate it, but I get it. Can I just make one request? Well, two, actually."

"What is it?"

"One, you will only take this on if my brother promises to help with the investigation."

Before I could protest, a voice cut into our conversation.

"I already promised her aunt that I'd help out, so that's condition number one met. What else do you want from her?" Detective Park stood at the door, carefully taking off his shoes while balancing a takeout tray of food in his arms. "I told Rosie we just ate, but she insisted I bring this. I'll put it in the fridge while you two finish your conversation."

He left the room while Jae mussed up his hair in frustration. "How does he always come in at exactly the right moment? Does he have to be so cool all the time? I need to take back that spare key. That way he has less opportunity to come to the rescue."

I hid a smile—Jae had grown up the geeky little brother to Jonathan's more athletic and dashing personality. According to Jae, he didn't start filling out and coming into his own until his senior year of high school, and the awkwardness of his younger self still came out sometimes.

I nudged the plate of cookies closer to him. "What was the other thing you wanted me to promise?"

"I'm onto you. You can't use sugar to soften me up every time, you know." He picked up a cookie, thereby negating what he'd just said, in my mind. "Anyway, my other request is that you never hide what you're doing from me. No omissions, no 'I know he'll get mad about this, so I'll just tell him about it later'—none of that. I want you to trust me enough to let me know what you're doing, even if you think it'll upset me. *Especially* if you think it'll upset me. Can you promise me that?"

That . . . was so not what I thought he was going to say. I thought he'd make me promise to drop the case at the first sign of danger, or that I wasn't allowed to investigate without him or his brother babysitting me. Maybe even put a restriction on the hours I was allowed to investigate, like I had to stop asking questions once the streetlights came on, as if I was a kid with a curfew (well, I still kinda sorta had a curfew, but that's neither here nor there). But all he wanted me to do was trust him? I was reminded, yet again, of how different he was from my past partners and wondered for the fifty millionth time what I'd done to deserve him.

I smiled at him. "Of course I promise. Just be prepared to be mad at me all the time now."

113

He smiled back. "I'm prepared. Not like it's going to be anything new, right, Longganisa?"

She licked his hand and snuggled her head against him. She always took his side.

"You better remember that, because I don't want you pouting later and acting like you didn't know what you were signing up for," Detective Park said, coming out of the kitchen and settling into a chair across from us. "Was that enough time for you two to work things out?"

Jae and I looked at each other and nodded.

"Good. Now Lila, your aunt said your godmothers told you all about the threatening letters—"

"Wait, letters? As in, plural? They only showed us one."

Detective Park let out a bone-weary sigh, a sound that anyone who'd spent considerable time around the Calendar Crew would be familiar with. A noise that conveyed annoyance and frustration and "wtf, I absolutely cannot believe those three but actually yeah, that tracks" in a simple exhalation.

I'd sent myself the photo of the letter from Ninang April's phone, so I showed it to him.

"This is just the latest one they received. They've gotten one every day since Divina's memorial service. They basically all say the same thing, though."

I took my phone back from him. "That's so weird. Why since her memorial? Why every day? Why a physical letter instead of an email or something?"

"I can't say anything about the timing, but I'm assuming they send physical letters to seem more threatening. There's something about holding an actual piece of paper in your hands, delivered to a place that shows the sender knows how to reach you, that makes the threat feel more real. Plus your godmothers don't check their email. I asked them to log in to their accounts to see if they'd received anything before Divina's memorial and they each had thousands of unread messages." Detective Park shuddered. "How they can stand seeing that notification every day is beyond me."

He seemed like an inbox-zero kind of guy and seeing my godmothers' chaotic email accounts (I mean, they still used sbcglobal.net, for goodness' sake) must've been a shock to his system. He looked like he was in physical pain as he recounted the story.

"Have you or the police learned anything from these letters? Potential suspects, threat level, et cetera?"

"I'm pretty sure it's either the woman who owns that other laundromat chain or the cheating hardware store guy. There's also a chance it's someone taking advantage of their vulnerability after the murder and vandalism to air out previous grievances."

"What do you mean by that?"

"Because of everything that's been going on, we all assume that it's connected to their new business and/or the murder. But there's always a chance that someone who ordinarily would've kept their issues with your godmothers to themselves is now taking this chance to kick them when they're down. Using the already fraught situation to mess with their heads, you know?"

"That's sick," Jae said, and I agreed.

"I'm not saying that's what's happening, but we can't rule it out. Unlike the SPPD, I like to keep an open mind when it comes to my cases instead of shutting down a line of investigation before it even starts."

I took a moment to study him. His tone was matter-of-fact, without a trace of the bitterness I thought he'd feel toward his former place of employment. But there was also something else there, something that I couldn't believe I hadn't noticed before.

"Do you miss it?" I asked.

It'd been a few months since he'd announced his retirement from the force, and even though he seemed happy with his decision, right now I could tell he felt a sense of loss. Being law enforcement was all he'd ever known, and it was hard to ignore how he lit up as we discussed the investigation.

Now it was his turn to study me. "You're just like your aunt, you know that?"

Nobody had ever compared me to Tita Rosie. Not favorably, anyway. She was kind. Selfless. Resilient. While I was—

"You're both thoughtful. You see a lot." He paused, gathering his thoughts. "I don't miss the force. Not exactly. You think you can change the system from the inside, and when you realize you can't . . . I left because I no longer felt the sense of purpose and fulfillment that I used to. And that still holds true. It's just that I don't really know what to do with myself now. I only really know how to do that one thing, you know?" He laughed. "Who knew I'd have to reinvent myself at my age?"

So weird to think he was twenty years older than me, and yet we both had arrived at a similar crossroads. Made him way more relatable. And maybe now it'd be easier for me to call him by his name rather than his old title.

"So, Jonathan," I said, "what should our next steps be? I'm assuming the police already talked to Ultima Bolisay and Glen Davis and came up with nothing?"

"Divina's time of death was somewhere between ten p.m. and midnight. Their spouses both vouched for them, saying they were home at that time, but who knows how reliable those claims are."

"You think their spouses may have lied for them? Glen Davis is getting a divorce, so I don't see why his soon-to-be ex-wife would cover for him."

"She could be holding it over his head as a bargaining chip. Blackmailing him to give her what she wants in the divorce," Jonathan said.

"Also, there's a chance they're not lying, per se," Jae added. "If Ultima or Glen snuck out after their partners fell asleep, it's not like they'd know. Especially if it's a couple on the outs like the Davises."

"Then we can't write them off just yet," I said. I stroked Longganisa's head, playing with the springy antenna on her headpiece while I thought about what this could mean.

"I'll keep an eye on the two of them to see if there's anything suspicious going on. Even if they're not killers, there's a good chance they're the vandals or letter writers," Jonathan said. "And they're potentially the most dangerous suspects, so leave them to me."

Jae looked at me. "What will you do? And do you need my help?"

I was about to brush aside his offer when an idea came to me. "Wait a minute. You own your dental clinic. You're part of the chamber of commerce too, aren't you?"

"Yeah, but I haven't attended a meeting since my first year here. My client list grew rather quickly and I didn't have time to keep up with the meetings. Didn't need to, honestly."

"Everyone there knows me and my godmothers. They're not going to talk freely around us. But you . . . you're fresh meat. And people love you. I bet you could get people who wouldn't bother giving me the time of day to open up to you."

His receptionist, Millie, liked to joke that Jae had missed his calling as a bartender or therapist since people loved telling him intensely personal things shortly after meeting him. Which was strange, considering how many people hated going to the dentist, and it's not like they could chat while he was working on their teeth. I would've assumed it was Millie exaggerating about Jae as always (she absolutely loved him, in a proud motherly way) if I hadn't seen his powers at work for myself. Just the other day, on one of our recent dates at a restaurant in Shelbyville, our server confessed some intensely personal (and honestly, rather graphic) medical issues she'd been facing. Mind you, this was in response to Jae asking, "And how are you doing?" after our server greeted us and introduced herself. She hadn't even handed over the menus yet.

I couldn't believe it'd taken me this long to think of using his powers for an investigation. Not that I was entirely comfortable with getting him involved. It's not like I didn't know how dangerous these cases could get.

"I'll gladly attend a meeting if you think it'd help," Jae said. "But you sure you're OK with it? Beth will probably be there."

Beth Thompson and Jae had had a thing last year, a fact that I tried to ignore since she was such a good customer. And honestly, we weren't together at the time, so it's not like Beth and I had beef or anything.

But still.

"It's fine. Beth knows we're together, and I trust you."

Jae and I must've looked into each other's eyes too long for comfort since Jonathan cleared his throat and stood up. "Well, that's that. I'll keep an eye on our prime suspects, and Jae will gather intel at the next chamber of commerce meeting. Lila, do you have anything planned?"

"I need to sit down with the aunties and ask them to make a list of who'd be angry at them, or the biggest pieces of gossip they'd heard recently, and maybe build a suspect list from there."

"Good idea, but you know they'll probably deny their involvement. The police have already asked them, and they insist it's either Glen Davis or Ultima Bolisay."

"You're handling those two, but Ninang Mae and Ninang June had asked Divina to become friendly with Ultima's daughter, Nabila. I'm going to see if I can find a way to talk to her one-on-one. Maybe have

Tita Rosie arrange something with the church outreach group or lure her to the Brew-ha Cafe somehow. I'll talk to Adeena and Elena to see if they have any other ideas."

"All right then, we all have our assignments. Make sure to check in regularly, and above all, be careful." Jonathan clapped a hand on my shoulder and affectionately messed up Jae's hair before getting up to leave.

I'd wanted to stay at Jae's longer, but my early start (not to mention the crushing pressure Ninang April put on me) had me struggling to keep my eyes open. He insisted I leave with his brother, who'd follow me home in his car to make sure I got there safely.

Too tired to do my usual ten-step skincare routine, I just took off my makeup, changed into my PJ's, and slid under the covers with Longganisa. It'd been a long day, but this was just the beginning. At least I had two powerful allies at my side, and tomorrow morning, I'd talk to two more. I was counting on the craftiness of Adeena and Elena to guide my next steps.

"Sleep tight, Longganisa. We've got a busy day of crime fighting planned for tomorrow."

Chapter Sixteen

"I'm all for luring Nabila to the cafe and pumping her for info, but how do you propose we do that?"

Adeena set our usual drinks in front of me and Elena, then helped herself to a buko pandan mochi Rice Krispie treat. I'd filled them in on everything I'd learned the previous day and how the Park brothers and I had split up the investigative tasks. All that was left was to figure out our side of the investigation.

"I like the idea of printing out discount coupons and distributing them on their side of town. Brings in new business, and since we'll be giving them out to everyone in that area, she won't think we're targeting her," Elena said.

Shady Palms was by no means a large town, but it's not like you could just walk from one side to the other in half an hour. Close to twenty thousand people called Shady Palms home and, like most places, people tended to stick to the areas they were familiar with. Ultima's laundromat chain was scattered throughout the North Side of the town, while Tita Rosie's Kitchen, the Brew-ha Cafe, and just about all the other businesses I frequented were on Shady Palms's South Side.

As such, I wasn't very familiar with the Bolisay family's part of town and I doubted they ever came by ours despite Tita Rosie having the best food in Shady Palms, not to mention being the only Filipino restaurant for miles around. Would a coupon really be enough to entice Nabila to enter (her mother's) enemy territory?

"Maybe we could also raffle off something and make it so that she wins and has to come here to pick it up?" I suggested. "I'm not sure how we could rig it so that she won, though."

"Leave that to me," Elena said. A mysterious smile crept across her face as she added, "It's been a while, but I'm sure my sleight of hand skills are still there. If Adeena prepares the prize box and you print out the coupons, I'll handle the rest."

Just two hours later, Elena returned to the cafe with Nabila Bolisay and her friend Teresa, the one we met when the church outreach group helped clean the laundromat.

I greeted them as Elena led them to me. "Welcome to the Brew-ha Cafe! This is your first time here, right? What brings you by today?"

"They're our grand prize winners! Can you grab the gift box?" Elena turned toward the women trailing after her. "And ladies, make sure you use your coupons while you're here."

Nabila and Teresa lined up at the counter to place their order with Adeena while Elena followed me to my office.

"I managed to catch them at the end of their shifts, so they should have time to spare. Let's make the most of it." Elena bent down to snap a leash on Longganisa, who was napping under my desk. "Time to break out the big guns. Nisa, work your magic and break down their defenses, OK?"

Elena was way more devious than we ever gave her credit for, and I loved it.

She led Longganisa, dressed in a bunny costume, over to the two women, while I brought out the gift box packed with our hand-roasted coffee beans, herbal teas, a branded reusable to-go cup, and a cookie assortment.

I handed the box to Nabila. "Congratulations! I hope you enjoy our Best Of sampler box and become a regular Brew-ha Cafe patron."

They were both sipping on drinks from our signature menu, the Nurse Bernie (a spiced ube latte named after Bernadette) for Nabila and a Brew-ha #1 for Teresa.

"Ooh, you've got good taste," I told Teresa. "That's my signature drink."

"It's so good!" she said. "I totally thought the coffee would overpower the pandan, but they work well together. This is so much better than that crappy chain coffee we usually get, right, Nabila?"

Nabila hesitated. "Um, it's fine, I guess."

Teresa rolled her eyes. "Your mom's not here. You can say what you really think."

"This is why I told you that I didn't want to come! I knew you'd be like this," Nabila hissed. "Anyway, it doesn't take two people to pick up a prize."

"But you were the one who won, so you had to be the one to pick it up. That's how these things work, right?" Teresa said, grinning at me and Elena.

"It's part of the rules, sorry," Elena said. "Besides, if you didn't come, you wouldn't be able to meet our mascot, Longganisa. Nisa, say hi to our guests."

Longganisa, the perfect little pup that she was, trotted over to Nabila and Teresa and posed like she wanted them to pet her. The two women obliged, cooing over her like she was the cutest thing they'd ever seen (which she probably was).

Adeena brought me an iced sampaguita matcha but was too busy behind the counter to sit with us, so it looked like it was up to me and Elena to question these two.

"I'm glad you were able to make it to our cafe. Tita Rosie introduced me and Adeena to Teresa, but we didn't get to talk much. And I've seen you around, of course, Nabila, but since I'm usually with the aunties, I could never find a chance to chat with you."

"You wanted to talk to me?" Nabila asked.

"Well, yeah. I mean, we're around the same age, right? But you went to the Catholic high school and live on the other side of town, so we never hung out."

"You're right. Most of the people I know from high school either moved or got married and have kids. Teresa and I are pretty much the only ones who've stuck it out here."

"Well, I for one would love to get to know you both better. We hold weekly events here and have a flower-arranging workshop planned for later this week, if you're interested."

"Flower arranging? That's an interesting choice for a cafe," Teresa said.

"Elena and her mom grow all our plants and flowers and have connections to some local florists who'll provide the supplies for free in exchange for advertising," I explained. "And our friend's daughter volunteered to teach the class. Naoko did both traditional and origami flower arranging as her talent for the Miss Teen Shady Palms pageant last year, and we thought she'd make a great instructor."

"That does sound pretty fun . . ." Nabila admitted.

"Look at you, actually admitting to something you know your mom would disapprove of," Teresa said, grinning at her friend.

"Not to be rude, but your mom's not going to have a problem with us hanging out, is she? Like, she's not going to come storming into the cafe and demand I stay away from you?" I made a big show of backing my chair away from Nabila.

"OK, I know my mom can be a lot, but this isn't *Romeo and Juliet*. Just because she doesn't like your godmothers doesn't mean she's going to boycott your coffee shop or challenge you to a duel."

"To be fair, Nabila, she absolutely would if she thought she could get away with it," Teresa said. "I love Tita Ultima, but you know how she is."

"It's not like that! She's only acting ridiculous because she'd had her eye on that property for years and Lila's godmothers stole it out from under her!"

"What?" Both Elena and I leaned toward Nabila.

"My mom's been wanting to expand her reach to the South Side for a while now," Nabila explained, subtly shifting to move away from us. "The property your godmothers bought is in the perfect location, but the owner refused to sell to her for years. And then suddenly your godmothers, who have no experience in our line of work, managed to buy the property. That doesn't seem suspect to you? Your godmothers must've done something underhanded to steal that property from my mom."

"It's not stealing if it was never hers," I said.

"Try telling my mom that."

"Well, whatever transpired is between the aunties and your mom. It has nothing to do with us, right?" Elena asked.

Nabila hesitated, but then Longganisa sat on Nabila's foot and looked up at her as if to say, *You sure you don't want to be our friend?*

Even if you weren't a dog person (do those exist?), there was no way you could resist that look.

Nabila reached down to scratch Longganisa under the chin. "I guess it wouldn't hurt to stop by once in a while. You know, to see Longganisa."

I smiled. "Longganisa and I appreciate that. Our pastry stock is getting low, so I need to get back to the kitchen. Congrats again on winning the prize pack."

Adeena followed me to the kitchen. "I heard your whole conversation and you didn't mention Divina once. Wasn't the whole point of getting them here to ask about her?"

I washed my hands and put on my apron. "Too soon. Don't you think they'd be suspicious if I start firing off questions about a dead girl the first time we talked?"

"Fair enough."

"I'm leaving it up to Elena and Longganisa to convince them to return soon. Once we get more familiar with each other, then I'll ask them about her."

"Elena and Longganisa really are the Brew-ha Cafe's secret weapons, huh?" Adeena asked.

"I honestly don't know how we'd make it without them."

Chapter Seventeen

The threatening letters continued coming every day, which made me wonder if the sender actually planned on making a move against the Calendar Crew. There was one instance where we thought the vandal had struck again, but it just turned out a kid got mad at the vending machine for eating their dollar, so they kicked the glass and accidentally broke it. However, with the threats not stopping and little progress happening in the investigation, my godmothers grew jumpier and jumpier each day. I couldn't stand seeing their mental health deteriorate like this, so I knew I had to do more.

Since their physical safety was in the hands of Jonathan and his friends, I decided to start driving past the laundromat at night to see if the vandal would strike again. The Calendar Crew had originally planned on having the laundromat open twenty-four hours for convenience, but Jonathan had convinced them to shelve that idea until the killer was caught. They closed every night at nine p.m., so my plan was to drive around the area shortly after closing time. Nothing too dangerous since I could just call it in if I saw something suspicious, but it still made me feel like I was doing something.

After I told Jae about my planned patrols, he gave me one hell of a lecture and it was decided that he would drive and I'd provide the road snacks each night. Great deal on my part since I hated driving but loved feeding people and spending time with him. Win-win for me, but I felt bad that instead of relaxing after a long day's work, he felt the need to babysit me, and I told him as much.

"Babysit you? Am I really that patronizing?" Jae's face fell. "I just don't want you to be alone in a potentially dangerous situation. If Adeena and Elena were with you, I wouldn't mind, but . . ."

"But what?"

"I don't know . . . I just thought it'd be cute. Like we're on a mission together or something." He blushed and swept his hair back with one hand so he didn't have to look at me. "We don't spend enough time together, so I thought this would be the perfect opportunity for late-night hangouts."

Oh. My. Gulay. Why was my boyfriend the absolute cutest?

And he was right, with the two of us owning our own businesses and me helping my family out all the time, it wasn't often that the two of us got quality time together. And since I lived at home with my old-school aunt and grandmother, it's not like I was allowed to sleep over at Jae's place. Add my random bouts of amateur sleuthing and I was amazed he hadn't left me for someone whose life wasn't absolutely bananapants. But instead of complaining about it (too much), he found other ways for us to be together. He wasn't perfect by any means, but considering my absolutely atrocious past relationship choices, I should be careful not to take him for granted.

After one of our nighttime cruises, we both decided that the sweets I'd packed weren't enough and I offered to treat him to a midnight snack at Stan's Diner. They weren't a twenty-four-hour joint, but they came pretty close, closing at two a.m. and opening at six a.m. six days a week.

Stan Kosta and his wife, Martha, provided the best food and experience you could ask for at a greasy spoon. They served honest, earnest food, and Jac, whose palate was a little less adventurous than mine, absolutely loved it there.

Stan and Martha greeted us like old friends and their server showed us to our favorite booth. We'd been there so many times we didn't need to look at the menu and immediately put in an order of Greek meatballs to share.

"We'll also split Martha's dessert of the day. I can't wait to see what it is."

Stan's Diner boasted one of the most impressive dessert cases I'd ever seen, lined with all-American classic cakes and pies as well as a few Greek delicacies Martha had learned from Stan's family. But she also had a daily special in rotation, usually to make use of seasonal or excess ingredients.

"That would be the strawberry rhubarb pie. Let me know when you're ready and I'll have Martha bring you over a nice, big slice." The server, a woman named Doris who was long past retirement age, winked at Jae and left to go put in our order.

"So that's why you love coming here, huh? You stepping out on me with Doris?" I teased, watching him turn red.

He'd been a bit of a late bloomer and could sometimes be oblivious to the effect he had on others around him, but even he knew how popular he was with older women.

"It's not like that. She just gives me extra-large helpings and will sometimes throw in a freebie, that's all . . ."

Sure enough, Doris soon returned with our order plus a large basket of French fries. "The meatballs come with bread, but I know how much you like fries, Lila. On the house for you and Mr. Handsome here." She smiled warmly at us and left so we could enjoy our meal.

"You're right, I could totally get used to that kind of service," I said, tearing off a bit of pita to scoop up a meatball and tzatziki sauce. "Ooh, he used lamb today! I bet this is his spring version."

I helped myself to some fries, which were not only fresh and crisp, but absolutely delicious dipped in the garlic sauce that accompanied the keftedes.

The meal passed quickly with long periods of silent eating punctuated by random bits of comfortable chitchat. Soon after Doris cleared our empty plates, Martha and Stan came to the table with plates of dessert.

"Mind if we join you?"

Stan slid next to Jae after we told them we'd love their company, and Martha set two dishes at each place. "Strawberry rhubarb pie was today's special, but there was a tiny bit of bougatsa left and I thought you'd enjoy it."

The crisp phyllo filled with custard and topped with cinnamon and powdered sugar was delicious and comforting, and I quickly abandoned my pie to focus on the bougatsa.

"Martha, this is amazing! Thanks so much. It's been a long day, so the extra sugar is much appreciated."

Martha laughed. "You sound like Adeena. Make sure to let her know that my Chocolate Overload cake is the special for tomorrow. I know it's one of her favorites."

I promised her I would, and made a note to myself to stop by the next day as well since I also loved that cake.

"How are your godmothers doing? We dropped off a casserole for April but haven't had a chance to chat with them," Stan said, gesturing at Doris, who poured us all some decaf coffee.

I doctored my coffee with a large glug of heavy cream. Sadly, the coffee was as atrocious as ever, and I wondered how to politely suggest becoming their coffee supplier. "Ninang Mae and Ninang June have rallied a bit and the laundromat seems to be doing OK, but I'm worried about Ninang April. She's still mourning her niece and has to deal with new business stress and all these ugly threats and vandalism . . . it's a lot."

"And I'm sure those vultures at the chamber of commerce aren't helping. Or those gossips at the church," Stan said, shaking his head in disgust.

Considering my godmothers usually were those gossips at the church, my sympathy only went so far. He was right though, there were people who seemed to delight in my godmothers' latest string of problems, even those who'd previously been friendly with them. Love how quick people are to turn on you in this town.

"Have you heard anything particularly interesting? Not, like, for gossip's sake, but to help narrow down motives and potential suspects," I assured him. "It's been a couple weeks and there's still no progress on either the vandalism or murder. I know these things take time, but it's making me anxious that my godmothers are still getting threats and there's been no real updates."

Stan studied me for a moment before shoving his untouched plate of bougatsa my way. I dug into the crispy creamy delight while Stan and Martha gathered their thoughts.

"I'm not one to speak ill of the dead, particularly since I never met the poor girl," Martha said, her eyes down as she picked at her pie, "but I heard she and Glen Davis were rather . . . close. He and his wife were talking about reconciling, then suddenly he was up to his old tricks. Or so it seems. I'm not sure what that girl's side of the story is. Not that she can tell us now."

Jae and I exchanged looks. Guess what Yuki had told us and Ninang Mae and Ninang June confirmed had already spread this far.

I'm surprised nobody else had told Jae about it—sometimes his receptionist or an older patient would share some hot goss with him, but I guess not in this case. That's not to say they didn't know anything. Maybe Jae could also use his powers to get the aunties at his clinic to gather info for him about my godmothers.

It's so weird; I was used to the Calendar Crew being the fount of knowledge about everyone in this town. But since this case was about them, I had to find other sources. It made me a little uncomfortable, like I was going behind their backs, but this was a necessary part of any investigation. I was trying to help them, not find ammunition against them.

"Did you ever see Divina and Glen Davis together? Do you know if she just talked to him at his store, or if they spent time together elsewhere?"

Martha's forehead wrinkled as she considered my questions. "I don't know if they were dating, if that's what you're asking. From what I've heard, she'd go to his store almost every day, claiming to need supplies for the laundromat or to fix something around the house or for a new art project. That's how Mrs. Davis found out about their friendship. She'd stopped by the shop to surprise him with lunch and found them being particularly chatty."

"She was finally ready to forgive him and he blows it over a girl who could almost be his daughter." Stan snorted. "It's all well and good to be forgiving, but I wonder how many times you can put up with the same humiliation before you move from 'forgiving' to 'foolish.'"

"Love isn't logical. You know that, dear," Martha said, admonishing him. "And it's not right for us to comment on their marriage like this. Nobody knows what it's really like behind closed doors."

Jae had been quietly making his way through his strawberry rhubarb pie (he'd also slid his bougatsa toward me when he saw how much I was enjoying it), but Martha's observation seemed to stir something in him. "When Mr. Davis's initial affair was revealed, he seemed to blame Lila's godmothers for it rather than admit he was the problem. If he got in trouble again because his wife saw him with Divina, do you think he blamed Divina for it?"

"Wouldn't be surprised if he did. He told everyone that his previous mistress was a Jezebel, and he never would've cheated if she hadn't tricked him." Stan rolled his eyes. "I don't believe in breaking your marriage vows, but people make mistakes. It happens, right? But you've got to take responsibility for those mistakes, and he's the type to push it on everyone else."

"What happened to his mistress? I thought Glen was leaving his wife for her."

"Oh, that reminds me!" Martha said. "Glen supposedly tossed his mistress aside to try and woo that girl, Divina. I was at the Honeybee Salon getting a perm, and that woman was crying about it to anyone who would listen."

"Was she one of the stylists?" I asked

"No, she was there getting a pedicure. I don't know her name, but I'm sure if you ask about her there, the staff will remember her." She took a sip of coffee and shook her head. "She carried on for quite some time—it was rather shameful, honestly. I hope she tipped her nail person well after subjecting her to that."

I thanked Martha for the information, and we ended the meal with idle chitchat and empty plates and Doris brought the check. While waiting for her to bring my card back, I started planning my next move. I finally had new, actionable information. If Glen Davis's former mistress blamed Divina for her affair ending, she might've retaliated against her. So I needed to go to the salon and find out who the mistress was and how to find her.

The Honeybee Salon was owned by my teenage apprentice, Katie

Pang (long story), and it wouldn't be the first time I'd gone there as
part of an investigation. I'd text Adeena and Elena later to see if they
could come with me to the salon—not only would going with other
people draw less attention to our nosiness and make it easier to gather
information, but it had also been a while since the three of us had
pampered ourselves. A spa day was just what we needed.

Or at least that's what I thought, until Jae said, "Hey, could I come
with you to the salon? I know you plan on going there for the investigation."

I stared at him. "You want to come with me to the salon? Why?"

"I like investigating with you. Besides, I haven't had a pedicure
since I lived in Chicago and I miss it."

"You used to get pedicures?"

"Yeah. I played basketball a lot and it made my feet kinda gross, so
my friend would take me with him when he got pedicures." He
shrugged. "It's relaxing and good hygiene to take care of your feet.
You're not going to get weird about it, are you?"

Doris had arrived during this exchange and stood next to me,
squirming awkwardly, so I asked her, "Are you OK, Doris? It looks
like you have something to say."

"What? Oh, don't mind me, dear. My hosiery is bunching, that's
all." She handed my card back. "Always good to see you two. Come
back soon, you hear?"

Jae and I made our way back to the car, and once I buckled in, I
turned to him. "All right, my fellow crime fighter. Let's go get our
nails did."

Chapter Eighteen

E xcuse me? Can you show me how to use the massage chair?"
Jac and I had arrived a little early to our appointment at the salon. Not so early that we inconvenienced them, just enough that they'd seat us and leave us alone to settle in and do a bit of eavesdropping before our pedicures. Jac was even more excited at the thought of getting a pedicure than I'd expected, wanting to get the full experience by settling into his massage chair and accepting the mimosa one of the assistants offered him.

The assistant blushed and showed him the controls for the chair and got to work filling the foot baths with hot water for the both of us. After she left, Jae and I soaked our tired feet in the deliciously hot water while sipping our mimosas and surveying our surroundings.

The nail section of the salon was near the front, with the haircut and styling area taking up the main part of the shop and a small waxing room at the back. The salon was configured in a way that managed to feel both spacious and cozy, so the massage chair I was sitting on offered the perfect vantage point for people-watching. The salon buzzed with energy as the stylists snipped and styled and chatted with their clientele.

I caught snatches of conversation, but nothing particularly interesting. Guess I'd have to rely on having a chatty nail technician, something I usually dreaded. Adeena excelled at the small talk that powered these kinds of interactions, but I'd never been particularly good at it. My favorite salon in Chicago played nature documentaries on a loop and the nail technicians mostly chatted amongst themselves if they sensed the client didn't want to talk. Instead of forced conversation with a stranger that got weirdly personal in the first five minutes, I could get lost in learning more about the animals in Patagonia or fun facts about capybaras (Did you know an adult capybara can weigh as much as an adult human and that they eat their own poop because of digestion issues? Gross but fascinating.).

Luckily, my boyfriend had mastered the art of mundane conversation, and when our nail technicians approached us, Jae took the lead. While I sorted through the nail polish selection (I'd forgotten to choose my color before sitting down, so my nail technician kindly offered me a ring of nail polish samples to browse through), Jae said, "It's been so long since I've had a pedicure! I used to get them every two weeks back in college, but I haven't been since I moved to Shady Palms."

"I love a man who takes care of himself," his nail technician said, gazing at Jae adoringly as she laid out her tools. "It's amazing to me how many men don't take care of their feet. Then they have all these issues once they get older."

"Do you get a lot of men here? The place I went to gets plenty of older guys as clients since the owner, this guy named Jimmy, was known as a wizard when it came to curing fungus and other foot hygiene problems."

Jae's nail technician (whose name was Jenny, according to her name tag) smiled. "I trained at a place like that, which is why pedicures and foot treatments are my specialty. Anyway, we don't get a lot of men here, which is a shame."

"There's that one guy who used to come with Clarissa all the time," my nail technician said. Jenny was the only one wearing a name tag (possibly since she was the head nail technician, according to said name tag), and I hadn't been paying attention when she introduced herself, so I didn't know her name. "I haven't seen him in a while, though."

"You didn't hear what happened?" Jenny asked. "Oh right, you were out last week. Clarissa came in here screaming and crying that some young harlot stole her man."

My nail technician snorted as she finished clipping my nails and got to work buffing them. "Wasn't that guy married? The irony of calling another woman a harlot."

Jenny grabbed a tool that looked like a cheese grater and got to work on Jae. "Tell me about it. She made a huge scene, and we had to apologize to all the clients who were there that day. We even sent them home with free samples to make up for it."

"That sounds tough," Jae said sympathetically. "It's nice to hear that you all care for your clients and their comfort, though. And I'm sure that woman is probably embarrassed about her outburst."

"I sure hope so," Jenny muttered. "We can't be dealing with outbursts like that every other Tuesday. We've had clients like that in the past, but they were people who only dropped in occasionally. This woman is one of my best clients and I don't want to have an awkward conversation with her about shop etiquette, but I will if it happens again." She worked for a while in silence before sighing. "Her beau was such a great tipper, too. I'm sure he was just trying to show off in front of her, but I wasn't going to complain."

"He was married but would still come to a busy salon with his girl-friend?" I asked. "That was rather bold of him."

"Tuesdays are our slowest day, so I guess he thought he was being slick. Slow doesn't mean empty, after all, so of course his wife found out."

"Are you talking about Glen?" An older white woman was getting into the chair next to Jae, assisted by another nail technician. "That pompous ass. Erica Davis is a saint for putting up with him all these years and I hope she takes him for everything he's got in the divorce."

"So, he's still married, had a girlfriend, and then left that girlfriend for another girlfriend? Am I getting that right?" I asked. I had to be careful to keep my voice at the right tone—I couldn't show how eager I was for information without rousing suspicion, so I went for curious with a touch of disdain.

Apparently that was the right move, since the new woman leaned over Jae to look at me and said, "I know, right? Glen's not even that good-looking. But he has just enough money and charm to woo young women."

Jenny snorted. "Young is right. According to Clarissa, the one he left her for is young enough to be his daughter."

"That poor girl," the new woman added.

"You know who the new girlfriend is?" my nail technician asked.

"I told you, Clarissa was screaming about it on her last visit. Though considering the circumstances, I wonder if Glen went back to Clarissa after all this . . ."

"He broke up with the new girl already?"

Jenny gave her an odd look. "Glen's new girlfriend was that girl who died a couple weeks ago."

My nail technician gasped and her hand slipped, leaving a glittery black nail polish smudge across my big toe. "No way! That was her?"

The older woman leaned over toward us again. "Rumor has it, Glen killed her because she found out some sort of secret about him."

"Really? The clients who were here when Clarissa had her breakdown think she might've been involved, too. Trying to get her man back, you know? Maybe she convinced Glen to do it?" Jenny said.

"Have you told the cops your suspicions?" I asked as my nail technician worked on repairing her mistake.

Jae's eyes widened and he subtly shook his head, but his warning came too late. The women all stopped talking at once and slowly turned to look at me.

"There's nothing to tell."

"We're just talking, it doesn't mean anything."

"Clarissa's a sweetheart, she wouldn't hurt a fly." Jenny eyed me suspiciously. "You better not run your mouth off to the cops or the papers or anything."

"Oh, no, I didn't mean it like that. I just, if you seriously think they had something to do with it—" I stammered before Jae swooped in.

"Sorry!" he said with a laugh. "My girlfriend listens to a ton of true crime podcasts, so she can take things too seriously sometimes. She didn't realize you all were just having fun." Jae grinned at the women, a real *aw shucks, ain't she cute?* kind of a smile.

Pretty sure every person within a twenty-foot radius swooned at that smile. Heck, it almost worked on me, and I was in on the whole plan. I mentally kicked myself again for not utilizing him better in previous investigations, but I wouldn't make that mistake again.

"Ohmigod, I love those podcasts too!" the older woman said. "Which one's your fave? I love . . ." and the chatter picked back up again.

Once our pedicures were done and we'd gotten as much information as possible from the people around us, as well as a list of podcasts and documentaries I absolutely *had* to watch, Jae paid (I covered the tip) and we headed back to the cafe. Once we got there, we told Adeena and Elena everything we'd learned.

"What's our next step, Chief?" Adeena asked.

"Jenny mentioned Clarissa comes in every other Tuesday to get her nails done, so do you know what that means?"

"Elena and I get to pamper ourselves next Tuesday?"

"Exactly. It wouldn't make sense for Jae and I to show up again so soon, plus you two deserve a break. Ask Joseph if you can expense it to the cafe's account. Tell him it's a team-building exercise or something. Maybe bring some coupons with you. That makes it official, right?"

We chatted about what we'd learned and what we hoped to learn the next day, the tension melting away from my body, the comfort of my loved ones coming together to help me and my family a more potent stress reliever than the best pedicure.

With them by my side, it was finally all coming together.

Chapter Nineteen

A aaaahhh! Lila, we need your help!"
A loud crash followed by Adeena's scream had me running out from the kitchen, where I'd been preparing the treats for our afternoon rush. An overturned shelf, several smashed gardening pots, and a bunch of dirt and fresh herbs littered the front of the cafe that was Elena's domain.

I beelined over to the crying kid and frantic woman standing in the middle of the mess.

"Is anyone hurt?" I asked, looking over the pair.

"We're fine. Just a little shaken up," the woman said. "I'm so sorry, this is all my fault. I was too busy chatting and wasn't watching him."

"I'm just glad you're both OK. What happened? I want to make sure there are no safety hazards here."

"I'm not sure, my back was to him," she started to explain when Elena joined us.

"These shelves are designed to be pulled out to make it easier to change the layout. The kid accidentally pulled a shelf all the way out, so everything on it fell off."

"I wanted to climb to the top," the kid said, starting to hiccup now that his tears had stopped. "I didn't mean to break it. I'm so sorry, miss."

"What have we told you about climbing?" the woman said sharply. "It's too dangerous! You could've hurt yourself. Or someone else if those pots had fallen on them."

"I'm sorry!" the kid wailed, bursting into tears again.

The woman sighed. "We'll pay for everything. We're really sorry about all this."

Elena bent down so she was eye level with the kid. "Do you promise not to climb onto things you shouldn't anymore?"

She held out her pinky to the kid, who hooked his pinky around hers. "I promise."

"Then everything is fine," she said. "I'll clean this up. Lila, could you grab some gardening pots and a bag of soil from your office? I can repot the herbs, but we should rethink this shelf design."

Adeena appeared and handed Elena the cleaning supplies. "I'll make a list of things we'll need from the hardware store to fix this. We can grab everything after work."

The hardware store? Jonathan had warned me not to go after Glen Davis since he could be dangerous, but after the chatter at the beauty salon the other day, I had to admit I was curious about the man. There was nothing wrong with me going to a suspect's workplace on a legitimate shopping trip, right? In broad daylight, I might add.

"If you don't mind me running a few more errands, I can pick up whatever you two need from the store once I'm done baking."

They agreed, so after I got Elena the replacement pots and finished up my afternoon chores, I was on my way to Davis's Ace Hardware.

• • •

Adeena and Elena had decided to build new shelving from scratch using Elena's uncle's workshop later in the week, but we figured it would be good to keep a toolbox around the cafe for basic repairs. I wasn't the handiest person around—my cousin Ronnie had been in charge of maintenance when he lived with us, and after he left, we usually got one of Ninang Mae's sons to help out—but Adeena and Elena were artistic and loved working with their hands. I figured my lack of knowledge around tools would be useful in my reconnaissance mission since I would naturally need help and could ask questions.

I lucked out that Glen Davis was on the floor when I arrived. I didn't want to head straight for him and make him suspicious, so I wandered up and down the aisles until I came to the toolbox section. As I picked up various models and pretended to inspect them, I studied Glen out of the corner of my eye.

The woman from the nail salon claimed he had charm and money but wasn't particularly good-looking, and she was right. Glen Davis was nothing special, but he had that bland handsomeness of a small-town Hallmark movie hero. Maybe somewhere in his forties, average height, broad-shouldered, and still strong, considering he took it upon himself to carry customers' heavy purchases to their cars despite having plenty of younger employees who could do it. But when he thought no one was looking, I saw him rubbing his back and groaning, heard his knees crack when he bent down to pick something off the ground. And I knew exactly how I wanted to play this.

"Excuse me? Can you recommend a good basic tool kit?" I waved Glen down and did my best to exude sheepish helplessness. "I need to fix a shelf at my cafe, but I don't have any tools."

"Don't worry, little lady, we've got everything you need right here."

Glen swaggered over and looked at the selection before picking up a pastel pink toolbox.

I wasn't sure what annoyed me more—the idea of "gendered" tool-boxes, as if different genders required different tools for maintenance, or the fact that a person couldn't just happen to like (or dislike) pink without having to deal with the internalized misogyny of it. *Wait, that's not why you're here, Lila. Focus! You just need a tool set that works and gets the man talking.* I smoothed out the expression on my face and smiled at him as I reached out to inspect the kit.

Glen was definitely not someone who twisted himself up over gender politics, considering he handed it over and said, "Cute, huh? It's new and very popular with all you DIY women. Got them a couple weeks ago when a customer asked for something more 'aesthetically pleasing.' She was the artsy type and—"

"And what, Glen?" an icy voice behind us asked.

We both turned around and a woman who could only be Glen's soon-to-be ex-wife stood glaring at us. Her glamorous appearance (full face of makeup, brown hair swept up in a chignon, matching cardigan and dress set with kitten heels, all *way* too much for a trip to the hardware store) contrasted oddly with the lunch box clutched in one trembling hand, which she shoved at his chest.

"You forgot your lunch. Again. I thought we could eat together, but it looks like you're busy seducing another young thing. You certainly have a type now," she added, her eyes narrowed as she studied me. "She looks just like the other one."

The other one? It took a moment to compute, but once it did, the look of fury on Glen's face matched my own—she was referring to Divina.

"Don't you start. Go wait for me in the back. I don't need you embarrassing yourself in front of my customers again."

"You mean you don't want me embarrassing you in front of a future mistress. But you do that just fine yourself. You think you're fooling anybody with that dye job?" the woman shot back before storming off to the back room.

Glen's hand moved toward his hair before pausing and redirecting to the back of his neck. "I'm sorry you had to see that. I'm going through a divorce and, well, you can see how that's going." He let out a hollow laugh. "And what she said to you was absolutely uncalled for. As an apology, I'll offer you a discount on that tool kit. How's that?"

I forced a smile. "I appreciate it. Who was she talking about though? I look like someone?"

"There was a woman I was friendly with. You both have the same, uh, complexion, I guess."

Same complexion. What a safe way to say "you all look the same."

"I see. And I'm guessing your wife was not so friendly with this woman?"

"What an understatement. I guess she felt threatened because we were in the middle of patching things up, and then she sees me making friends with a younger woman and jumps to all these conclusions." He rolled his eyes. "I tried to explain that we were just talking, but she didn't want to hear it."

"It's such a shame when a man and woman can't be friends, just because other people misunderstand their relationship."

I really did think that since it constantly happened with me and Terrence, one of my oldest and closest friends. But something told me that true friendship wasn't what Glen had in mind for him and Divina.

"Thank you! Try telling that to my wife. Anyway, it's a moot point now that . . ." He trailed off, as if finally realizing how much he'd been oversharing with a stranger. Though I could easily finish that thought for him.

It was a moot point now that Divina was dead.

He cleared his throat. "How about I ring you up so you can get that discount? Is there anything else you need today?"

"I think that's all for now, but I'll be sure to come back for my next DIY project. Thanks so much for your help, I really appreciate it."

After checking out, I drove to a few other stores to pick up more cafe supplies and it was closing time by the time I made it back to the Brew-ha Cafe. I filled them in on what I'd witnessed as we locked up.

"I don't know if any of that counts as a clue, per se, but if Glen and his wife were trying to patch things up and his wife was hostile toward Divina, there's a chance that one of them cut Divina out of the picture for the sake of their marriage," I said, wrapping up my account.

"It's not much, but it's still something," Adeena said. "I made our nail appointments for next week, so hopefully we'll run into that Clarissa woman there. We'll let you know what we find out."

After we said our goodbyes, I sat behind the wheel of my car for a few minutes, unable to muster the energy to even turn it on. For some reason, the day felt like it had been fifty hours long and it wasn't close to done yet: I was about to have dinner with the Calendar Crew.

Chapter Twenty

What's so secret that you didn't want your tita and lola around?"
Ninang June set a large platter of steamed fish on the table. Ninang April and Ninang Mae followed with rice, sautéed vegetables, and bowls of sawsawan for dipping. As much as I loved the more elaborate dishes Tita Rosie prepared at the restaurant, for the everyday, this was the type of simple home cooking that we enjoyed when it was just us.

I dribbled a mix of patis and calamansi over my fish. "The investigation has stalled. Between Divina's death, the vandalism, and now these threatening letters, it's hard to say if it's all connected through one person or if it's different people with different scores to settle."

"Again I ask, why are you meeting us alone instead of our usual family dinner?"

"I know you all like to think that your gossip is harmless—"

"That's because it is—"

"But we have to consider that maybe something you've said had consequences you hadn't intended."

Ninang Mae shrugged. "If people don't want to be talked about, they should've behaved better. Why shouldn't there be consequences for their actions?"

"But don't you see how the same could be said for all of you?"

Ninang Mae looked at me blankly, but the other two busied themselves with their food.

"People don't like having their business aired out in public. It would be one thing if you took the person being affected aside and told them. You'd be meddling in stuff that's not your business, but at least you're trying to be discreet. But the way you do it, half the town knows by the end of Mass."

"I don't see what the big deal is—"

"Mae, just because you don't think it's a big deal doesn't mean other people think the same as you. That's what Lila's trying to say, isn't it? That's why you wanted to meet us?" Ninang April looked up from her plate. "You thought we'd be more honest if it was just us."

Ninang April was as straightforward as Ninang Mae, but she at least had tact. She thought before she spoke, and though her words often stung the most, it was usually because she hit too close to the truth you were conveniently avoiding (not that I was projecting or anything).

I nodded. "I thought it'd be easier since none of us would have to worry about politeness and could just be real about what's happening."

Out of respect for my grandmother (due to age hierarchy) and my aunt (due to her soft heart), it was common for us to be careful how we spoke around them. Even my godmothers, though they could only censor themselves so much.

Ninang June said, "That's fair. What do you want to know?"

"Out of all the tsismis you've spread lately, who's been most affected by it? Other than the Davises." I glanced between Ninang Mae and Ninang April. "Back when you two had that argument in the church, you mentioned people who'd gotten fired or publicly humiliated. Do you think they might have something to do with this?"

To Ninang Mae's credit, she didn't react defensively this time and sat thinking it over before responding. "I doubt it. Father Santiago intervened with the kid who got fired. We had him work off his debt to the church and even wrote him a recommendation letter for college when we saw that he really was sorry. As for that dollar store plastic surgeon, he's doing just fine. I think he's practicing in Miami now."

Ninang June added, "That former news anchor is a really successful romance author now. I remember her telling Mae that she didn't appreciate how it was handled, but she was grateful to finally leave the profession."

Ninang Mae nodded. "The only reason she got plastic surgery to begin with was the pressure she felt to look young and beautiful since she was on air. When she no longer had to worry about that, she was able to pursue what made her happy."

"I haven't read her books, but I've heard they're good. She wouldn't tell me her pen name because she said her books are really . . . how did she put it? Steamy? Spicy? Anyway, there's some content she didn't want me reading," Ninang April said with a laugh.

"But those are the best scenes!" Ninang Mae insisted.

Ninang June agreed with her, and they both started discussing their favorite couples and situations and all the things you never, ever wanted to hear coming out of your godmothers' mouths. I stared down at my fork and wondered if I could jam it into my brain to make me forget this part of the conversation.

I also made a note to get the author's name after dinner.

All that aside, I felt better about my godmothers and how they'd handled those situations. Even though I knew cruelty was never the point when they gossiped, it was nice to be reassured their hearts were in the right place.

And just as I thought that, Ninang Mae said, "But if you want something *really* juicy, then . . ." and started reeling off a list of all the embarrassing, sordid, and sometimes downright shocking things the citizens of Shady Palms were getting up to.

Ninang April and Ninang June both tried acting like they were above it all, but soon they were jumping in to correct Ninang Mae or interject their own opinion on the matter.

"No, Mae, it was his cousin's wife that the mailman had the affair with, not his wife's cousin."

"Oh, and that one clerk, you know the one, he's up to six children now. He doesn't have time for the two kids he has at home, but he's going around impregnating how many women, Diyos ko!"

"How much is that woman getting sued for? You know the one, we reported her for selling that sauce on her social media that wasn't FDA approved and all those people got sick? She's part of Mary Ann Randall's crowd."

I'd started zoning out (how the heck did my godmothers know so much about what everyone in our town was getting up to?) but that last bit of information jumped out at me.

"Wait a minute! Did you say you reported a member of the PTA Squad and now they're getting sued?"

"One of the church outreach members bought a jar of that sauce to be supportive and it made her so sick, she ended up in the hospital. I told her that if that woman's selling unsafe food, she needs to be stopped. So we reported her, and the member that got sick is suing to cover the hospital costs and other expenses."

"I'm surprised you didn't hear about it. When the scandal broke out, it was all over the *Shady Palms News*. That PTA woman had quit her job to start selling that sauce and other food products, but when it all fell apart she couldn't get her job back."

"Last I heard, some of the PTA members took pity on her and employed her as an assistant of sorts, running errands for them and doing odd jobs around their houses."

"Good on Mary Ann for not abandoning one of her friends, I guess. Anyway, do you remember that woman's name? She's probably our best bet if Glen and Ultima are cleared."

"Helen Kowalski," Ninang Mae said promptly. I knew I could count on her to never forget a gossip target's name.

"Why is that name familiar?" I asked as I jotted it down in my phone notes.

"She's Mary Ann Randall's best friend," Ninang June said.

Mary Ann Randall was the head of the PTA Squad, a group of moms with a lot of time on their hands and the need to be involved in every little thing. Even though the PTA Squad had finally accepted me and made the Brew-ha Cafe their new hangout spot, Mary Ann still didn't like me and blamed me for her daughter not being named Miss Teen Shady Palms last year. Which is why Helen Kowalski was suddenly familiar to me—she was the mother of another contestant that year.

I made a note to reach out to both of them—Helen for her alibi, and her child, Leslie, to see how they were doing. Luckily, our cafe apprentice, Katie, knew Leslie, so I could ask her to set up a meeting. Not like I could hang out outside Shady Palms High School in the hopes of running into them. Not if I didn't want to look like a creeper, anyway.

"This is great! I'll let Detective Park know about this when I see him tomorrow. And I should text Amir, too. He probably knows about the lawsuit and can give me some background info on it."

Finally, a new suspect with a tangible connection to my godmothers. Here's hoping it proved to be the lead I needed.

Chapter Twenty-One

"It's been a while since we could all enjoy breakfast together. I'm looking forward to this feast."

Jonathan picked up his mug and smiled at Tita Rosie and Lola Flor as they set platters of Filipino breakfast meats (longganisa, tocino, tapa, and sardines), fried eggs, and garlic fried rice on the table for DIY silog platters—the breakfast of champions, and the favorite way to start the day for me and the Park brothers.

Breakfast at Tita Rosie's Kitchen with my aunt and grandmother had long been part of my daily schedule, and along the way, we'd added Jonathan and Jae to our breakfast ritual. Adeena and Elena would usually join us, but since they were leaving early for their mani-pedi reconnaissance, they were handling the morning service while I caught up with my family. Not that our breakfast party was any smaller than usual since Izzy and my cousin Ronnie, Tita Rosie's only child, joined us this morning. Ronnie and I had had a rather tempestuous relationship in the past, and it was only recently that we started mending things between us. It was still a little awkward—you couldn't exactly erase decades of drama and trauma in a few short months—but I loved seeing the smile he brought to Tita Rosie's face. Plus, Izzy was a very welcome addition to the family, so it was worth putting up with him for now.

"Hey Cuz! I heard you got involved in another murder beef. You really need better hobbies."

. . . I'd spoken too soon.

"Considering my 'hobby' saved your sorry a—um, butt." Tita Rosie had thrown me a look so I changed my wording. "You should really be a whole lot nicer to me. I could always use more groveling in my life."

He rolled his eyes but smiled since he knew I was right. "How about I contract you to cater all the wine tastings we're hosting this season? We'll handle the cheese and charcuterie, you take care of the rest."

I lifted my mug of tsokolate in a toast. "Done. Let me know when to stop by to sign the contract."

"How about later tonight? Marcus's shift starts at four and you could stop by mid-shift with some snacks for him. He's been really down lately and I'm sure he'd appreciate it. Don't worry, we'll expense it," Ronnie added, heaping his plate with garlic fried rice, two eggs, and a pile of tocino.

"How's the investigation going?" Izzy asked as she ladled the sardines in tomato sauce over her rice. "Marcus keeps playing it off like he's totally fine and has everything under control, but he's clearly about to snap, he's so tightly wound up."

I relayed everything I learned from the Calendar Crew yesterday and finished up with, "So my next move is to talk to Katie and see if she can help me meet up with Leslie. I also want to talk to Helen, but I need to get her alone. She won't open up to me in front of the PTA Squad."

I glanced over at Jonathan, who was busy loading up his plate with all the meat. "Any ideas?"

"I remember when that scandal broke. You might want to look up the *Shady Palms News* articles from that time. And talk to Amir, too. He wasn't involved in the case, so he should be able to speak freely about it. He might have insight the rest of us wouldn't."

He added one more slice of tocino before saying, "As for meeting with Helen Kowalski, she frequents your cafe. Your job is to find a way to sit down with her when she's alone. I'm sure you'll find a way. My side of the investigation isn't going very well, I'm afraid. Our only suspects both have alibis for the time of Ms. de los Santos's death. Not ironclad alibis, mind you, but still hard to either prove or disprove. We need something more concrete."

Lola Flor had been quietly eating her breakfast, her usual look of discontent on her face, but something about Jonathan's statement made her face pucker, as if there was a bad taste in her mouth. She looked at my aunt. "Rosie, can you make me a cup of coffee? The fancy stuff Lila brought is too bitter for me."

Tita Rosie studied her mother. Lola Flor obviously had something to say and wanted Tita Rosie out of the room, which was odd. It's not like she'd ever been shy about speaking her mind before, and certainly not in front of her daughter. But Tita Rosie knew that if Lola Flor needed her to be out of earshot, she must've had something questionable to share. "Of course, Nay. Does anyone else need anything while I'm up?"

The rest of us shook our heads and waited until the kitchen door closed behind her before turning our attention to Lola Flor.

"You can't tell Rosie about this. It's an anonymous tip." Lola Flor looked around the table, gazing into everyone's eyes to gauge if we'd keep her secret. "Ultima Bolisay runs a gambling den beneath one of her laundromats."

My eyes narrowed—Lola Flor had sworn to my aunt that she quit gambling months ago. "How do you—"

"Don't ask how I know. The important thing is, you can use this information to either confirm her alibi or put some pressure on her for Divina's investigation. The penalty for illegal gambling is way less than for murder. Even if she's not the killer, she might know who is."

"I'm guessing certain kinds of information get traded at this establishment?" Jonathan said.

My grandmother nodded. "You should question her. I bet she'd be willing to strike up a bargain."

"I'm not a detective anymore, remember? I'm just going to call this in and say I received an anonymous tip. Detective Nowak will handle it."

Lola Flor smiled, an action so rare and somehow scary that Ronnie and I both shivered. "If you're not a detective anymore, you're not obligated to report it, right? Look at it this way: At best, they'll shut her down and you'll lose an excellent resource. But if you talk to her and she's innocent, you can gain her trust. She'd make an exceptional informant."

Ronnie stared at our grandmother. "I thought I was the shady one in the family, but Lola's got me beat."

"I don't know what that means, but if you're comparing yourself to me, I don't like it. My plans are smart. Yours are just greedy," Lola Flor said sharply.

Says the woman with a gambling addiction, but that was an issue for the therapist she refused to see. I wasn't foolish enough to say that out loud.

Lola Flor glanced at the kitchen, where Tita Rosie was still waiting and presumably not eavesdropping. "Jonathan, think over what I told you. Now, go get Rosie and reassure her everything is OK. But not a word to her about what I said, do you understand?"

Jonathan nodded and made his way to the back while Lola Flor glared and gestured at us to keep eating. Jae added more longganisa to my plate and winked at me before turning back to his own food.

By the time Tita Rosie and Jonathan made it back to the table, we were all chatting and acting (semi)normal. Tita Rosie set a cup of instant coffee in front of Lola Flor and a takeout box in front of me. "Adeena and Elena couldn't join us, so I packed up some mamon and turon for them since those are their favorites."

I thanked her, and the breakfast party soon drew to a close. Jae had to open his clinic and Jonathan went to go check on my godmothers, but Izzy and Ronnie followed me back to the cafe.

"Man, I knew Lola Flor liked gambling, but who knew she was involved in some underground ring?" Ronnie said.

I shook my head. "Tita Rosie and I were so proud of her for giving up the casinos, but I guess that's because she was just getting her fix at Ultima's."

Adeena popped up next to us. "I only caught part of that, but I am absolutely demanding that I get the full story."

"Shouldn't you be working?"

"It's fine, Katie's got it."

The teen was hard at work behind the counter, assisted by Elena.

"I was hoping to tell you and Elena together to save time, but I don't want to leave Katie by herself."

"Don't worry," Izzy said. "I worked as a barista for most of college. I'd be happy to help out while you debrief. You probably have to go over your plans for the afternoon as well, right?"

Once I'd checked in with Katie and Izzy had washed her hands and donned a Brew-ha Cafe apron and cap, the rest of us headed to the kitchen so I could catch up on baking while letting my partners know what I'd learned.

"—and yeah, that's pretty much it," I said, popping loaves of pandan zucchini bread in the oven. "I don't know if Jonathan is going to take Lola Flor's advice, but it seemed like he was thinking about it."

"It's a tough choice. He seems like a by-the-book kind of guy, so I'm sure the idea makes him uncomfortable. But since he's not a cop anymore, there's no reason to dismiss Lola Flor outright. This is probably a soul-searching moment for him. Made worse since he can't talk to Mommy about it." Ronnie bit into a piece of turon, the caramel coating of the fried banana spring roll shattering and leaving little sprinkles everywhere. "Elena, I know these were meant for you, but I might have to steal them all."

Elena laughed and set several cans on the table. "Good luck with that. But it's the perfect pairing. I've been trying to come up with a beer that would satisfy sweet tooths like Adeena's, and this is the first sample of our banana bread beer. I based the flavor profile on Lila's salabat banana bread. Tell me what you all think. It should pair well with the turon and mamon."

Banana bread . . . beer? Oh my gulay, that sounded so weird but so good. Too bad Jae and I both had work. He was more of a cider guy, but he loved trying craft beers with interesting flavors. And I managed to get into enough incidents without mixing alcohol and dangerous kitchen tools. But maybe just a taste would be fine.

Either we'd all been spending way too much time together or Elena's bruha powers extended to mind reading because she said, "Don't worry, I have a couple cans stashed aside for you and Jae. You know you're two of my most important taste testers. Adeena's not really helpful when it comes to this—she just likes to be included."

"I'm sorry that I don't like things that taste yucky," Adeena said. Rather than sipping from the can, she'd poured some of the contents into a squat glass and was gingerly dipping her tongue into her drink, like a cat lapping up water.

"Do I dare ask what you're doing?" I said, grabbing a glass for myself and pouring a small amount from Adeena's can. I liked to take a good sniff before tasting, and that was easier to do from a glass than from a can.

"This way I can taste it without having to swallow it if it's gross. It passes the first test, so I guess I can drink some."

I shook my head at her ridiculousness and raised the glass to my nose. The banana was definitely there, but I also got ginger, cinnamon, cayenne, and something else I couldn't quite identify until I took a sip. "Mmm . . . you nailed all the spices from the salabat banana bread, but there's a nice sweetness that's not from the banana. Toffee or dates?"

Elena grinned. "Yes to both. By the way, Ronnie, this is part of the dessert line I was talking to you about."

Though they operated separately, Elena ran the tiny microbrewery that was connected to the Shady Palms Winery with two of her cousins. Their signature lager was on tap in bars throughout the area, and she was working on developing a line that not only complemented my cousin's wines but also worked here at the Brew-ha Cafe since we had a liquor license.

Ronnie nodded his approval, and while everyone but me drank (Adeena and Elena only had another half hour on their shift, so it was fine), we gossiped a bit about who we thought patronized Ultima's gambling den and what kind of dirt we could get on them, then brainstormed ways to corner Helen Kowalski to get her to talk. Adeena promised to talk to Amir about the case before bringing the conversation around to the mission she and Elena were on once they clocked out.

"Do you think Clarissa will actually be there today? And willing to spill to random strangers about Divina while getting her nails done?" Adeena grabbed the empty cans and rinsed them out before tossing them in the recycling bin.

"I'm not exactly expecting you to get a murder confession out of her. Just see if she ever met Divina, or if Divina was actually dating Glen, or if Glen was ever violent . . . stuff like that. We know so little about Glen, even with my visit to the hardware store yesterday. This is our best chance to talk to someone who could tell us what he's really like. Well, without approaching his wife, but that's a bit of a touchy subject considering she thinks I'm his next conquest." I gave Adeena a pointed look. "No scaring her off though. We don't want her to know that we consider both her and Glen serious suspects."

Adeena gasped in outrage and Elena laughed, putting her hand on her girlfriend's shoulder. "I'll run interference if she's being too obvious. Don't worry, Lila. By the end of the day, we'll get every last drop of tsismis possible from our little paramour."

Elena's smile, so sweet, so devious, made me glad yet again that she was on our team.

G reat work today, Katie!"
It was closing time at the Brew-ha Cafe, and my teenage apprentice and I were locking up. Katie Pang was in her last year of high school and had been an utter godsend since she started working with us in the fall. As we cleaned, I tried (yet again) to gently push her to attend an out-of-town university so she could experience life outside of Shady Palms, but she'd vetoed that.

"I still own the Honeybee Salon, and even though Beth helped me hire people to manage it, I want to stick close by. Mom taught me all about hair, so I thought I'd take a quick cosmetology course at Shelbyville Community College for my first year, and then a more intensive business management degree online." Katie stacked the clean mugs behind the counter. "Plus, I'm going to spend the summer interning with Beth. And since Joy made it into the University of Chicago, like she'd always dreamed, I plan on visiting her every month. She can be in charge of expanding my worldview."

Joy Monroe was Katie's best friend and the server at Tita Rosie's Kitchen. With both our shops losing our helpers, it was probably time to start looking for their replacements. Yet another thing to add to my Worry Pile.

"By the way, you know Leslie Kowalski, right? I heard there was some drama with their mom last fall. How are they doing?"

"You're talking about that botulism in a bottle thing, right? Leslie told their mom not to do it, but she wouldn't listen. I guess Mrs. Kowalski saw someone making big money on TikTok doing it, so she thought she could do the same." Katie rolled her eyes. "I don't know why she was even on TikTok to begin with. Anyway, I think money might be tight at their house since Mrs. Kowalski can't get her job back. I heard Leslie was putting college on hold to work for a bit first."

I shook my head. That poor kid, having to pay for their mom's mistakes. Then it dawned on me. "Do you think they'd want to work here? We were looking for your replacement anyway, and we're at a point where we can pay our employees."

Katie came to us through the apprenticeship program at her high school, so she worked for us for school credit and work experience, not money. Even when we'd offered to pay her, she refused, stating she had more than enough money from her inheritance, and we should save that money for when we needed a full-time employee. I guess that time was now.

Her eyes lit up. "That would be great! They used to come here all the time but had to stop since their family couldn't afford it anymore. They'd be a great replacement. I'm happy to help train them, too."

I scribbled a note on the back of a business card, telling Leslie to text me to set up an interview time. "Could you give this to them next time you see them? Tell them what we talked about and not to stress if they don't have a résumé since I'm assuming this is their first job."

"Awesome, thanks, Lila!" Katie glanced at the clock after taking the card. "Don't you have to go to the winery to sign a contract or something? You can go ahead, I've got this. I'll talk to Leslie about the job, and if they're not interested, I'll spread the word about there being an opening here once I'm gone. So stop worrying and handle your business."

I smiled as I grabbed my bag and woke Longganisa from her nap beneath my desk so we could leave. The youths were gonna be all right.

Chapter Twenty-Two

Business wrapped up quickly at Shady Palms Winery and I found myself with unexpected time on my hands. As Ronnie and Izzy had asked, I'd prepared some sweets for Marcus and had planned on spending some time with him before calling it a day, but he'd called in at the last minute.

"This makes me even more worried about him," Izzy said. "He's been taking days off to help with the laundromat, but he always lets us know in advance. He didn't even say he was sick or anything, just that he couldn't make it today and that one of the other security guards would be taking his shift."

I gnawed on my lower lip, wondering if there'd been a new development that the aunties hadn't told me about yet. "I'll swing by his place and check up on him. I still have to give him these snacks anyway."

"Let us know how it goes. And give him this letter." Ronnie handed me an unsealed envelope. At my curious glance, he said, "If he needs time off, but is worried about the money, I want him to know we've got his back. He'd never come to me about it, so I figured I'd lay out some options for him and he can work out the details with Izzy."

Dang. I guess my cousin had turned into a pretty decent guy after all. I looked over at Izzy, who was smiling at him, and once again marveled at the power of a good, strong partner. Which reminded me . . .

After saying goodbye to Ronnie and Izzy, I headed to my car and made a call. "Hey Jae! You free tonight? I'm out on some errands right now but was hoping we could grab dinner after."

He laughed. "When did you become a mind reader? I was craving some of Miss Nettie's hush puppies. If you pick me up, I'll keep you company on those errands and then we can head to Big Bishop's BBQ."

My stomach rumbled as it remembered it had been way too long since it'd gorged on copious amounts of good Southern comfort food. "I'll be there in twenty."

After I picked up Jae, we headed to Ninang Mae's house, but nobody was home and Marcus wasn't answering his texts. I texted Ninang Mae and she said he'd helped out at the laundromat earlier and was probably just napping, leaving Jae and me with time to kill. It was too early for dinner, so I flicked through my notebook to see if I could fit in a quick investigation before we ate.

I wanted to wait till Leslie got back to me before approaching their mom. I hoped that they could give me some insight into the situation, maybe even help me get their mom alone so I could talk to her in private. Jonathan was handling Ultima and the (alleged) gambling ring. Glen Davis had moved down the suspect list, but wasn't completely off of it. But what excuse could I use this time to visit his hardware store?

I was about to ask Jae when I suddenly remembered why I'd wanted to patrol with him in the first place. The vandal. They'd used spray paint to deface the window, walls, and laundry machines, and they must've bought it somewhere. Glen's hardware store was as likely as anywhere else.

"Jae, do you know anything about spray paint?"

Sorry, but it's illegal to sell spray paint in Shady Palms." Jae had helped me concoct a story about needing spray paint for the new shelves Adeena and Elena were building for the cafe, but not only was Glen Davis not at his store, one of his employees had completely eliminated any chance of me tracking down the vandal through their purchases.

"I thought that was just in Chicago? I didn't realize it extended all the way out here," Jae said.

"As far as I know, the mayor heard about the city ordinance in Chicago and decided to adopt it a few years ago to fight against our graffiti problem," the store clerk explained. "Not that it's helped any. You could go to literally any other town or suburb in the area to purchase it since it's only illegal to buy, not to own. All it's doing is making sure that our customers take their business elsewhere to buy it."

We thanked them and left.

"Well, that's oh for two," Jae said, buckling himself in. "No Marcus and no paper trail for the spray paint. What do you want to do next?"

"I could really use a win right now. Let's head to Big Bishop's BBQ."

Big George and Nettie Bishop were longtime friends, feeding and watching over me, Adeena, and Terrence since our high school days when we'd hang out at their restaurant almost every day after school. The smell of frying catfish and collard greens and cornbread swirled around me as I entered Big Bishop's BBQ, as welcoming and familiar as the hug Nettie greeted me with.

"Lila! It's been too long since I've seen you. And you too, Dr. Jae. How are we doing this fine evening?"

"Better now that I get to see you again, Miss Nettie. And enjoy some of Big George's barbecue, of course." That earned Jae an extra strong, maternal hug.

"What can I get for you?"

"I was thinking of the brisket special, but that catfish smells so good and it's been a while since I've had it," I said, poring over the menu that I'd memorized almost a decade ago.

"How about I get the brisket special and you get the catfish? That way we can share," Jae said. "I'll have the mac and cheese and coleslaw for my sides."

"No sweet tea?" Nettie asked, hiding her smile.

Her restaurant was the first place Jae had tried real Southern sweet tea and he'd almost choked the first time he sipped the delicious, syrupy sweetness. As a dentist, he could be a bit of a goody-goody, extolling the virtues of boring things like flossing and not eating too many sweets. Though he did make an exception for my desserts. As he should.

George stopped by our table as we were finishing our mains. "How was it?"

"You fishing for compliments, Big George? Because I think it's pretty obvious that we hated it," Jae said, gesturing at our clean plates.

George ruffled Jae's hair. "You think you're funny, don't you? Sounds like someone doesn't want sweet potato pie."

Jae and I both gasped. Nettie's sweet potato pie was legendary in Shady Palms.

"Stop teasing them, George. You know I'd never let them go

unfed," Nettie said, setting plates down in front of us. "Eat up, baby. I know you been running yourself ragged helping out your aunties."

"You're the best, Miss Nettie," Jae and I said before digging in to our pie.

"How are your godmothers doing, by the way?" Big George asked. "From what I've heard, it's a nasty business."

"What've you heard?"

He glanced around his crowded restaurant and leaned close. "There are some people saying that your aunties are getting their just deserts."

I knew there were people who thought that, but hearing those words coming from Big George's mouth was such an attack, I actually reared back.

"Not that I agree with them!" he was quick to clarify. "I'm just telling you what I heard."

"What you heard was people not caring that a woman died so they can dunk on my godmothers."

He had no response for that.

"Did you at least hear something useful? Something that could help us find the killer?"

He shook his head and started to apologize, but Nettie cut him off. "Lila, I understand that you're upset, but there's no reason to take that tone."

"I'm not trying to take a tone, Miss Nettie, I just—"

"Just what? Just hoped that we'd be 'useful'? I'm sorry we can't help your investigation, but we were asking after your godmothers to be neighborly. See if they needed us to send over food or wanted some company." She started clearing our empty plates. "Maybe you should remember that next time you try interrogating your friends and neighbors."

Jae put his hand on mine and raised his eyebrows at me.

I sighed. "You're right. All that's been going on has me frustrated and upset and I was taking it out on you, Big George. I'm sorry."

He smiled at me and ruffled my hair this time. "I know you didn't mean it. And the way I said it was probably insensitive. I just meant to warn you that people were being nasty about your godmothers and for them to be careful who they trust. That's all."

I smiled back. "I appreciate that." I tried to fix my hair but gave up when my curls refused to cooperate. "I just can't believe how quick people were to turn on them. I get that they're annoying gossips and have spread a couple rumors here and there, but to be happy about their misery? It's messed up."

"I do agree that all the schadenfreude is concerning," Miss Nettie said. "But I'm sure that there are people in this town who think that your godmothers have done more than just spread a few rumors."

"It's just talk—"

"It's never 'just' talk. Don't forget that words have power, Lila." Miss Nettie sighed and shook her head. "Even ones that aren't true. *Especially* ones that aren't true."

"'A lie can run round the world before the truth has got its boots on,'" Jae quoted. "I know the aunties think they're just having harmless fun, but . . ."

He trailed off, likely trying to spare my feelings, but I urged him to finish. "But what?"

"It's not harmless to the people whose lives they've destroyed."

I scoffed. "Melodramatic much?"

"You know I'm right. And until they learn that, people are going to continue turning on them." Jae smiled encouragingly. "But if anyone can change them, it's you."

Chapter Twenty-Three

Because of our twice-thwarted investigation attempts, even with our detour and relaxed dinner, Jae and I still had some time before our patrol, so Jae helped me shop for cafe supplies and take Longganisa for an extra-long constitutional along the Riverwalk. It had been such a fun, peaceful, normal night that I hated to ruin it by going out on our nightly patrol (plus these late nights were wreaking havoc on my skincare routine), but I wouldn't feel right if we skipped our duty and something actually happened. Still, tonight would be an early night in, just a cursory pass or two around the laundromat area and then I'd be in bed by ten.

Of course, nothing ever works out the way I plan.

We were just about to call it a night when Jae suddenly pulled to the side of the road across the street from the laundromat. "Lila, do you see that?"

The streetlights illuminated the parking lot in front of the laundromat but not the entrance, so I had to squint to make out the hooded figure dressed in black in front of the door.

"Is that our vandal?"

I reached for the door to let myself out, but Jae stopped me. "Wait! We don't know if they're dangerous. You call the police and I'll call my brother. I know you want to stop them, but it's safer for us to watch and wait."

Grumbling at how smart and practical and right my boyfriend was, I did what he said. My call ended before his, so I could hear Jonathan giving him orders. Orders that I totally would've followed if, in that moment, I didn't see Marcus's car pull into the parking lot and Marcus jump out and run toward the shadowy figure.

"Jae, that's Marcus! We have to back him up!"

There was no oncoming traffic, so Jae quickly maneuvered the car into the parking lot and we joined Marcus, who'd managed to subdue the figure before they could use the can of spray paint that lay at their feet.

Marcus pulled back the hood and revealed . . . a white woman I didn't recognize.

I was hoping for a *Scooby-Doo* reveal—like Marcus would take off the woman's hood and we'd all gasp because it was Old Man Winters who used to run the haunted amusement park. Or at least something more dramatic, like me actually knowing who the person was.

She seemed to know me though. "You! Why are you here?"

I studied her to see if maybe I was mistaken. She looked to be in her forties, average height, no makeup, oversized glasses, brown hair pulled back in a bun. In other words . . . plain. She could've been any random woman I passed by on my daily routine.

"I'm sorry but . . . who are you?"

She did not like that question and tried to launch herself at me, but Marcus had a firm grip on her and she didn't get very far.

She wouldn't answer any of our questions after that, but luckily, Jonathan arrived before the police and was able to identify her.

"That's Erica Davis, Glen Davis's wife."

"Wait, that's her?" I asked. When I saw her at the hardware store, she'd been all done up and looked nothing like the woman standing in front of me. "So, you were the one behind all the vandalism?"

She stared defiantly at all of us. "Who told them to interfere in my marriage? Did they think it was funny to humiliate me by letting the whole town know my husband was cheating on me?"

Marcus frowned. "Wait a minute. My mom told me that you hadn't known your husband was having an affair."

She narrowed her eyes at him. "So?"

He looked taken aback. "What do you mean, 'so'? My mom and her friends were trying to help you. They didn't like that he was doing all this behind your back."

"And who asked for their help? 'Cause I sure as hell didn't. We were perfectly happy before they meddled. So what if he stepped out once in a while? I'm the one he loved! He never would've left me if it wasn't for them . . ." Erica dissolved into tears and Jonathan had to catch her as her knees gave way. "Why couldn't they have just minded their business? None of this would've happened if it weren't for them." She pounded on Jonathan's chest as she sobbed, and he took it, just calmly holding her by the shoulders until the police arrived and took her away after questioning us.

Marcus stared after her long after the police left. "That woman killed Divina and tried to destroy my mom's business because she's upset my mom and the aunties told the truth about her shitty husband? But she doesn't blame him at all? How does that make sense?"

"I know it's cliché, but the truth hurts. Many people prefer a happy lie. It's easier." Jonathan put his hand on Marcus's shoulder, and that's when I realized Marcus was trembling. "Your mom and her friends may come across as annoying busybodies, but they're also women who believe in the truth. Their values don't allow them to sugarcoat things. Not everyone will like that, but I find it admirable."

Marcus looked up at him, then reached into the pocket of his windbreaker and pulled out an envelope. "I found this when I was helping at the laundromat earlier."

Jonathan opened up the printed letter and Jae and I crowded around him to read the message:

> Congrats on making your new business a success!
> It would be a shame if someone destroyed it, the
> way you destroyed my life.

"I showed it to my mom and the aunties, but they tried to brush it off as a prank and refused to report it," Marcus explained. "You were already gone for the day, so I figured I'd tell you tomorrow and called off work to keep an eye on everything. I was just coming back from the hospital where I warned Ate Bernie about it when I saw that woman in front of the laundromat."

"This isn't the first threatening letter they've received. It's one of the reasons I've been keeping an eye on them. They likely didn't want to bother reporting it since they reported the others and the SPPD hasn't done anything about it yet," Jonathan said.

Marcus inhaled deeply through his nose and exhaled slowly through his mouth several times, a move Sana taught us to better manage our emotions. "I am so glad I left the SPPD. Anyway, this means it's over, right? We caught the vandal and killer."

"We still don't know that Erica Davis is the killer," Jonathan said. "But for now, we can rest a bit easier knowing a major threat has been neutralized. I'm going to the station to make sure this is handled properly. You should all go home—it's been a long night."

"I'll go with you," Marcus said.

Jonathan nodded, then turned to Jae and me. "Lila, good work calling in the incident right away. Hopefully this is the end, but either way, there's nothing more for you to do tonight. Jae, make sure she gets home safely."

He patted Jae on the back then headed to the police station with Marcus. I was still too stunned to function, so Jae drove me home, the two of us quietly going over the events of the night. He parked the car and walked me to the door, but before I could go in, he pulled me into his arms.

"I'm so glad everything worked out," he said, running his fingers through my hair, gently caressing the waves before leaning down for a kiss. "I have to borrow your car to get home, so I'll swing by to pick you up for work. Get a good night's sleep, OK? It's over now."

I returned his kiss and went inside, robotically making my way through my bedtime routine. As I snuggled in bed with Longganisa, I repeated those words to myself.

It's over now.

Chapter Twenty-Four

W ell, that's anticlimactic. And after Elena and I went on our super secret spy mission and everything."

Adeena set my iced sampaguita matcha latte in front of me (I was quickly getting addicted to them and wondered if I could convince her to add them to the permanent menu) and the malunggay-strawberry herbal blend that Elena had finally perfected in front of her girlfriend before sitting down with her usual lavender chai. She'd come in all excited to make her report when I interrupted her to tell her that Marcus, Jae, and I caught the vandal the previous night.

"First of all, your 'super secret spy mission' involved foot massages and free mimosas. Don't act like you were cracking safes and stealing blueprints or anything like that."

Adeena sighed. "Why don't we ever get mixed up in something cool, like an art heist? I would be so good at heisting. For our next case, can we make sure there's a part where we infiltrate a fancy party and I get to have a sexy, dangerous ballroom dance scene?"

"It's probably not relevant now, but do you want to know what we found out from Clarissa?" Elena asked, wisely ignoring Adeena and her antics.

"I promise not to fall in love with my target during our dance, if that's what you're worried about. That's too cliché, even for me."

"Yeah, you might as well since you went to the trouble of gathering the information. Plus you never know when it might come in handy," I said to Elena.

"I know you two hear me."

Elena took a sip of her tea. "Well, the most important thing we learned is that Clarissa has an alibi for the time of Divina's murder. One of her coworkers just retired, so her company had a big goodbye dinner for them. Afterward, Clarissa and a bunch of her coworkers went out for drinks. I was able to confirm this since they went to a bar that one of my cousins works at and they were able to check the records and verify the time she was there based on her credit card purchases. Plus, she got sloppy drunk and talked the ear off of one of the bartenders there, so they remembered her."

Adeena must've gotten tired of being ignored since she finally added something useful to the conversation. "The other thing we learned is that Glen Davis is a piece of work. He promised Clarissa he'd leave his wife for her, but everyone in the salon said she was a fool for believing him. He probably wouldn't have taken that next step toward divorce if the aunties hadn't outed the affair. Anyway, Clarissa thought they'd finally be together for real but then he started ignoring her for Divina. And when Divina died, he went crawling back to his wife."

"Was Divina actually seeing him?"

Elena shrugged. "Hard to say. Clarissa says no, and that Glen was just trying to make her jealous. Others say that Clarissa is just deluding herself. The most popular opinion was that he was chasing her, but

Divina was leading him on. You might have to talk to him yourself to get a definitive answer."

"I promised Jonathan he could handle that side of the investigation, but now that there's technically no more investigation, I guess it wouldn't hurt to get his side of things," I said.

Jae would hate that, but since I learned he hated it marginally less if I dragged him along on these excursions, I knew what we'd be doing later.

Or at least, that's what we would've been doing if Bernadette hadn't called me mid-shift to let me know that Ninang April was in the hospital. Katie and Joy weren't supposed to work that day, but I called both of them in so that Lola Flor and I could head to the hospital ASAP. Tita Rosie stayed behind to run the restaurant with Joy but would close early and head over after the dinner rush.

Once we got to the hospital, we ran into Ninang Mae, Ninang June, and Jonathan in the lobby.

"What happened? Is Ninang April OK?"

Ninang Mae started to answer but burst into tears before she could get anything intelligible out. Ninang June put an arm around her and said, "She's still in surgery. Bernie's going to keep us updated."

"Was she in an accident or something?"

My godmothers glanced at each other before looking over at Jonathan. He ran a hand down his face, weary in a way I hadn't seen in a while. "With Erica Davis in custody, April insisted on moving back to her house and ending the constant supervision. She was supposed to move her things from June's house this morning and start a later shift at the laundromat, but she never showed. Mae asked me to stop by April's house to see what happened and I found her in the living room. She had head trauma, so I called an ambulance and rode with her to the hospital. Your cousin was working the ED when we arrived and said she'd alert everyone while I talked to the police."

"Head trauma?" Lola Flor asked, her voice sharper than usual. "She was attacked?"

"I believe so. The front door was unlocked when I arrived and there were signs of a struggle," Jonathan said. "She was likely struck on the head with a blunt object, but I didn't see anything that could've been used as a weapon near her, and Detective Nowak tells me they didn't find anything either."

"She hadn't been home in a while. Maybe a burglar thought the house would be empty and she surprised them in the middle of their theft?" Ninang Mae suggested.

You could tell that she desperately wanted that to be true. But Jonathan wasn't the type to give false hope.

"That's certainly possible," he said. "But highly unlikely."

"You think it's connected to Divina's murder," my grandmother said.

He nodded. "As does Detective Nowak. He believes the killer either has it out for the family specifically or that April found important information regarding her niece's death and they wanted to silence her."

"Either way, it means the case isn't closed," I said.

That statement, obvious as it was, made a heavy atmosphere even heavier, and we all sat in silence until Bernadette found us hours later to give us an update.

"She's out of surgery, but she hasn't woken up yet. Until she does, it's hard to say anything definite." Bernadette was doing her best to keep the emotion out of her voice and stay professional. "They're not going to let anyone see her today, but there'll be police surveillance outside her room to make sure she's safe. You should all head home and get some rest."

But the ninangs refused to listen to her until Ninang April's doctor came by and repeated what Bernadette said. "We'll keep you updated if there are any changes in her condition. But there's nothing you can do for her right now. The best way to help is to stay strong and healthy. Now go home."

Tita Rosie had joined us by this point and insisted that Ninang Mae and Ninang June accompany us home for a meal. Too tired and hungry to fight her, we all headed to the house.

I had a feeling we'd end up here, so I prepared a few dishes at the restaurant before meeting you at the hospital."

Tita Rosie and Lola Flor set platter after platter on the table, basically a replay of everyone's favorite comfort foods. She'd had me invite Adeena and Elena to make up for always leaving the cafe during work, and she'd also had us contact Jae and Marcus to let them know what was going on. Bernadette would be joining us after her shift ended, so it was going to be a pretty full house.

We were just missing Ninang April.

It was so weird to see Ninang Mae and Ninang June without her. The Calendar Crew was always a trio; you either saw them all together or not at all. Longganisa usually avoided them, but maybe because she sensed their sadness, she'd been extra clingy and snuggly with them. Jae and Adeena were also doing their best to be charming and entertaining, while Elena, Marcus, Jonathan, and I helped my aunt and grandmother put the finishing touches on dinner.

Once everything was set and we'd taken our places around the table, Lola Flor said a quick grace, thanking God for the food and praying for Ninang April's swift recovery. And with that one sentence, Ninang Mae and Ninang June's resolve vanished and the two of them broke down in tears. There are few things more uncomfortable than watching your godmothers sob into their bowls of nilaga.

I glanced over at Lola Flor and was shocked to see that her eyes were as red as my godmothers'. She met my gaze and jerked her head toward Ninang Mae and Ninang June, and it was like I could hear her voice in my mind.

What's wrong with you? Go comfort them.

I got out of my seat and put one arm around each of the women, hugging them close. They clung to me, crying into my shoulders like children while I squeezed them tight and murmured words of commiseration and consolation.

"I know. It's all so awful, isn't it? You've all had so much to deal with lately, but you don't have to go through it alone. We're here for you." I hugged them close and took a few deep breaths, hoping they would mimic my slow, intentional inhalations. "This isn't the end, though. Ninang April will fight through this and we'll all be together again. And in the meantime, we need to work together to catch whoever did this."

Ninang Mae clung to me for another moment before grabbing a napkin to wipe her face. When she finally faced me, her eyes burned with resolve. "Lila, you have to get them. I'll do whatever it takes, whatever you need me to do. We have to make them pay for what they've done to April."

"Yes, put us to work. Please. I can't just sit around doing nothing," Ninang June said as she pulled herself together.

I looked over at Jonathan. Now that I'd rallied the team, I wasn't quite sure what to do with them. As if he understood my hesitation, he nodded at me and took charge.

"We need to check on Glen's and Ultima's alibis and canvass April's neighborhood to see if there were any witnesses. Maybe one of her neighbors saw an unfamiliar car in the driveway, or someone lurking in the area." Jonathan looked around the table, trying to divvy up the assignments. "Mae and June, I'm sure the neighbors all know you. It'd be natural for you to ask questions, considering the circumstances.

And I'm sure most will be sympathetic since they know how close you are. I'll talk to Glen Davis and Detective Nowak. Lila, you know Mrs. Bolisay's daughter, right? See what you can find out from her."

"I thought you were in charge of Ultima," I said. "Why do you want me to talk to her daughter?"

"I looked into that, uh, anonymous tip I got about her," Jonathan said. "Everyone I talked to at that location backed Ultima's alibi, but it was pretty obvious they were on their guard around me. Ultima is wary of me right now, and she's clever, so I think the best way to handle her is to go around her. At least for now."

That made sense to me, so I promised to try and meet with Nabila soon.

"Rosie and I will talk to the parishioners at St. Genevieve," Lola Flor declared.

"And Father Santiago, as well," Tita Rosie added. "I hate to think about it, but there's a chance that the attacker was someone from our community. The church is our best place to look for them."

"What about us? We want to help too," Adeena said, gesturing to herself and Elena.

"You can talk to your brother and see if he's heard anything about the case," Jonathan said. "And I'm hoping at least one of you can accompany Lila when she visits Mrs. Bolisay's daughter. I don't want anyone talking to any potential suspects alone."

"I'll talk to Millie and see if she has any gossip to share," Jac said. "And I'll set up a meeting with Beth and Valerie to ask about the chamber of commerce members."

"I'll check in with my cousins to see if they heard anything. They work in just about every bar in Shady Palms and Shelbyville, so if anyone with loose lips has been chatting up the bartenders, they'll know about it," Elena volunteered.

With an action plan in place, you could feel the tension in the air slowly dissipating, and our dinner ended with the usual love, laughter, and leftovers for everyone to take home.

"Do you think your brother's OK?" I asked Jae as we chatted in his car, not ready to say goodbye yet. "I know why he left the SPPD. And I admire him for having such strong convictions. But it kind of feels like he was meant for this, don't you think? That was the most talkative I've seen him in a while."

"He really comes alive at moments like this, doesn't he? I noticed it too. You're right, but I don't know what the alternatives are. He hated working for the police department here. But he's not going to want to move anywhere else for work. He came to Shady Palms to be closer to my parents in their old age, and now he has your aunt. There aren't really a ton of options left for him." Jae shook his head. "I hope he finds his purpose soon. Seeing him like this is kind of unnerving. And for all his faults and issues with the system, he was a force for good as a detective."

I sighed and leaned my head against his shoulder. "This town could use a force for good."

Jae smiled down at me. "At least it has us."

Chapter Twenty-Five

Join me as we pray for our members in need, including April Lucero, Nolan Matthews, and Neil Michael. We also remember our dear departed friend, Divina de los Santos. Her memorial photo is still in the meeting room, and her loved ones would appreciate any notes of condolences and friendship."

Father Santiago wrapped up the Sunday Mass, and everyone started making their way to the church basement meeting room for refreshments and mingling. My family paused to light candles for my parents, Divina, and now Ninang April before joining everyone downstairs. Ninang Mae and Ninang June hovered by Divina's portrait, which had a few cards in front of it. At least some of the parishioners cared enough to leave their condolences.

"We should collect these before we leave," I said to my godmothers. "Maybe we can read them to Ninang April later. I'm sure she'd appreciate it."

"That's a good idea," Ninang June said. "Maybe we shouldn't hang around this table then, in case anyone wants to leave a card. I'm sure some people would feel awkward doing it knowing we're watching."

"You think?" Ninang Mae asked. "I figured people would want to make a big show of doing it, so that everyone knows how kind and thoughtful they are."

I couldn't discount that, considering how many of these community niceties were just for show. Still, Ninang June had a point. But how to phrase it without being rude?

Luckily, Lola Flor had no such qualms. "June's right. Besides, neither of you are particularly popular at the moment, so it might be best to circulate and gather information, then meet back here before we leave."

Ninang Mae sucked at her teeth, but otherwise stayed quiet and walked off with Ninang June. I spotted Nabila and Teresa next to the refreshments and went over to join them.

"How's it going?" I asked as I poured myself a cup of coffee from the church's metal urns. I took a sip and did my best not to make a face so as not to insult the aunties who'd brewed the coffee.

I must not have been very successful because Nabila and Teresa started laughing.

"Kind of hard to choke down if you're used to the quality at your cafe, huh?" Teresa said, wrinkling her nose as she sipped at the anemic-looking brew in her cup.

"It's not that bad," Nabila said, adding tons of sugar and powdered non-dairy creamer to her cup.

"Yes, that's why you're doing everything you can to make sure you don't actually taste the coffee, right?" Teresa smiled at her best friend, then leaned toward me, lowering her voice as if sharing a secret. "She finished all the cookies from that gift pack the same day she got it. She's been wanting to go back to your cafe, even if she can't bring herself to admit it."

"You're the worst, you know that, right?" Nabila muttered, her ears red. She wouldn't meet my eyes, instead looking around the room as if plotting her escape.

"Are you two free after this? I plan on heading to the cafe for a few hours. Longganisa is there, and I need to put the finishing touches on my Sangria Sunday contribution."

"Oh, I probably shouldn't . . ." and here Nabila's eyes strayed again.

I followed her gaze and realized she was looking at her mom, who was busy talking to someone else and not glancing our way. Was she worried that her mom would see us talking together?

There was an awkward pause before Teresa asked, "What's Sangria Sunday?"

"Oh, it's something my friend Sana hosts every Sunday. She runs the Mind & Body Wellness Studio in town and also coaches women of color entrepreneurs."

"That sounds pretty cool," Nabila admitted. "I've been meaning to check out some of the classes there. I swim a few times a week, but I want to try something new."

Lightbulb moment. "Why don't you two join us? You don't have to be an entrepreneur to hang out and Sana's always happy to meet potential studio members."

When Nabila hesitated again, I added, "I'm bringing malunggay Basque cheesecake and Adeena and Elena are preparing the nonalcoholic drinks for our hangout. And since it's at the fitness studio, nobody has to know you were hanging out with me."

I thought she'd be embarrassed that I pointed that out, but she actually sighed in relief. "You're right, that's perfect. Mommy's always telling me to lose weight and that I should network more, so she can't complain about me going. I just won't mention you."

I wasn't sure if I should be sad, amused, or alarmed that this grown adult was so afraid of her mother that she had to lie about what she was doing so that her mom wouldn't know she was spending time with the goddaughter of her archnemeses. But was Ultima controlling enough to order Nabila to do her dirty work? Or were her mommy issues so strong that Nabila would do whatever it took to protect Ultima and the family business?

Here's hoping Sana and the others could draw her out more, because there were clearly some issues at play here, and I needed to know if those issues were the reason Divina was dead and Ninang April was in a coma.

This sangria is fantastic! I can't believe you all do this every week." Nabila, armed with a giant glass of sangria and a hefty slice of my malunggay Basque cheesecake, smiled at all of us gathered around Sana's living room. Yuki couldn't make it because she was helping Naoko with a school project, but the rest of us had managed to assemble for our weekly hangout.

"We don't all always make it, especially Yuki since she's married with a kid. But at least one or two members of the group manage to come so I'm not stuck drinking alone," Sana said, topping off Nabila's glass. "I make it a point to schedule nothing at this time, so unless it's a true emergency, I'm always available. It's the only way I can guarantee myself some time off. But I know that's not practical for everyone."

"We are nowhere near that level of work-life balance yet, but at least we get plenty of wine out of it," Izzy said as she pulled a few bottles out of her tote bag.

"When you run your own business, it's easy to forget that everyone needs and deserves time off," Elena said, handing Adeena a slice of cheesecake. "It's tough trying to make that work, especially when you're fairly new."

"We're not there yet either, but we're close!" Adeena slid a forkful of cheesecake into her mouth and moaned. "Lila, I know you said you used malunggay powder, but I swear it tastes like I'm eating a matcha and white chocolate cloud. This is so good."

I grinned. "Isn't it great? With the powder, there are so many possibilities for drinks and desserts. I'm sure Elena could use it in some of her bath and body products too."

"Drinks and herbal products? Are you trying to muscle in on our territory, Macapagal?" Adeena puffed herself up to look big and threatening, which didn't really work considering she was only five two and wearing a goofy T-shirt with a cutesy cartoon frog saying, "I like soup!" (same, little frog, same).

"Don't worry, I know when to stay in my lane." I started to say more when I noticed Nabila and Teresa staring at us. "What's up?"

"Oh, you two just seem like such good friends. I was wondering how long you've known each other," Teresa said.

"I kinda knew who she was when we were kids, but we went to different schools," Adeena said. "We didn't start hanging out till freshman year of high school."

"I went to St. Genevieve for grade school," I explained. "I didn't really have many friends there outside my family, but Bernadette is a year older and Marcus is a few years younger. I think he was in class with you, right, Nabila?"

She nodded. "He was a bit of a clown, but I remember him being a sweet kid. He always followed you two around like a baby duck."

I laughed. "Yeah, looking back, we were a pretty insular group. I mostly kept to myself or hung out with family. I didn't really break out of my shell till high school."

"I wouldn't exactly say we were friends back then," Bernadette said. "You were just the snobby, annoying kid my mom made me compete against all the time."

"She's only saying that because I usually beat her," I said in a stage whisper before raising my glass to her. "It's fine, you were the popular one. At least you have that going for you."

Bernadette grinned and clinked her glass against mine. "To my best frenemy."

We both drank to that, then Bernadette got up to refill her plate. Teresa took her place next to me. "I find it hard to believe you didn't have any friends in grade school. You seem so popular now."

I choked on my wine. "Me? Popular? Not really. I mean, you'd think so considering I was Miss Teen Shady Palms back in high school, but really, a lot of that was luck and practice, not popularity. Winning the pageant actually made me more unpopular since a lot of people thought I didn't deserve it."

She studied my face. "Were you bullied?"

"Not as a kid. Bernadette was right when she called me a snob. I was mostly alone because I felt like I didn't fit in and that nobody in my classes understood me or my dreams. I thought I was better than everybody." I grimaced remembering how I used to be. "But in high school, there was a girl named Janet who *hated* me. She was dating my friend Terrence and assumed there was something going on between us. She only stopped tormenting me because he broke up with her when he found out how she was treating me. After that, it was mostly passive-aggressive petty stuff. But for a while, she made my life hell."

"Do you still see her around town? She wasn't someone who went to school with us, was she?" Nabila asked.

I hesitated, wondering how much to share without violating anyone's privacy. I'd had a brief and very unpleasant reunion with Janet after I returned to Shady Palms. She was currently in jail for her part in a certain tragedy that happened the previous year, but last I heard she was taking her rehabilitation seriously. Terrence was still engaged to her, but I knew it was a delicate situation. He was a great guy and didn't want to abandon her in her time of need, but I thought it was cruel to drag things out considering he'd told me they'd grown apart long before the mess that led to her arrest. But that was his business and I trusted and respected him enough to leave it alone.

"I saw her when I first came back, but she's not in town anymore," I said, finally settling on something neutral yet true.

"That's good," Nabila said. "Bullies are the absolute worst. I'm glad you don't have to deal with her anymore."

That was rich coming from her, considering what a bully her mother could be. But there was no point in antagonizing her—not right now anyway. Not when I needed to get to know her better.

"How about you two? How long have you been friends?" I asked, gesturing between her and Teresa.

"I moved to the States when I was twelve," Teresa said. "I had some relatives here in Shady Palms, so I stayed with them and they enrolled me at St. Gen's. That's where I met Nabila."

"Oh, so I was already in high school when you arrived. And you both went to the Catholic high school as well?"

They nodded and Teresa added, "When I found out the Bolisays were also Bicolano, it was like being back home. They made me feel so welcome."

Nabila added, "Her relatives moved away our junior year, but my mom convinced them to let her stay with us so we could complete high school together. Said she'd had enough big changes in her life and could use the stability."

"That was so nice of her," I said. Not at all like the Ultima I knew.

"My mom's a good person," Nabila said. "I'm sure your godmothers have brainwashed you against her though."

I didn't know it was possible to choke on a piece of cheesecake considering it was so soft, but that statement almost took me out. It took the glass of water Sana poured me and a couple pounds on the back from Bernadette before I could speak again.

"Brainwashing? You're one to talk. You can't even be seen next to me without your mom throwing a fit. Do you really wanna go there?"

Nabila crossed her arms. "Whatever. Your godmothers are nothing but attention seekers anyway. I bet they made up most of this stuff to get everyone back on their side."

Elena and Adeena had to physically restrain Bernadette, who was cussing Nabila out and looked like she was about to punch her in her filthy, lying mouth. I jumped in to make sure Bernadette didn't get in trouble, but the more I called Nabila out for what she said, the angrier I got.

"You think my godmothers had Erica Davis vandalize their business on purpose?"

"Well, it just seemed—"

"Did they also set up Divina's murder? Put Ninang April in a coma as a publicity stunt? Is that what you're really saying to us right now?"

Now it was Sana and Izzy's turn to hold me back as I got closer to Nabila, my pointer finger jabbing at her face to emphasize each question.

Nabila's gaze darted around the room, trying to find an ally. Even Teresa wouldn't look her in the eye.

"You know I owe your mom for everything. But that was way too far. Lately . . ." Teresa trailed off and it looked like she was gathering her courage. "I feel like I don't know either of you anymore. It's like an obsession."

Nabila's nostrils flared as she turned on her supposed best friend. "An obsession? You really want to go there? You?"

Sana placed a gentle hand on both of the girls' chests and separated them. "I'm sorry, but I don't appreciate you bringing all this negativity into my home. I'm going to have to ask the two of you to leave."

That seemed to bring them to their senses and they started apologizing profusely, but Sana had had enough. "I understand, but I still would like you both to leave. You're welcome to my studio and even to another Sangria Sunday, but right now, I think it's best for everybody for you to go so we can all cool off."

"We're really sorry," Teresa said as she pulled Nabila to the door. "Come on. Don't you have anything to say?"

Nabila bit her lip and studied the rest of us in the room before lowering her head, yanking the door open, and rushing out. Teresa just sighed and followed her out.

"Well, that was something," Sana said, pouring more wine in her glass. "Not exactly how these Sangria Sundays are supposed to go."

"I'm sorry. I'm the one who brought them into your home, and all so I could get closer to them for an investigation." I reached out to get more sangria; then, remembering I had to drive and figuring I needed to cool down anyway, I pivoted to the water pitcher instead. "Not that it did any good. All we learned is that Nabila is delusional and will accept anything her mom says, no question. Which I kind of already knew."

"I don't know, I thought your conversation opened up some possibilities," Elena said. "Think about it. She was being insulting when she hinted that your godmothers set up the vandalism, but what if it was her mother whispering in that woman's ear that pushed her to do it? Or maybe she ordered her daughter to get close to Divina, just like Auntie Mac and Auntie June tried to make Divina get all friendly with Nabila and something went wrong?"

"What are you saying? Ultima is the mastermind behind everything and she's just pulling the strings to get everyone to do her bidding?" I asked.

She shrugged. "Or Nabila is so messed up, she did it on her own thinking it's what her mom would want. I wouldn't be surprised if either theory turned out to be true."

She had a point. But how to get close to her after everything that just went down? The things she said weren't exactly something she could just take back and all would be forgiven.

Bernadette voiced exactly what I was thinking. "After what happened tonight, I don't think she's gonna get all buddy-buddy with us again. I highly doubt she's gonna just show up for my Zumba class and be all, 'Hey, remember how I said your mom was using all these tragedies to lie and get attention? My bad, totally didn't mean it!'"

"Teresa seemed a bit more reasonable. She owes the Bolisays a great debt, but she also realized that Nabila was out of line," Adeena said. "She might be our way in."

I nodded. "Good point, we should definitely work on her. I wish there was a way to get close to Ultima though. If she really is the mastermind, I think talking to her or at least observing her would really help the investigation. But Jonathan said he's handling her and she knows what I look like, so I can't be directly involved."

"Did he ever check out that illegal gambling ring your grandmother mentioned?" Adeena asked.

I rolled my eyes. "Yeah, but you've met him. Everything about Jonathan screams 'Cop!' The people there clammed up around him. Ultima claimed she was there the nights Divina died and Ninang April was attacked, and everyone backed up her alibi, but who knows if they were just covering for her."

"So then we need someone to go in there that would fit in and that Ultima either doesn't know or, even if she did, wouldn't arouse her suspicion that they were there," Elena said.

"She'd probably recognize Jae, and Amir is just as bad as Jonathan when it comes to his law-abiding appearance," I said. "She'd also know both of you and of course Bernadette and Marcus as well. Maybe Terrence? But I think he's still out of town."

I was thinking out loud and hitting dead end after dead end until

Izzy came forward to refresh my water glass. I grabbed her wrist. "Of course. Why didn't I think of this before?"

Bernadette smacked herself on her forehead. "You're right! He'd be perfect."

"Uh, what's going on? Why are you two looking at me like that?" Izzy asked nervously.

"We need someone who looks shady enough to be completely at home in an underground gambling ring, but is still on our side. Who do you think perfectly fits that bill?" I asked.

I could see the moment it clicked in everyone's heads and I grinned. "I hope Ronnie's kept his card shark skills sharp. He's going to need them."

Chapter Twenty-Six

After coming up with the foolproof plan of getting Ronnie to go undercover at Ultima's illegal gambling den, I might have hit the sangria just a touch too hard.

"Sorry about this, Jae! She kept insisting that she wanted to see you, so I figured you could help her sober up. We can drop her car off for you, though," Adeena said as she and Elena passed me over to Jae.

"I'm fine, there's just something wrong with my shoes, that's all," I said, pulling them off. "I think the heel is loose. I should get these fixed."

"Of course, babe," Jae said reassuringly as he took my shoes and handed me a sports drink. "Let me carry these for you. I brought you a Pocari Sweat. Are you hungry at all?"

I twisted the cap off the bottle and started gulping down the drink. "Mmm, grapefruit and electrolytes. And yeah, I'm craving something salty. Let's go to the grocery store and get some snacks."

"With no shoes on?" Adeena asked, trying to hold back a laugh. "Or are your heels magically fixed now?"

I glared at her. "I'm sure I'll manage."

Sana disappeared for a moment and came back with a plain pair of flip-flops. "Will these work? My shoes are too big for you, but these shouldn't be too bad."

Considering Sana was at least five inches taller and two shoe sizes bigger, I didn't see this going very well, but she was right. There was maybe an inch gap in the toe and heel areas, but they weren't so comically big that I was going to be tripping over my own feet. I was less likely to break an ankle while wearing them than my heels, at any rate.

"Thanks, Sana, these are a big help."

"No worries. You can keep them or toss them when you're done. Those are just the cheap flip-flops I bring with me to the salon when I get a pedicure. I've got a stack of them in my closet."

With my footwear handled, I was able to make it down the stairs (Sana lived above her fitness studio) and to Jae's car with no problems. I told him all about the argument I had with Nabila and our new plan to send Ronnie to spy on Ultima and see what he could find.

"Wow, that's one heck of a productive hangout. Is that why you drank so much even though you have to wake up early tomorrow for work?" He pulled into the grocery store parking lot and gave me a look. "I hope you don't have a hangover after all this."

I wasn't sure if I should be annoyed or touched by how he was trying to look out for me, so I figured some light teasing was in order. "Unlike you, I'm still in my twenties, so I'll be fine. Get me another sports drink and a bunch of salty carbs and I'll be ready for my morning run with Longganisa."

He clutched at his chest in fake pain. "Well, since this old man needs to sleep soon, maybe I should drop you straight at home and let your aunt and grandmother help you."

"Nooo, I'm sorry! I'll treat you to your favorite seaweed snacks and those honey butter chips you love."

He leaned over for a quick kiss. "Acceptable. Now let's go, I'm hungry!"

We wandered up and down the mostly empty aisles, filling our basket with whatever snacks looked yummy and easy to eat on the park bench outside the store. Jae was off in the refrigerated section looking for more sports drinks and I was searching for salted cashews when I bumped into Glen Davis—literally. My overly large flip-flops and current lack of coordination sent me crashing into him after I spotted him and swiveled my head too suddenly in his direction.

He dropped his basket to catch me, holding me just a little too long and a little too close for comfort. "Hey, it's you! The girl who was looking for a tool kit. Are you OK?"

After steadying me, he leaned in so close I thought he was going to kiss me, so I threw my hands up to block his face.

"Whoa! Personal space."

"Oh, sorry, I just thought I smelled alcohol on you." He let go of me. "Are you drunk? Do you need a ride home?"

I didn't know if it was the liquid courage or just the look on his face as he very unsubtly checked me out, but suddenly this man seemed so disgusting to me and it made me sick to think of him with Divina. I had to know his connection to her.

"You'd like that, wouldn't you? Get me in a car alone with you? Did you say the same thing to Divina? Pretend to be all sweet and thoughtful to get on her good side?"

His eyes flew open and his head jerked back as if I'd punched him. "Whoa, what's this about? And why are you bringing up that girl?"

"I know you were trying to cozy up to her until your wife found out about her. And now she's dead. What a coincidence, right? Unless it wasn't a coincidence." Now it was my turn to lean in too close and make him uncomfortable. "Maybe you were upset your plans to reconcile with your wife were messed up, so you took care of the problem. Or maybe your wife stumbled across her one day when she went to vandalize my godmothers' laundromat. Decided to get rid of the threat herself. Then again, maybe you two did it together. You know, as a sick couple's bonding activity instead of just going to therapy or whatever."

Glen's head whipped from side to side, either looking to escape or for some backup, but I couldn't stop.

"Were you two in on it? After all, you're each other's alibis. Mutually assured destruction, right?"

"That's enough!" Glen yelled. "First you get my wife arrested, and now you want to pin murder on us too? Well, it's not gonna happen! We're both innocent."

"Oh, I know what happened. You found out that she was only talking to you to help out her aunt and the laundromat, didn't you?"

His entire body stiffened and I knew I hit a sore spot—his bruised ego. "She tried to play me like a fool! Cozying up to me, all beautiful and worldly and fascinating, making me feel like . . . anyway, it doesn't matter. All we did was talk. Ask anyone, they'll tell you they only ever saw us chatting in public and nothing else. I never did anything with her and I sure as hell didn't kill her. I just want to forget about her."

"Yeah, that's the problem. Everyone wants to just forget about her. She's just an inconvenience to you and the SPPD, isn't she? But she was a person. She had a family who loved her. Like my Ninang April, who keeps blaming herself for everything."

"Maybe she should! Maybe her big mouth finally caught up to her and both she and Divina paid the price!"

"So you admit it? That these women wronged you and you had to make them pay."

"I'm not admitting nothing!"

At this point, another late-night shopper wandered into our aisle but turned tail and ran as soon as they saw our confrontation. Knowing it was only a matter of time before the staff came over to calm us down or kick us out, I started to lay it on real heavy.

"Everyone knows it was either you or Ultima Bolisay and she has an actual alibi. She admitted to her gambling den and has several witnesses saying she was there the night Divina was attacked." I was technically bluffing since I didn't quite believe Ultima's alibi, but I wasn't lying either. "But the only alibis you and your wife have are each other. Pretty sus, huh?"

His face twisted in confusion. "What does that mean? Suspicious? If you want suspicious, I suggest you poke around Ultima's alibi. Just because she was there part of the night doesn't mean she was there the whole time. I know for a fact she puts her husband in charge at least once a week while she handles some business. Though I think her daughter's doing it now since he's in the hospital."

"What kind of business?"

"You won't get more out of me without a warrant or a hell of an incentive."

He started to walk away, but I grabbed his arm. "Wait, I'm not finished talking to you!"

"Let go of me, little girl, or I'm going to make you wish you had." Glen raised his other hand at me, but before he could do anything, he was yanked away.

"Hey there, what's all this?" Jae stood between me and Glen, his posture and tone carefully controlled. He had a slight smile on his face and his voice was polite, so it was easy to overlook his threat level until you looked into his eyes. "Are you threatening my girlfriend?"

"Oh, uh, hey there, Dr. Jae," Glen said, reminding me that Jae was one of the few dentists in town so everyone knew him. "It wasn't a threat, I just got a little hotheaded, that's all."

"And why is that?"

"She accused me and my wife of having something to do with that girl's death. I don't know who raised her, but that's not exactly polite conversation, is it?"

I swear the air around us dropped a few degrees, the chill in Jae's eyes was so strong. "Your wife tried to destroy her family's business, someone she knew was killed, and now her godmother's in the hospital. You think politeness is what she needs to worry about right now?"

Glen started to sputter. "I mean, I'm sorry for their losses and all, but what my wife did has nothing to do with me. I didn't do anything."

"In that case, why don't you tell us where you were Wednesday morning?" I asked. Even if he didn't kill Divina (which I still wasn't sure about), there's a chance he was the one who attacked Ninang April.

"I'm at my store every weekday from eight to four. If you don't believe me, you can talk to my employees and check our security cameras." Glen crossed his arms. "And before you start wondering if I go out and kill people on my lunch breaks, I've been eating in the break room or my office for a while now. Which you'll also see on the camera. You satisfied?"

"I will be once I look at those videos." I got the call about Ninang April around two p.m. that day, so if he was telling the truth, those tapes would definitively rule him out.

"Fine. And Dr. Jae, for what it's worth, tell your girl to be careful. Someone clearly didn't like those women sticking their noses into other people's business. If she's going to do the same, she better watch her back." Glen bent down to pick up his shopping basket. "Not a threat. Just common sense. I'll be seeing you."

"How condescending." I imitated Glen's voice. "'Dr. Jae, tell your girl' . . . as if I wasn't standing right there."

I moved to pick up my own shopping basket, but Jae stopped me. "Lila, despite how he said it, he's right. You know how dangerous this can be."

"We're in public! And I knew you were around—"

"We're in public and he still raised his hand to you. You can't predict how people will react if you press them too hard." Jae grasped my hand in his. "Promise me that you won't interrogate people alone. That you'll always make sure to have backup anytime you do this. *Promise me.*"

I caressed his cheek, usually so soft and smooth, now tense and rigid as he clenched his jaw. "I promise."

He closed his eyes and leaned into my touch. "Good. Now let's go pay for these snacks. I'm hungry, and we've got a lot to plan for tomorrow."

Chapter Twenty-Seven

Ay April, you'll never believe what she did next. So then . . ."

Ninang Mae prattled on and on to a comatose Ninang April, catching her up on all the latest gossip in Shady Palms. It had been several days since her attack, but even though her surgery was a success, Ninang April still hadn't woken up. We'd taken to visiting her every day, sometimes individually, often as a group, and chatting with her so she wouldn't be lonely. Or at least, that's what we told ourselves. I know on my part that I did it to try and regain some sense of normalcy, some hope that if we just kept talking to her, she'd eventually answer back.

Ninang Mae and Ninang June sat on one side of the bed and Tita Rosie and Lola Flor sat on the other, the former clutching her rosary and the latter holding Ninang April's hand. Bernadette, Marcus, and I stood apart from the group, watching our elders and not speaking. Ninang April had a private room, so we were able to gather like this every day without anyone complaining about the crowding or noise.

But every day, this one-sided vigil got heavier, the conversation more forced, the outcome more bleak. Was it time to come to terms with the fact that we might lose her?

I wasn't ready for that. I didn't know that I'd ever be ready for that, but certainly not when the person who put her in this hospital bed was still on the loose.

"I need some fresh air," I said. "Do you all need anything? I might stop by the cafe for some coffee and to check on Longganisa."

"I'm fine, anak, but maybe you can bring some coffee for the staff room? I'm sure the doctors and nurses would appreciate it," Tita Rosie said, her fingers rubbing the rosary bead she'd paused on. She eyed the three of us hovering by the door. "Bernie and Marcus, why don't you go with her? She'll need help carrying everything. Bring snacks too, OK?"

The three of us silently made our way to my car. It wasn't until I pulled in to the plaza that housed the Brew-ha Cafe, Tita Rosie's Kitchen, and Dr. Jae's Dental Clinic (it was all very convenient) that Marcus said, "I don't know how much more of this I can take."

I pulled into a parking spot, and Bernadette and I both turned around to look at him in the backseat. He had his head down and was staring at his hands.

"Marcus?"

"I thought it was all over when I caught the vandal. I thought my mom and everyone would be safe. Now Ninang April might never wake up and Ate Bernie's mom and mine could be next. The police have made so little progress, and it just feels like there's nothing I can do. Are we just supposed to wait around and hope that the worst doesn't happen? 'Thoughts and prayers' our way through this?"

Tears dripped down onto his hands as he let this out. Bernadette and I unbuckled our seat belts and moved around to the back where we sandwiched him in a tight embrace, the two of us holding him as he cried.

"I needed this," he said, his hands clutching our arms that were wrapped across his chest. "Thanks. I've been trying to stay strong in front of my mom, but sitting in that room just felt like the breaking point, you know? I couldn't do it anymore." He wiped his eyes and smiled up at Bernadette. "Sorry to put this on you, Ate Bernie. I know you're struggling as much as me."

She ruffled his hair. "No worries. My job at least keeps me busy enough to pretend I'm doing something useful for the family. You're the one who's had to go to the laundromat every day and fill in for Divina and now Ninang April. Of course you had to let it all out."

"You could cry too, you know. No need to act tough in front of us," I said.

"You'd like that, wouldn't you? As much as I'd love that kind of release, you both know I'm secretly a robot and crying is impossible," Bernadette joked. "Anyway, let's go load ourselves with chocolate and caffeine before we have to head back to the hospital."

"Ate Bernie . . ." Marcus and I both said.

"Look, someday I will learn emotional intelligence and then it'll all be over for you heauxs. But until then, I just need you to feed me, OK?"

Laughing, the three of us made our way into the cafe and were greeted by Adeena, Elena, Katie, and Joy, who was helping at the cafe today since Tita Rosie's Kitchen was closed.

"Ate Lila!" Joy threw her arms around me. "I feel like I never see you anymore. Are you all done at the hospital? How's Tita April doing?"

She was so adorable that I patted her on the head even though she was three inches taller than me. "Why hello there, Miss Soon-to-Be-College-Student. How's it going?"

Ever since her early admission acceptance to University of Chicago, Joy had spent more time working to save up money before she moved away. So even though she was right next door, it wasn't exactly easy to chat with her while she dealt with the increasing popularity of Tita Rosie's Kitchen.

"And no, we're just on a snack run. The three of us are taking a breather before heading back with coffee and sweets for everyone. How are things here?" I moved behind the counter to box up a bit of everything for my family and the hospital staff, then loaded a platter with everything chocolate we had on display while Joy filled me in on the rather uneventful day. "That's good. Oh, could you put in an order for an iced Brew-ha #1 for me? Thanks."

I made my way over to Bernadette and Marcus's table and set the sweets in front of them. "As per your request, all the chocolate we have on offer."

There were pandan cheesecake brownies, red bean brownies, ube chocolate chip cookies, ube Oreo mochi Rice Krispie treats, brown butter chai chocolate chip cookies, Mexican hot chocolate cookies, and a champorado parfait, the last of which was still in the experimental phase. I didn't usually make so many chocolate offerings in one day, but I guess subconsciously I felt the need for chocolaty comfort as much as Marcus did.

"I know things look bad right now, but there's about to be a break in the case. I just know it." I crunched on an ube Oreo mochi Rice Krispie treat and momentarily lost myself in the various flavors and textures that played so well together. "If nothing else, Ronnie's supposed to infiltrate Ultima's gambling den soon. We're just waiting for Jonathan to finish some things up on his end."

Bernadette's face scrunched up the way it did anytime her ex-boyfriend's name came up. "Pinning our hopes on Ronnie doesn't exactly fill me with confidence."

"Don't worry, Jonathan was able to get some equipment from a private detective buddy of his. We'll be listening in as backup," I reassured her.

"Whoa, that actually sounds like fun. Count me in," Marcus said.

"Don't you work tonight?"

"Yeah, but I can call off for this."

Bernadette and I leveled looks at him. "How many times have you called off this month?"

"Not that many."

"And how many times is 'not many'?" Bernadette pressed.

"I just think—"

"Marcus, I'm glad you want to help, but we've got this covered. If this doesn't work and we need a new angle for the investigation, you can get in on that," I promised. "Right now, keeping a job with a steady paycheck is what will help your mom the most."

Marcus sighed. "Fine. But if you ever need me, either of you, make sure to call me. I got your backs, OK? I want you to know you can rely on me."

Bernadette reached out to hold one of his hands and I held his other. She was probably thinking the same thing as me: our (figurative) little brother was all grown up now.

W e dropped off the boxes of coffee and sweets in the staff break room and made our way back to Ninang April's room to relieve the aunties of their vigil. They weren't staff, so they weren't allowed into the break room, but since Bernadette worked there and Ninang June used to be head nurse, they pulled some strings and were able to use an empty meeting room to relax in rather than be forced to convene in the noisy cafeteria.

Bernadette, Marcus, and I took our places around Ninang April with Lola Flor, who stayed in the room after saying she wasn't hungry.

"Lola Flor, can I at least get you some water? You need to stay hydrated if you want to be strong for Ninang April," Bernadette said.

Lola Flor agreed, and while Bernadette filled a plastic cup from the pitcher on the side, I moved my chair closer to Lola Flor.

"Has the doctor been in yet?" I asked.

She nodded. "No changes, but her brain waves remain strong, so they're going to continue hoping she wakes up soon."

Bernadette tried to hand Lola Flor the water, but my grandmother didn't seem to see her. All her attention was focused on Ninang April's still form. "Lola Flor, are you OK?"

Lola Flor blinked and looked up at Bernadette, then over at me and Marcus, who leaned toward her in concern. She let go of Ninang April's hand to accept the water.

"I'm fine. Just lost in thought." She sipped the room temperature water and avoided meeting our eyes. "How's the investigation going? Did Jonathan give you an update?"

"I'm supposed to meet up with him and Jae later. But as far as I know, nothing worth mentioning."

"What is taking them so long? I knew it would go downhill once Jonathan left the force, but are they so incompetent that one person leaving makes that much difference?"

"Detective Nowak says it's tough because the only clue they have is a matching pair of fingerprints at both the laundromat and Ninang April's house that don't belong to any of us and aren't in the system, so they can't trace it. All their suspects seem to have alibis and there were no witnesses and no working security cameras. This goes for both Divina's case and Ninang April's," Marcus said. He'd been in contact with Detective Nowak more than anyone else because he'd not only been close to Divina, but his mom was connected to the case and he'd worked at the SPPD once upon a time.

"I thought there were no prints at the laundromat?"

"Apparently, they were able to recover a partial print later on. And it seems to match the one at Ninang April's house."

"I'm meeting with Jonathan later because he said he might've found someone who can help regarding Ninang April's case," I said. "He said it might be nothing and to not get my hopes up, but I'm not giving up. We're close. I know we are."

Lola Flor looked at me, then back at Ninang April. "You better be."

She stood up and left the room without another word or glance at me and my cousins.

"She's taking this a lot harder than I thought she would," Bernadette said. "I know they're the two that are the most alike, but I didn't think they were that close."

I'd never thought about it, but she was right. Tita Rosie may have been her daughter, but the one who was most like Lola Flor when it came to the way she thought, spoke, and acted was Ninang April. Despite never saying it, I knew Lola Flor loved my aunt. Of course she did. But did she see Ninang April as another daughter figure? Considering how deeply she still felt the loss of my father, her younger child, was Ninang April a sort of stand-in for him? I was only eight when he and my mom died, but from what I remembered, he was nothing like Lola Flor, personality-wise. He wasn't quiet and reserved like Tita Rosie—in fact, he was loud and outgoing, a real entertainer and charmer, just like my mother. Who my grandmother hated. Maybe that's why Lola Flor gravitated to Ninang April—both of her children were so different from her and seemed to reject the way she'd raised them. And I was sure the fact that Ninang April had no family here drew in my grandmother as well.

I looked over at my godmother. *Please wake up, Ninang April. You're not alone here. And there are people who need you.*

So please wake up.

Chapter Twenty-Eight

H ey Leslie, thanks so much for taking the time to meet with me."
I'd finally arranged a time to meet with Leslie Kowalski for
their Brew-ha Cafe interview. I'd kept putting it off since things had
started happening in the investigation, but we were still a few days
off from Ronnie checking out Ultima's gambling ring and I didn't
want to stop the momentum. I figured now was the time to meet with
some of our dark-horse candidates to see if they were connected to either case.

"Thanks for this opportunity! Especially since I don't have any work
experience." Leslie Kowalski handed me their résumé and sat down in
the chair across from me. "I know you said I didn't have to bring a résumé, but it's one of the assignments they make all seniors do."

When I first met Leslie, I remembered them as a drab wallflower,
always hiding behind their more outgoing best friend, Sharon (Mary
Ann Randall's daughter). I learned there was more to them during
their Q&A portion of the beauty pageant, and appreciated the spark I

saw in Leslie when they had a chance to stand on their own. We were meeting in my office for privacy, but I also hoped it'd help Leslie relax since Longganisa was in her bed beneath my desk. When I saw them smile down at Nisa, I knew we'd have a good interview.

"You may not have official work experience, but you're a member of the cheer team and have done plenty of charity events with them. Can you tell me a bit more about some of these events?" I asked, pointing to the section they'd listed under "Volunteering."

"We do a lot of fund-raising at the school, you know, for uniforms and transportation to competitions and things like that. But we also hold bake sales, food and clothing drives, and things like that to raise money for the community center and food bank. We're hoping to eventually raise money for college scholarships, but that might take some time to organize."

"That's amazing! I didn't realize the cheer team was so community-oriented. It's sure changed since my time at Shady Palms High."

They smiled, glowing with pride but not for themself. "It was all Sharon. She's always been like that. She sees what needs to be done and then she sets out to do it, no matter how hard. I hope she becomes a community organizer—she'd do so much good. Her mom's not into that idea, though. No money or prestige."

I'd planned on asking about Leslie's mom after the interview was officially over, but they gave me an in I just had to take. "Mary Ann is very much a go-getter. I hope Sharon stays true to herself and follows her own path. And maybe her mom will come around eventually."

Leslie made a face like, *yeah right, I'll believe it when I see it* (and honestly, I agreed). I said, "OK, I know Mary Ann is a tough sell, but from what I hear, she's being a good friend to your mom right now."

Leslie looked at the floor. "How much did you hear?"

"Just that your mom had some legal and financial troubles over a product she was trying to sell, but she's doing her best to get by and Mary Ann's helping with that."

They made a *pssht* noise with their lips. "Yeah, she's helping, all right. By making my mom her servant and acting like she should be grateful about it."

"There's no shame in being a domestic worker," I gently chided Leslie, "but if your mom feels like she's being taken advantage of, that's a different story."

They flushed. "Sorry. I didn't think about how that sounded. I didn't mean that my mom's too good for that kind of work. And the fact that she's willing to publicly support my mom after her humiliation says a lot for their friendship. I just . . ."

"How's your mom doing? Has she accepted the situation, or . . . ?"

"It was pretty bad at first, not gonna lie. She said some, um, not-so-nice things about your godmothers for getting in her business."

I grimaced. "I was afraid of that."

"But it's not like that now!" They were quick to reassure me. "She doesn't have a grudge against them or anything."

"How can you be sure? I'm not accusing your mom of anything," I quickly added. "But there's been a lot of bad stuff happening around my godmothers lately."

Leslie looked sad. "A few months ago, I want to say around Christmas, my mom was doing really bad. I think she felt guilty she couldn't get me or my siblings the gifts she knew we wanted. But she didn't want to admit that she was the problem, so she just drank and ranted about how unfair life is. Finally, our family doctor sat down and had a talk with her. Told her that she knows my mom didn't have any ill intentions, but she needs to understand that someone could've died because my mom couldn't be bothered to research food safety."

"And she finally accepted it?"

They nodded. "It scared her. Before, she was too mad to take the claims seriously. But she respects our doctor, and after that talk she started researching the case and realized how lucky she was that her business got shut down early before she could do any permanent damage."

I would have to talk to Helen Kowalski before I could officially cross her off my list. Obviously. Just because I didn't want this kid's mom to be the killer or attacker didn't mean I could let my guard down. I'd been fooled before, after all. But I had to admit that hearing Leslie's side of the story definitely helped.

"I'm glad to hear that." I cleared my throat and looked down at their résumé to reorient myself. "Anyway, sorry to get so off track. Getting back to the interview, what kind of tasks were you in charge of for the fund-raisers?"

Leslie looked relieved that we were no longer talking about their family's private life. "Um, all kinds of things? But my favorite is definitely the bake sales. Sharon's great at selling, so she and the rest of the squad usually handled that while I did all the baking."

"You like to bake?" Consider my interest piqued.

"I *love* to bake!" They leaned toward me, face lit up with excitement. "I used to bake all the time with my nana when I was a kid. My mom doesn't really like it. She prefers cooking, but she has to look good in front of all the other moms, so she has me prepare her dessert contributions for PTA events and parties."

They paused and thought for a moment. "I know that a big part of this job is customer service, so I don't want it to seem like I don't know how to handle sales. Sharon's been having me help with that stuff more at fund-raisers since she thinks it's good for me. And I'm always happy to learn new skills."

They were sounding better and better as an employee. Adeena, Elena, and I were cross-trained in each other's areas so that we could all handle making drinks, baking and assembling desserts, talking knowledgeably about plants and beauty products, etc. Elena was good at everything, so I trusted her with my basic recipes. Adeena, however, could really only handle popping ready-made dough into the oven. Training someone to help me out in the kitchen would not only make our business run smoother, but it'd allow me to run errands and take time off with a clearer conscience knowing someone could hold my spot down for me.

I leaned toward them. "I know graduation's coming up soon and you have a lot going on, so why don't we start you off with training and maybe the occasional weekend? Once you're ready, we'd be happy to take you on full-time."

Leslie's hands flew up to their face. "You mean I've got the job?"

"I'll need you to come back later this week to fill out paperwork, but yes. Welcome to the Brew-ha Cafe crew!"

They let out a shriek so piercing that Longganisa started howling and Katie ran into my office. "What's going on? Is everything OK?"

"I've got a job!"

"Oh, that's great!" Katie hugged them. "By the way, your mom's here. Said she needs the car."

Leslie deflated at that, but I figured it was now or never to talk to Helen. "Hey, that's great! Katie, could you ask her to come here? I'd like to talk to her about Leslie's position. And Leslie can give the good news about their new job."

Helen Kowalski was a forty-something-year-old white woman whose style, like much of the PTA Squad, consisted of dressing head to toe in faux luxury athleisure wear (a specialty of the local Thompson family corporation). She had the same drab coloring as Leslie (or I guess technically Leslie got their drab coloring from her), but at least Leslie had a spark to them. You could sense intelligence and humor and life when talking to them. I couldn't say the same for their mom.

"Helen! So good to see you. I think Leslie has something to tell you."

I nudged an extremely uncomfortable-looking Leslie forward. "Hey mom. Guess what? I've got a job!"

Helen reacted in a way that I can only describe as surprised-blinking-guy gif. "You what? Why didn't you tell me you were applying for jobs?"

I raised my eyebrows at Leslie, but they looked so miserable I directed my response to Helen. "I hope it won't be a problem. I already promised Leslie that their training won't interfere with graduation and we have a full-time position waiting for them once they're ready."

"Full-time position? How much are you paying? Minimum wage?"

"Minimum *living* wage," I said.

There was a difference between the two, and the other Drew-has and I had promised each other that we would only take on new staff if we could offer a proper living wage. If we couldn't afford to give our workers proper pay, we didn't deserve to have their labor. Simple as that.

I assumed Helen was asking these questions because she was being snobby and thought her child deserved to work at a fancier, higher-paying job, so my jaw legit dropped when she asked, "Do you have any other open positions? I'm looking for a job, too."

"Mom!" I thought Leslie was going to melt into a puddle on the floor, they looked so horrifically embarrassed.

"I'm sure you don't want to be stuck working with your mom, but you know our situation. And considering who your godmothers are, I'm betting you know our situation, too," Helen added, waving off Leslie's concerns and giving me a knowing look.

"About that . . . Leslie, I'm sorry, but could you give us some privacy? Don't worry, I'm definitely keeping that position saved for you," I assured them with a smile.

Leslie skulked off, closing the door behind them.

"Helen, I understand things are rather tight right now and I sympathize. But I've heard that you hold a grudge against my godmothers and I'm not comfortable working with someone who wishes my family ill will."

"Wait, who told you that? I may have been upset with your godmothers at first, but that's because my life was falling apart and it was easier to blame them than deal with it. I'm in a better place now. And while they may be a tad bit nosy for my taste, they ultimately saved me. If I'd kept selling that sauce, who knows what might've happened?"

OK, so either Helen and Leslie colluded on this story before the interview or Helen was telling the truth. Still, though . . .

"Mind telling me where you were the night before opening day of the Big Spring Clean? And also your schedule from last Wednesday?"

Helen looked confused, but took her phone out and opened up her calendar. "Let's see, that first one . . . Leslie had a cheer competition out of town. Mary Ann thought it'd be fun to book a hotel and watch the kids perform. Like a mini getaway."

I made a note to double-check that with Leslie and maybe Katie, but if true, then Helen didn't kill Divina.

"As for that other day, I was all over town running errands for Mary Ann. I spent most of that morning getting her an oil change, according to this." She showed me her calendar, which corroborated her story. I'd make sure to have Jonathan call the mechanic to verify it.

"I'm glad to clear all that up. Unfortunately, we don't have the funds for a second full-time employee opening yet. Maybe in—"

"I'll take part-time. Whatever you have available. Do you offer delivery? I could be your delivery person so you don't have to handle it yourself."

Even more convincing than the desperation in her voice (OK, so maybe the desperation moved me a teensy bit—I'm not made of stone) was her offer to do delivery. Since my baking occurred mostly in the morning and maybe a stint in the early afternoon to refill our cases, I was usually the one tasked with delivering catering orders and picking up supplies. Hiring someone whose sole job was to handle all those tedious tasks would not only free up more cafe time for me, it would also allow us to expand our services and offer delivery to all our customers rather than just our large catering orders. I may not have wanted someone who got called out for food safety issues doing any of the food prep, but if she was just driving, I didn't see any issues. And to top it off, if Helen was out doing delivery work, she wouldn't be working inside the cafe most of the time, which should be a huge relief for Leslie. I didn't want them to be scared off from the job before they even started. Win-win-win.

"You know what, Helen? That's a fantastic idea. If you're willing to take a food safety course, we can take you on as a part-time employee in charge of all the delivery orders. Does that work for you?"

She didn't even flinch when I mentioned the food safety course, just nodded so hard she looked like a bobble head. "Yes! When can I start?"

I needed to break the news to my partners that I'd hired another employee and expanded our services without consulting them. I should probably text Terrence, too, to update our website and app to reflect the changes we were making.

"I need to talk to our tech guy about changing our website and app first. I'll text you once my partners and I figure out a schedule."

Helen wrote down her contact info and left my office with a bounce in her step that hadn't been there before. That I didn't think had ever been there. Pleased with not only crossing something off my investigation list, but also improving the business and doing a good deed as well, I clipped Longganisa's leash to her collar and headed out to let Adeena and Elena know we had some new Brew-has on staff.

Chapter Twenty-Nine

H ey Cuz, we've got a bit of a problem."
It was the night of Ronnie's big undercover sting operation (I know that's not the correct word, but it sounds so much cooler and my cousin likes feeling important) at Ultima's gambling den, which was conveniently located below her flagship store. It'd been less than an hour since he'd arrived at the location and he was already calling me with problems. This did not bode well for our investigation.

"Ronnie, are you in trouble? If so, get out of there and contact Detective Park!"

"Aww, are you worried about me? You're so sweet. I guess we really have gotten closer these last few months."

My heart had started racing at the thought of my cousin in danger, and it still beat in double time, but this time in anger and frustration instead of panic.

"On God, I will sic Bernadette on you if you don't tell me what's going on."

"Sorry, sorry! What I meant was, there's a problem with the original plan but it could also be an opportunity. I've already talked to Detective Park about it and he told me to call you."

I waited for him to tell me why Detective Park wanted him to call me, but I guess invoking his ex-girlfriend's name put a bit of a scare in him and he didn't say anything else until I prompted him.

"And . . . ?"

"Oh, right. So I'm supposed to be observing Ultima and learning more about her, maybe try to talk to her, right?"

"I repeat, and . . . ?"

"But she just left. One second, she was there talking to one of the card dealers and then it was like she bamfed out of there."

"Bamfed?"

"You know, like teleported. It's the sound Nightcrawler made when he—"

"Ronnie, can you get to the point? Ultima is gone, so what? You're done early?"

"Detective Park is tailing her to see where she's going, but someone arrived to take her place. One of the regulars said it's her daughter. I know you sent me to avoid being seen by Ultima, but with her gone, I figured you might want to check this place out yourself. I'll continue working the card tables and you do whatever it is you do."

Nabila was there? Well, I guess that answered the question of whether she knew about her mom's side hustle or not. After our little blowup at Sana's, I wasn't sure if I should risk being seen at her mom's gambling den. Then again, wouldn't that be the perfect place to catch her off guard? She wouldn't want me blabbing all over town about her mom's illegal activities, so I could use this opportunity to push and ask some awkward questions. Or was I just putting myself in unnecessary danger?

"If you're worried about the daughter too, I can handle this myself.

Considering I've never met her, I doubt she knows who I am," Ronnie said, correctly interpreting my silence.

"No, it's too dangerous with Detective Park gone. You should have some backup. Just let me call Jae and we'll figure out a new plan."

"Sounds good, Cuz. You go ahead and call Dr. Muscles. I'll continue cleaning up around here. These Shady Palms fools still haven't learned how to play cards."

Shaking my head, I hung up on my cousin to call my boyfriend. "Jae? I'm gonna need your help. How good are you at card games that *don't* have fantasy creatures on them?"

T o be honest, when I heard about Ultima's gambling ring, I figured it would just be, like, a really big poker night. You know, a bunch of guys smoking around several card tables. This is . . . I don't even know how to describe this."

Jae and I stood near the entrance of the gambling area, taking everything in. It wasn't as if Ultima had installed slot machines (though I did see a few video-gaming machines lining the walls) or had cocktail waitresses wandering around in skimpy outfits à la Las Vegas, but considering this was hidden underneath a laundromat, the decor was . . .

"A lot," I said to Jae. "The only way to describe this place is 'a lot.' I guess I shouldn't be surprised considering Ultima is just as gaudy as my godmothers, but this much red and gold is legit hurting my eyes. And is that an actual bar area in the back?"

It was. In addition to the bar and requisite poker tables, there were also areas dedicated to mahjong (naturally), pusoy (of course), blackjack, dominoes, and a bunch of other games I didn't recognize.

"Whoa, they have Go-stop! I used to play this with my mom and grandparents all the time," Jae said, making his way to a table with beautiful tiny cards decorated with flowers. I'd seen them in K-dramas before and had always wanted to try playing, but I'd looked up the rules once and couldn't figure it out. I'd never been particularly good at card games.

"I'm gonna look around, maybe meet up with Ronnie. Have fun," I said, giving him a quick kiss. "Let me know what you learn."

Jae settled himself at the Go-stop table and I made my way to the pusoy section, knowing that's where I'd find Ronnie. He excelled at just about all card games, but Filipino poker was his favorite.

He was right where I thought he'd be, but one look at him let me know he was holding court at the table, and I didn't want to have to listen to him brag and/or talk smack. I kept on walking until I saw Nabila alone behind the bar. Perfect.

"Can I get an amaretto sour, please?" I said, sliding onto the bar stool in front of her.

Her hands stilled on the glass she was polishing. "What are you doing here?"

"The same as anyone else here, I imagine. Grabbing a drink, enjoying some illegal gambling, all that good stuff."

Nabila slammed down the glass. "What're you trying to pull? Is this a raid? Are there cops surrounding the building or something?"

"First of all, I'm honored that you think a little ol' cookie baker like me could be leading a raid. Though you lose points for assuming I'm working with the SPPD. Like I'd want to be anywhere near one of their bumbling operations."

Her eyes narrowed, but she motioned at me to keep going. "Second, I'm just here to talk. There's no gotcha moment. I don't have, like, a video camera inside of my hat or a wire recording our conversation."

Ronnie was wearing a wire, which was how Detective Park was keeping tabs on him, but she didn't need to know that.

"What do you want to know?" she asked as she got to work on my drink.

I watched Nabila's quick, confident movements as she mixed the cocktail and idly wondered if the Brew-has and I should sign up for a bartending course. The Brew-ha Cafe had a liquor license, which we mostly used to sell Ronnie's wine and Elena's craft beer. But if we offered specialty cocktails and mocktails, that would open us up to a whole world of nighttime events we could be offering.

"Where'd you learn to mix drinks?" I asked.

She paused, the orange slice garnish in her hand hovering above my glass. "That's what you want to know?"

"Among other things."

She stuck the orange slice on the rim, plunked a maraschino cherry in the glass, and slid it in front of me. "Not all of us got to go away to college like you did. Some of us were stuck at home helping out our family business and learning random skills from YouTube to get by."

"How long has your mom been running this joint?"

She shrugged. "Since I was in high school. Maybe even before that. My dad was the one in charge since my mom was so busy with the laundromats. But then he got cancer and is always in and out of the hospital, so my mom took this over and got me involved."

"Do you like working here?"

"It's more interesting than the laundromat."

I looked around the large open space and noticed what looked like a kitchen next to the bar area. "You serve food here too?"

"We all gotta eat, right? If we offer food, it means our customers are more likely to stay here longer. We have free small snacks for everyone, as well as simple pica-pica they can order." She nodded toward a menu on the wall. "My mom and I make everything ourselves."

Pica-pica are finger foods, basically anything you can eat easily with your hands. At Ultima's place, this meant sandwiches, siopao, and Spam musubi. They seemed to avoid the messier barbecue sticks and other typical fried Filipino finger foods, probably to avoid getting grease and sauce all over their cards.

"I'll have a Spam musubi as well."

She headed to the kitchen without a word and returned with my delicious, plastic-wrapped treat. I handed her the money for my drink and snack and took a bite while pondering what direction to take the conversation.

"Your family's laundromat is super successful and now I find out you've got this gambling thing going, too. Why is your mom so threatened by my ninangs and their one shop?"

Considering her outburst last time I dared to criticize her mom, I expected Nabila to erupt defensively. Instead, she leaned her forearms against the bar top and sighed. "That's a good question. I know it seems unreasonable to most people. Even I think she goes too far sometimes. But you have to understand she wasn't always like this. Competitive, sure. But the old her welcomed competition, if only so she could prove she was the best."

I took a sip of my amaretto sour, relishing the perfect mix of sweet and tart that flooded my tongue. "So what changed?"

"My dad got sick. We almost lost him at one point; he had to be resuscitated. And it's like my mom realized her life could change, that she could lose everything she cared about in an instant. That's the sense I got, anyway." Nabila helped herself to a cherry from the jar next to her. "There's also a more practical side to it. Having cancer is expensive. Especially if you want to afford good treatments and private rooms, which we obviously do. So my mom's become more and more obsessed with making money, making sure we're all taken care of. She's not greedy for the sake of being greedy, despite what you all may think."

"I understand why it's so important to your mom to protect her family's assets," I said. And I did. But how far would she go to do so?

"I know what you're thinking and you can stop right there. My mom didn't kill Divina or hurt Tita April."

"How do you know that? Her alibi is shaky at best."

"She was in Chicago when Tita April was attacked. My dad had an overnight hospital stay for a treatment he can't get here and she stayed with him. The cops already confirmed that."

Fair enough, though I needed to ask Jonathan to confirm that with the SPPD. "And the day Divina was killed?"

"She was here."

"All night? Didn't leave even once?"

"Nope."

"How can you be sure?"

"I was here. And I can assure you, she stayed here the entire time."

I nodded and let it go. I didn't have to say anything after that anyway—we both knew it was the first time all night that she'd been less than truthful.

Y ou guys learn anything?" I asked Ronnie and Jae.
      Jae and I had followed Ronnie to his condo since it was closer to Ultima's side of town than mine. We didn't bother going up though—it was late and a quick parking lot debriefing was all that was necessary.

"Glen Davis didn't kill Divina," Ronnie said. "One of the guys at the pusoy table saw them together the night she died. Glen had brought her with him, but I guess they got into an argument because he told her to find her own way home and she stormed off. He spent the rest of the night getting drunk, and the guy I talked to had to drive him home. A few of the regulars confirmed it after I talked to them separately. Whoever Divina left with the night she died, it wasn't Glen."

"That matches what I heard," Jae said. "Apparently, it's not often you see women around the place, especially not young, pretty women. So these guys took notice. Before that night, the only young women they saw around the place were Ultima's daughter and some other girl they knew worked for the Bolisay family."

"Did anyone see who she left with?" I asked.

Ronnie and Jae shook their heads.

"The only other thing I heard was that she ran into the kitchen after she and Glen got into that fight," Ronnie said. "Probably for privacy since the rest of that spot is a big open space. Nobody remembers seeing her after that."

"Do you think there's a door leading outside from the kitchen?" Jae asked. "That might be how she slipped out without anybody seeing her."

"Pretty sure commercial kitchens all have external doors. It's how we receive shipments and take out the garbage and stuff. Of course, it's not like we can expect everything in an underground operation to be up to code, but if they're preparing food there, it makes sense," I reasoned. "Divina rode there with Glen, so she didn't have access to a car. There's a possibility she left alone and hitchhiked or walked to the laundromat, but I seriously doubt it."

"So you think she got a ride with whoever was in the kitchen?" Jae asked.

I nodded. "Which means it had to be either Ultima or Nabila. Nabila said she and her mom were the ones that prepared the food, so there'd be no reason for anyone else to be in the kitchen."

Jae agreed, then yawned. "Sorry about that. I had an early start today and didn't expect to be out so late."

We both bid Ronnie goodnight and got into Jae's car to head

home. "Sorry to spring this on you, but I really appreciate you coming with me. You can sleep in tomorrow. Jonathan and I will exchange info over breakfast and we can fill you in at a later time."

"And skip out on your family's cooking? Never!" Jae said. "I'll see you bright and early tomorrow morning. I have a feeling we're about to crack this case and I wouldn't miss it for anything."

Chapter Thirty

W e finally have a break in the case," Jonathan announced at breakfast the next day.

Jae and I had just finished recounting what we'd learned yesterday, and I puffed myself up thinking what a good job we'd done. What Jonathan said next at first deflated my ego before buoying me back up.

"One of the neighborhood kids near April's house remembers seeing a car pulling out of April's driveway the morning she was attacked."

"That's fantastic! Why did they just now remember? Is there any way to ID the car?" I asked.

"When Mae, June, and the SPPD questioned the neighbors, they only talked to the adults. But one of the neighbors came forward after their kid told them about a flashy car with a weird license plate." Jonathan shook his head. "Apparently the kid is learning how to read and loves to read signs and license plates and everything around her. So when she accompanied her mom to the laundromat, she read the store sign and told her mom it was just like the license plate on the car she saw at April's. ULTIMA1."

"So it was Ultima! Did you learn anything when you followed her the other night?"

"Good news, bad news time."

"Bad news first to get it over with, please."

"Well, the bad news is that we can officially cross Ultima off the suspect list. When pressed about her car being at the scene of April's attack, she showed us proof that she was visiting her husband at the hospital in Chicago at the time of the attack."

I could've kicked myself—Nabila had told me as much the night before. I hadn't realized I was holding out hope that she'd lied, but at least on this she'd been honest.

"Well, what about Divina? Maybe someone else attacked Ninang April, but she took care of Divina."

Jonathan shook his head. "I've been tailing her for weeks and last night I finally figured out her little secret. The reason her illegal gambling ring can exist without worrying about police interference is because she's been paying off one of the cops at the station to look the other way. When I showed her the picture I got of her handing off the bribe, she opened up really quick. Showed me her logbook where she tracks all the payments, and it matches both her bank withdrawals and that officer's statement. She was meeting with him the night Divina died."

"Wait, the cop she's bribing admitted to what they're doing? Why?"

Jonathan smiled. "I have my ways. Anyway, the good news is that even though we know it wasn't Ultima or her husband, it was likely someone in her household or close staff if they had access to her car."

I thought back over both Nabila's defensiveness and loyalty to her mom. "Nabila. Her daughter. It has to be her."

"We have no way to prove who was driving just yet," Jonathan cautioned. "That kid only saw the car and license plate; they didn't see who was inside. Other than the unidentified prints in the house, there was no other evidence."

"So what you're saying is, I need to either prove she was driving the car that day or find a way to get her prints so you can compare them to the ones found in the house. Right?"

Jae turned to me in alarm, and Jonathan held out his hands. "Hold your horses. Because we have a witness placing the car at the scene, we might be able to convince the Bolisay household to get fingerprinted to see if there's a match."

"Why 'might'? If they have the witness account, what else do they need?"

"Because it's just a witness account, and from a child, no less, there might not be enough probable cause to arrest and fingerprint her."

"Couldn't they just ask her to volunteer her prints?"

My godmothers had been quietly absorbing all this new information, but they both burst into laughter at my naive question. "Do you think Ultima would let her daughter do that without a warrant or some kind of legal counsel? I wouldn't."

Everyone else was quick to agree and I sighed as I pictured Amir's face at hearing that we had finally absorbed his advice not to speak to the police or give consent for searches or anything like that without a lawyer present. I couldn't complain (I mean, yay for personal rights and all), but it sure did make investigating tough sometimes.

Then an idea came to me. "Wait, I got it! At church, we always go down to the basement for refreshments and socializing. What if I just 'happened' to pick up a cup that Nabila was using? Could you try to get fingerprints from that?"

Jonathan looked uncomfortable. "To legally be considered evidence, no, because of chain of custody, but—"

"But you're not with the police anymore," I pointed out. "Even if it can't be entered as official evidence, if you find a match, that could give me some ammunition to use against Nabila next time we talk."

Jonathan looked around the table, his gaze finally resting on Tita Rosie, who smiled at him. Not trying to push him one way or another, just supportive as always.

He sighed. "All right, let's give it a shot. If nothing else, we might get enough for me to make an anonymous tip or something that could justify a court order for the production of records. Just be careful, OK?"

I rolled my eyes. "I was in a literal underground gambling ring last night, Jonathan. I think I'll be just fine at church."

O K, so how are we doing this? Do you want me to provide a distraction while you and Ate Bernie grab her cup or what?"

I'd informed Bernadette and Marcus of my plan and they both promised to provide backup. Maybe a little too enthusiastically on Marcus's part.

"Don't make this weird, Marcus," Bernadette said. "Nabila's already suspicious of Lila, so I'll be the one to offer getting refills or throwing out their cups or whatever. Just make sure to stick with Lila and keep the conversation going so no one notices what I'm doing."

The three of us worked the room, making small talk with various parishioners since it would be too obvious if we headed straight toward Nabila. Besides, she was sticking annoyingly close to her mom and there was no way we could get a proper conversation going with Ultima around.

An opportunity presented itself when I saw Teresa gathering the notes and cards in front of Divina's portrait into a small tote bag. I signaled to my cousins where I was heading and that they should soon follow.

"Hey Teresa, what's up?"

She whirled around and sighed when she saw it was me. "Oh, Lila, you scared me. I was spacing out and didn't hear you coming."

Considering she was in a church surrounded by people and I hadn't exactly snuck up on her, that was a bit strange, but I guess I couldn't fault her for being jumpy with a killer on the loose. Unless there was something more to her behavior. Nabila was her best friend. Would Nabila have confided in her all the terrible things she'd done? And if not, did Teresa at least suspect her friend's involvement? I didn't know either of them well enough to sense if something was amiss, but considering how tight they were, it's hard to imagine that she didn't hold even the tiniest suspicion. Adeena and Elena would know almost immediately if I'd committed such a terrible act and vice versa, even without words. We just knew each other that well.

"Are you OK?" I asked.

"I'm fine. Father Santiago just asked me to collect the cards to give to Tita Mae and Tita June."

"Oh, right. They wanted to take the cards to read to Ninang April. I'm sure they'll appreciate the help."

Before Teresa could respond, Nabila joined us. "There you are, Teresa! I was wondering where you'd gone. I've been trying to sneak off to the refreshment table for forever."

"Oh, sure. Let me just drop off this bag and I'll join you." Teresa headed toward my godmothers, leaving me and Nabila alone. I thought Nabila would follow her, but it seemed she had some things she wanted to clear up.

"You haven't been running your mouth, have you?" Nabila asked.

"Why hello, Nabila. So nice to see you too. Lovely sermon from Father Santiago today, wasn't it?" I smiled at her and she rolled her eyes.

"Fine, social niceties it is." She thought for a moment. "Are you going to see Sana later? For your sangria thing?"

"Probably. We're supposed to go see Ninang April after this, but I'll probably stop by Sana's later. Why?"

Nabila fidgeted. "I wanted to apologize to her. For my behavior last time. But I doubt I'm welcome anymore. So could you ... ?"

"If you want to apologize, don't you think you'd best do it in person?" Bernadette said. She and Marcus arrived, both with a cup in each hand. Bernadette held one out to me. "Want some juice?"

I accepted and took a sip as Teresa rejoined us. Marcus glanced down at the cups in his hands before offering them to Nabila and Teresa. "Would you like these? I can go get more."

Teresa eagerly accepted, blushing as her fingertips brushed against his in the handoff. "That's so sweet of you, Marcus! Thanks."

"Yeah, just *so* sweet. Thanks, Marcus." Nabila smirked at her best friend. "Actually, I'm craving some meryenda. Teresa, why don't you go with Marcus and grab me something to eat? I'll wait for you here."

"Oh, um, OK. If you don't mind me keeping you company, of course," Teresa said to Marcus.

He smiled at her. "Of course I don't mind. I've been wanting to ask you about that one show you told me about anyway, you know the one ..."

Their conversation faded as they made their way to the refreshment table, but Bernadette, Nabila, and I watched them fondly.

"She has a crush on him, doesn't she?" Bernadette asked.

Nabila laughed. "She is *so* obvious, but Marcus somehow hasn't noticed yet."

"Marcus is a good guy, but he can be a little oblivious," I admitted. "Good luck to her."

"I hope he either figures it out or she gets the courage to make a move, because watching them is insufferable. Though I guess I'm happy she's back to her usual self," Nabila murmured, almost to herself.

My ears pricked up at that. "Has she been acting strange lately?"

If Teresa had been acting different around her best friend, it could signify that she knew what Nabila had done and was uncomfortable around her.

Nabila pursed her lips as if thinking it over, but Teresa and Marcus rejoined us before she could say anything more. The five of us chatted about nothing important for the next half hour or so (with Marcus easily and smoothly taking Teresa's and Nabila's cups with him in supposed search of a garbage can) until it was time for us to visit Ninang April in the hospital. I excused myself to use the bathroom before leaving and ran into Nabila on the way out.

"Oh, sorry!" I said, sidestepping so she could go in, but she forced a napkin into my hand.

"I need to talk to you. This is my number. Please text me as soon as you can."

Without waiting for a response, she entered the bathroom. I stood there, staring at the napkin in my hand, until Bernadette and Marcus came looking for me.

"Lila? What's taking so long? The others went on ahead and told us to hurry up."

Glancing over my shoulder at the bathroom door, I hurried the two away and into the church parking lot. "Nabila gave me her number. Said she needed to talk."

Bernadette eyed the napkin still clutched in my hand. "Then you'd better meet her. But not before talking to Detective Park first."

• • •

"Ijust want to go on record as saying that I don't like this and I think it's a bad idea," Jae said, watching his brother attach some sort of device to me that would allow him to listen in on my conversation with Nabila.

"I promise to make sure the door is unlocked and not stand within easy grabbing distance, as you so kindly warned me. At any sign of trouble, I'll run. But I think this is it. I think Nabila's finally ready to confess."

I thought back to how she acted during our conversation at church, watching Teresa so carefully while they were with our group. At first, I thought she was just trying to matchmake between Teresa and Marcus. But I also noticed she kept her eye on her friend even when she was just with me or Bernadette. She already said Teresa had been acting strange around her. Why would she need to observe her so closely if she wasn't worried that Teresa might accidentally let something slip about her?

Jonathan added, "I have a trusted friend on the force on standby in case we need him, and you and I will be stationed at the front and back doors. I don't like it either, but this is the most I can do."

Jae moved as if to hug me, but thought better of it as if remembering the wires. He took my hands in his instead and said, "No unnecessary risks. Just in and out, if possible. OK? And let us know as soon as you need help."

I squeezed his hands tight and leaned in for a kiss. I normally wouldn't do this in front of Jonathan and Tita Rosie, but it wasn't like I'd have a chance when I got to Nabila's, and I could use the comfort and strength his presence gave me. Lola Flor had stayed with the aunties at Ninang April's bedside, but Tita Rosie joined us at the house when she learned of our plan.

She smiled at our open affection. "I'll be waiting for you here. Be careful, ha? And I hope this will finally lead us to justice."

"H ello?"

I stood in front of the Bolisay family's front door. I'd already texted Nabila, telling her I was there, but she hadn't responded and she wasn't answering the doorbell either. Maybe it was broken? I knocked a few times, but still no one came. I jiggled the doorknob and found it unlocked.

"Jonathan, I'm going in."

I had one of my AirPods in so I could communicate with him if necessary without looking too obvious (I hoped), and after I got his go-ahead, I entered the Bolisay house to see if I could sneakily find some evidence before looking for Nabila.

Leaving the door unlocked behind me, I made my way through the entryway and stopped in the living room to look around. The Bolisay house was way bigger and more nicely furnished than mine, featuring furniture that hadn't been purchased and wrapped in plastic before I was even born. Framed photos arranged on a mantel above a fireplace (an actual fireplace!) caught my attention. I was only able to study them long enough to note that they were all Bolisay family photos, with many of them featuring Teresa, when I heard the murmuring of voices down farther in the house.

As I edged closer, I realized "murmur" was too soft a word to describe the confrontation taking place in what I soon saw was the kitchen. The intensity of Nabila and Teresa's exchange made it clear to me why no one had bothered to answer the door—considering Nabila was clutching a huge kitchen knife that she kept trained on Teresa, I wouldn't be surprised if they hadn't even heard me.

"Nabila, let's calm down and rethink this, OK? It doesn't have to be like this. You know I'd do anything for you and your family."

Teresa had her hands out in front and was addressing her best friend in low, even tones, the way you would a cornered animal. Oh no, did Nabila realize that Teresa had figured out what Nabila had done to Divina and Ninang April?

Teresa stepped forward and Nabila backed away, one hand pointing the knife at her friend and the other clutching a bundle of fabric, though I couldn't make out what it was from this distance.

"Jonathan, can you hear me? She has a knife! And she's pointing it at Teresa! What do I do? No one else was supposed to be here!" I hissed into my earpiece.

"Lila, stay where you are," Jonathan's voice said in my ear. "Do not engage. Detective Nowak is on the way. Just stay hidden and record what you can."

"Got it," I said. Unfortunately, I said it out loud, just as there was a lull between Nabila and Teresa, and both women turned toward my hiding spot.

"Who's there?" Nabila yelled out.

"Get out of there, Lila! Get out!"

I sprinted to the door, not bothering to see if she was coming after me, but screeched to a stop when I heard a crash and her scream. "Help me! Please, someone help!"

"Lila, don't—"

But I was already running back to the kitchen, and this time it was Teresa with the knife and Nabila was holding out her bloody hands. Did Teresa take the knife away when Nabila was distracted and cut her with it? Teresa had the knife in one hand and clutched a scarf close to her with another.

A very familiar scarf.

"Lila, you saw everything, right?" Teresa said, and my eyes flicked away from the scarf to her scared face. "You saw how she was threatening me, right?"

"Don't listen to her, Lila! And stay away!" Nabila shouted. "Go get help!"

My eyes went back and forth, back and forth between them, trying to get the scene in front of me to make sense. Until I remembered why that scarf in Teresa's hands looked so familiar. And then it all clicked into place. I'd been close. So close. But not quite there.

"It was you. Wasn't it, Teresa? You killed Divina."

Chapter Thirty-One

"I don't know what you're talking about," Teresa said. "I didn't even know Divina, why would I kill her?"

"You were the one in the kitchen at Ultima's gambling den that night, right? When she got into that fight with Glen and had to find her own way home." I glanced at the scarf in her hand. "She was always forgetting her scarf at the laundromat. So she must've asked you to stop there first so she could get it. I mean, why else would you be holding her scarf now?"

"I found it in Nabila's room!" she said. "And when I confronted her about it, she pulled a knife on me. You saw her."

"That's a lie! I only pulled the knife 'cause I found the scarf in your room and you got all scary when I asked you about it," Nabila shouted.

"She's been acting so strange lately, but when I saw the scarf, I finally understood," Teresa said. "She must've killed Divina to protect her family's business. And somehow Tita April figured it out, so she attacked her, too. I heard people talking in the laundromat, saying the police saw her mom's car pulling away from Tita April's house the day she was attacked."

"Why are you doing this?" Nabila's eyes filled with tears. "It's bad enough with everything you've done, but now you want people to think I'm a killer? That I attacked one of our elders? Do you really want me to go to jail for your mistakes?"

Teresa wavered at that. But then Nabila stepped forward and Teresa was instantly on her guard again. "Stay back. Both of you stay away from me. I didn't do anything."

"You can lie all you want, but we saved the cups you were both using at church earlier. Which means we have both of your fingerprints. Once we see which fingerprints match the unidentified ones at the laundromat and Ninang April's house, we'll know exactly who did all this."

Teresa backed away, her head whipping back and forth between me and Nabila as if we'd planned this. "You're lying. I would've noticed. When did you . . ." She trailed off, trying to remember when it could've happened, and I saw the moment her heart broke. "Marcus. Marcus took the cups away, saying he was going to throw them out. But he was just saving them for evidence, wasn't he?"

Tears glittered in her eyes. "Even him. She couldn't even let me have him, could she?"

"Give it up, Teresa. We know what you did."

She backed away, still clutching the knife, but didn't look like she was preparing to attack us.

"You knew Divina, didn't you? Back when you were kids," I said. "There was a childhood photo of Divina, her friend Clara, and two other girls from their middle school on Facebook. The same photo that someone printed out and left in front of her portrait. It was in the tote bag with all the cards you'd gathered for Ninang April."

She still refused to give in. "You have no proof that it's me in that photo."

"I can prove it," Nabila said. "I've known you since you first moved here. I'm sure I'd recognize you once Lila shows me the picture. So will anyone in my family."

Teresa deflated when she realized the truth behind her best friend's statement. "You're right. It's me and my cousin in that picture. We all grew up together."

"What happened between you and Divina?"

"She was over at my house one day and she accidentally . . . she walked in on my mom doing drugs in the bathroom."

I raised my eyebrows—I'd heard how strict the drug laws in the Philippines could be and could tell this was not going to end well.

"She told her parents what she saw, and some of our friends, too. Her parents reported it, and my mom was arrested. Word spread about her being in jail, and the kids at school were just . . ." She shut her eyes. "I thought they were my friends. I thought it would be OK since it wasn't like I was the one who did something wrong. But the bullying was nonstop."

"Divina bullied you?"

"No, but she didn't stop it and she definitely didn't apologize for what she did. It all got so bad that my dad decided to send me to the States to live with some distant relatives. He figured at least I'd have a new start without being labeled the daughter of a criminal."

I had many thoughts about the unjust laws levied against substance abusers, but now wasn't the time, so I held my tongue. "She was just a kid. I'm sure she didn't know what would happen. She probably just thought she was doing what was right."

"I wanted to give her the benefit of the doubt, too. It'd been almost a decade; she must realize that there were consequences for what she'd said. I wanted her to admit it. I wanted that closure, I guess. So when she came into the kitchen looking for a ride, I volunteered. She wanted to stop by the laundromat and then be dropped at your place. She said she had something she needed to tell you."

So that's why Ninang April thought she was at my house the night before she died. She must've texted Ninang April to say that's where she was heading.

"What did she want to tell me?"

Teresa glanced at Nabila. "She wanted to let everyone know about Tita Ultima's gambling den. When Glen Davis brought her there, she realized she had the perfect piece of ammunition to get him and Tita Ultima to leave Tita April and the others alone. I guess she wanted to ask you the best way to get the news out since she thought having the aunties spread the rumor themselves would reflect badly on them."

"And she told you all that? Knowing your connection to Nabila and Ultima?"

She looked down. "I may have let her think I was sympathetic to her cause. She'd come snooping around before, pretending that she wanted to be friends, so I let her think Ultima was using me just like Tita Mae and Tita June were using her."

"What happened when you got to the laundromat?"

"My cousin, the other one in the photo, she told me about Divina's scandal and how she was being sent away. She sent me the link to that IG account and I saw that she hadn't changed. Not at all. Just spreading rumors around so she could seem important. Do you know what she said to me that night? 'I'm just telling the truth. It's not like I'm making any of this up. If people didn't want me to talk about them, maybe they should act right.'" Teresa laughed. "Can you believe that? Miss High-and-Mighty. In her mind, she's always the good guy. As if the truth is so simple."

Teresa looked down at the scarf in her hand. "But if she hadn't opened her mouth, my mom wouldn't still be in jail and my dad wouldn't have had to die sick and alone. I never got to see him again. My mom wasn't hurting anyone. And now she wanted to ruin Tita Ultima? The woman who took me in after I lost my family? I couldn't let her do that. Why couldn't she have just minded her own business?"

"I'm so sorry, Teresa." I paused, wondering how to phrase my next question. "It'd been a while since you'd seen each other, but you were close once. Did she recognize you?"

She laughed again, the note of hysteria in it making the hair on my arms stand up. "No. And that's the point. She ruined my life, and she couldn't even remember who I was! I would rather she laugh in my face and say something awful to me. But no, she kept insisting that she hadn't done anything wrong, that she was a good person, that I must be misremembering what had happened. I just wanted her to acknowledge what she'd done. I wanted her to acknowledge that what she was trying to do to Tita Ultima would have major consequences. But she refused to take responsibility and I just got so mad! I pushed her. That's all I did, just a quick shove, but she stumbled and fell against the table and I . . . I didn't mean to kill her, I swear."

"If it was an accident, why didn't you call for help? She could've been saved!"

"I saw how hard she hit her head and she wasn't responding to me. I figured it was too late." Seeing the look on my face, she yelled, "I panicked, OK? It's not like I meant for this to happen! I'm a good person. I go to church every Sunday. I was protecting Tita Ultima. I'm not a murderer! I don't deserve to go to jail for someone like Divina de los Santos!"

She claimed she'd panicked, yet evidence showed that she'd taken the time to wipe down the area, leaving only that partial print behind. Not only that, but considering the message I found next to Divina, she must've gone out to get spray paint, returned to make it look like Divina's death was related to the vandal, and then stolen Divina's keys to lock up behind herself.

I said as much, adding, "So you did all that, but you're a good person, which means you don't deserve to go to jail. And Divina was a bad person, so it was OK for you to kill her?"

Teresa's eyes darted around the room, either looking to make a run for it or making sure Nabila and I had no way out after her confession. "I didn't say that."

"Didn't you? You're certainly thinking it. You called Divina 'Miss High-and-Mighty,' but I know your type, Miss Holier-Than-Thou. You attacked Divina because you claim she wouldn't take responsibility for what happened to you when you were a kid, but what are you doing now? Trying to place all the blame on her."

"Careful, Lila," Jonathan's voice in my ear suddenly warned me. "Don't push her. The place is surrounded, so just keep her talking until they're inside."

I forced myself to calm down. "Why did you take Divina's scarf?"

"I used it to wipe down the surfaces in the laundromat so they wouldn't have my fingerprints." She caressed the scarf. "I should've thrown it away; I know it was foolish to hold on to it. But it was so beautiful. I couldn't bring myself to just toss it in a dumpster. I'm glad I kept it, though. If only because—what's that noise?" Teresa edged toward the window and glanced outside. "Cops! Why are the police here?"

Her head whipped toward me, finally noticing the AirPod in my ear. "Have you been on the phone this whole time? Who's been listening?"

She stalked toward me with the knife, and I dodged around the kitchen island to keep it between us while I tried to calculate how long I'd need to keep this up before she caught me or the cops broke in to stop her. Surprisingly, Nabila stepped between us.

"Teresa, you need to get out of here! Now!"

That drew Teresa up short. "What?"

"They'll probably be at the front and back doors, but not the basement. Go out through that way and I'll try to stall them as long as I can. Now go!"

Teresa stared at her best friend as what she was trying to do sank in. "You'd help me escape?"

Nabila didn't answer, just grabbed her arm and started dragging her toward the basement door, but Teresa dug in her heels.

"What are you doing? We don't have time for this!"

Teresa set the knife down on the kitchen island and hugged Nabila. "I'm sorry. I'm so, so sorry."

The two of them were still clinging to each other, with Teresa apologizing over and over through her tears, when Detective Nowak and a few other cops burst into the kitchen.

Teresa pulled away from Nabila and put her hands up. "It was me, it was all me. She had nothing to do with it."

Detective Nowak moved to put handcuffs on her, but I stopped him. "Wait, Detective Nowak! She's already confessed to Divina's murder, but there's just one last thing I need to know. Why did you attack Ninang April?"

Detective Nowak studied me, then glanced over my shoulder. I turned around to see Jae and Jonathan standing a few feet away observing the scene. A look passed between Jonathan and Detective Nowak and then the detective nodded, pulling a recording device out of his pocket. "Go ahead."

Teresa sighed. "It was a stupid slip. I ran into Tita April when she was moving back into her place and I offered to help her carry stuff in. After we finished bringing in her luggage, I noticed a stack of boxes in the corner next to a couple of suitcases. She saw me looking and said she was packing up Divina's things to send back home to her parents.

The only thing she couldn't find was Divina's special scarf, which her parents wanted to frame."

I looked over at the scarf on the kitchen island and had a vague idea of where this was going.

"She looked so sad, and the next thing I know, I'm telling her I have it and can give it to her next time I see her at church." She shook her head. "I messed up. And Tita April's no fool. 'Divina was wearing it the day she died. Why do you have it?' When she said that, I knew it was over unless I shut her up. So I just grabbed the nearest thing and hit her in the head."

Teresa grabbed my hands, moving so suddenly Detective Nowak and Jonathan both jumped to my defense, but I shook my head at them. She stared into my eyes, begging me to understand. "I didn't plan any of this. I swear to you, I never wanted to hurt them! Not really."

I tore my hands away from her. "But you did. Just like Divina hadn't intended for you to face the consequences for her gossip. You got hurt anyway. And just like Divina, what you did can never be undone. Worse than her, actually. You killed someone. Ninang April might never wake up again. And after all that talk, you tried to pin your crimes on your best friend, who was willing to cover for you. I feel sorry for you—I do."

I stepped away from her and signaled to Detective Nowak that he could take her away. "But I'm not going to forgive you. You don't deserve it."

Chapter Thirty-Two

It was the day of Ninang April's flight back to the Philippines to deliver Divina's ashes to her parents. Tita Rosie and I had wanted to be part of the airport drop-off group that afternoon, but we'd been away from our businesses way too often over the past month. Besides, there was no real point since we'd just be saying goodbye at the door. Instead, we hosted a goodbye brunch so our friends and family could say one last farewell to Divina and wish Ninang April a safe trip.

They also came to see Lola Flor, who'd be joining Ninang April for a portion of the trip. It seems the familial fondness I observed that Lola Flor had for Ninang April was reciprocated, and Ninang April had offered an all-expenses-paid trip in exchange for Lola Flor's company and moral support. At first, I couldn't imagine going to Lola Flor for company or support, but now that I was an adult, I was starting to finally understand the many ways she was kind, even if her kindness was different from Tita Rosie's. Lola Flor accepted the free plane tick-cts but waved away Ninang April's offer to pay for everything else as long as Lola Flor got to spend some quality time in her hometown. She hadn't been back since she'd moved to the States forty-plus years ago, and the excitement she tried to hide about the upcoming trip was absolutely adorable.

It felt like half the town had turned up for this breakfast party: Adeena and Elena, Ronnie and Izzy, Amir and Sana, Yuki and her daugher Naoko (Akio never socialized), Terrence, Katie, Joy, Leslie, Father Santiago, Tita Lynn, the church outreach group, and, of course, our extended family, Ninang Mae and Marcus, Ninang June and Bernadette, and the Park brothers.

Because there were so many people with various dietary restrictions, Tita Rosie and I went all out setting up three different food stations. The first table was our usual DIY silog platters, where diners could create their own dishes from their choice of two kinds of rice, six kinds of protein (including vegan options), either fried or scrambled eggs, and sawsawan. The table next to it was the porridge party, with three savory versions (arroz caldo, lugaw, and goto) and two sweet (champorado and ginataang mais) plus various toppings. And the final area was my absolute fave, featuring my desert (or should it be dessert?) island food: the crepes station.

Stacks upon stacks of cooked crepes that you could stuff with savory fillings to make lumpiang sariwa, as well as shredded green jackfruit adobo and/or chicken adobo crepes. There were also various cut-up fruits (cut-up fruit = love), ube halaya, minatamis na bao, and whipped coconut cream, plus calamansi and panutsa (my spin on the classic lemon and sugar combination) to round out the sweet offerings. The Brew-ha Cafe and Shady Palms Winery provided the beverages, so you had your choice of coffee, tea, tsokolate, and various juices to make your own mimosas using Shady Palms Winery's specialty sparkling fruit wines.

And, of course, platters of mamon. Divina's favorite, and our small way of honoring her.

The party was still going strong two hours later, but we needed it to wind down since the Brew-ha crew and I needed to open the cafe and Ninang April and Lola Flor had to head to the airport soon.

Ninang April stood up and clinked her water glass to get everyone's attention. "First of all, I just want to say thank you for all your support this last month. Every time I thought that nobody cared, that me and my family had been forsaken, the people in this room stepped up to prove me wrong." She looked up at the ceiling, blinking away tears. "Nothing will ever bring back my niece. But now Divina can rest in peace, and her parents and I can begin to move on. Thank you all again, and now join me in a toast and a farewell to someone who left us too soon: To Divina."

"To Divina," we all said, raising our glasses and drinking to her memory.

"I have something I'd like to announce as well," Jonathan said, allowing a few moments of respectful silence before speaking and standing up.

I glanced over at Tita Rosie and Jae to see if they knew what this was about, but they looked as bewildered as I felt. Considering the last time he did something like this, he was announcing his retirement from the force, I knew this was going to be something big.

Oh my gulay, was he going to propose to Tita Rosie? I started dreaming about Tita Rosie in a beautiful dress and Jae in a tux and the amazing cake I would make for her, before bringing myself back down to earth. No, this was a party to honor Divina and Ninang April. He wouldn't do that. But then what kind of announcement would be appropriate here?

"Most of you know that I retired from the SPPD a few months ago.

I've spent this time doing a bit of soul-searching, wondering what my next move was going to be. During that period, I lent a hand to some friends in need during a dark and tragic time." Here he smiled sadly at the Calendar Crew, his eyes on Ninang April. "And what I learned was, I may have become disillusioned with the police force, but I still love helping people in need find justice. I talked to a private detective friend I have in Chicago, and he's agreed to let me work as a remote branch of his agency once I get my PI license. I'm also free to take on my own clients, so please come to me with any of your private investigator needs."

Everyone burst into applause and crowded around him as they chatted excitedly about what private investigators actually do and what it would mean for the people of Shady Palms to have Jonathan's services available. Once the crowd around him dispersed, the Brew-ha crew and I walked up to give our congratulations.

"I just got used to calling you Jonathan and now you're going to become a detective again?" I jokingly bumped him with my shoulder. "Now what am I supposed to call you?"

Jonathan smiled. "You can keep calling me Jonathan since a PI isn't quite the same as my previous title."

I smiled back. "We'll play it by ear, Private Detective Jonathan Park."

"With a name like that, he should have his own theme music," Adeena said, and started humming some James Bond–esque tune.

"Honey, he's not a spy. Wrong music genre. It should be something that gives strong 80s Miami vibes. Like, can't you see him posing under those fake palm trees on Main Street while heavy guitar or a sexy saxophone plays?" Elena turned to Jonathan. "Do you think you could grow a heavy mustache for the aesthetic?"

As we all laughed and joked, Jae came behind me and wrapped his arms around me, resting his head on my shoulder. "I think Elena's onto something. I kind of want to write my brother's theme music. Is that weird?"

"Just about everything in our lives is weird, don't you think?"

"Yeah," he said, planting a big kiss on my cheek. "I wouldn't have it any other way."

"Neither would I." I raised my glass to him and then to Jonathan and raised my voice. "Here's to the next adventure that our very weird lives will bring."

Those around us clinked their glasses and cheered at that statement, cheered for Divina and Ninang April and Jonathan, the celebration a symbol of closure as well as next steps. As I looked around the room at all the wonderful people in my life, I knew that as long as I had them, I'd be ready for whatever came next.

Acknowledgments

You'd think with this being the fourth book, everything would get easier (including writing this section) but it just gets difficult in a different way. *Murder and Mamon* marks the beginning of a new contract, a new arc in Lila's journey, and in many ways, a new start to my life as a writer. The Tita Rosie's Kitchen Mysteries was originally sold as a three-book deal. I had no idea if my books would resonate, if they would sell well enough for me to continue writing them, or if I'd even have any new story ideas past my original ones. I'm so happy that the answers to those questions were yes, yes, and YES!

As always, huge thanks to the team that makes this all possible: my wonderful agent, Jill Marsal; my editors, Angela Kim and Michelle Vega; and the rest of my Berkley team: Dache' Rogers, Tina Joell, Anika Bates, and Tara O'Connor, as well as Vi-An Nguyen for continuing to give me the best covers ever. I'd also like to thank Ann-Marie Nieves and the rest of the Get Red PR crew for all their amazing help.

Shout-out to the Berkletes who've been there with me since the beginning of this pub journey, as well as to the new crew—you've made these last few years not just bearable, but unbelievably fun. I don't know how I'd make it through publishing without you all.

Thanks to my writing groups, such as Sisters in Crime, Crime Writers of Color, Banyan: Asian American Writers Collective, my BIPOC writers Zoom group, the Pitch Wars crew, my Chicagoland kidlit writer peeps, and many more. Special shout-out to Kellye Garrett for being an amazing mentor, friend, and petty DM buddy. You're the best and the world better recognize that.

Much love to my IRL besties, who keep me grounded and remind me there's a world outside of writing: the Winners Circle (Kim, Jumi, Linna, and Robbie), Amber and Aria (and Matt), and Ivan aka Snookums. And to my DnD group, Ye Olden Girls, for all the support and laughter you've brought me these last few years.

Huge thanks to my family, who have always supported me and make an amazing street team, especially my husband, who manages to be the best wife guy (without being weird about it) and continues to believe that I'm capable of anything and everything. I love you so much!

And finally, to my readers. You are all the best and I appreciate the many ways you support me, but need to especially recognize my Ko-fi Pamilya-tier members: Tim and Kristen Sorbera, Katie Davidson, Christine Bradfield, Elisabeth Rossman, Sarah A. Rose, The Reyes-Chow/Pugh Family, Maria Reyes Doktor, Sam Bertocchi, Joanne Mosqueda Garces, Eliose Celine A. Labampa, Faye Bernoulli Silag, Eleanor Jane Hayes, Krystina Madriaga McHale, Maria Remedios Boyd, and Alexandra Cope. Thank you all so much! Until next time, my ubaes. ♥

Recipes

Tita Rosie's Arroz Caldo

Despite its Spanish-sounding name, arroz caldo is a Filipino rice porridge with a Chinese influence. It's similar to Chinese congee, Korean jook/juk, Japanese okayu, etc. The dish is hearty, warming, and comforting, and thanks to its flavor base of chicken and ginger, it's a rather healthy dish that is often served when someone is feeling under the weather. If Tita Rosie were a dish, she would probably be arroz caldo.

SERVES 4

Ingredients:

1 thumb-size piece of ginger, peeled and thinly sliced*
½ onion, chopped*
1 pound bone-in chicken pieces (drumsticks are perfect)
2 chicken bouillon cubes**
1 to 2 teaspoons minced garlic*

1 cup uncooked white rice***
2 tablespoons fish sauce (patis)
Black pepper
5 to 6 cups of water***

Toppings (optional):

Hard-boiled eggs, sliced
Fried garlic
Fried shallots
Green onions, chopped
Lemon or calamansi slices
Patis

*This is a great pantry/budget meal, so if you're out of fresh ingredients, you can sub in ginger paste or powder, garlic paste or powder, and dried chopped onion or onion powder.

**Bouillon cubes are common in the Philippines, so that's what's often used, but these can be replaced with chicken broth or stock, if you prefer.

***All types of white rice work here except for basmati (too mushy) and glutinous/sweet rice (too sticky). You can even use leftover rice (perfect for takeout rice that's gotten dry); you just need to reduce the liquid and cook time accordingly.

DIRECTIONS:

1. Heat some oil in a pot and sauté the ginger and onions until the onions soften and the ginger is fragrant.

2. Add the chicken to the pot and sear on high heat until all sides are brown.

3. Crumble the bouillon cubes into the pot and add the garlic, cooking until the bouillon melts and the garlic is fragrant.

4. Add the uncooked rice, patis, and black pepper, and stir so that the aromatics are evenly distributed and the rice is coated in the oil and chicken fat.

5. Pour in the water and bring to a boil, then lower to a simmer.

6. Cover the pot, with the lid slightly askew so steam can escape.

7. Simmer, stirring occasionally, until the chicken is fully cooked and the rice has reached the level of softness and consistency that you like, roughly 30 minutes. If you prefer your porridge thicker, cook until more of the water evaporates. If you like a thinner dish, add more water and adjust the seasonings.

8. Dish out and serve with your choice of toppings. Enjoy!

Lola Flor's Mamon

Mamon are individual Filipino chiffon cakes that are light and fluffy, simple yet delicious. They're often topped with butter and sugar and come in various flavors and toppings (cheese probably being the most common, and my favorite), but they're tasty all on their own. Adeena's and Divina's (RIP) favorite meryenda.

Ingredients:

Dry ingredients:

1 cup cake flour*
⅓ cup granulated sugar
½ teaspoon baking powder
½ teaspoon salt

Wet ingredients:

6 egg yolks
¼ cup vegetable oil**
¼ cup water

Meringue ingredients:

6 egg whites
¼ teaspoon cream of tartar
½ cup granulated sugar

Toppings (optional):

Butter
Sugar
Grated cheddar cheese

*If you don't have cake flour (I never do), use this easy substitute: Measure out one cup of all-purpose flour, remove two tablespoons, and add two tablespoons of cornstarch. Whisk/sift together and you've got cake flour!

**Mamon are chiffon cakes, which utilize oil to get that light, airy texture (think angel food cakes). If you want, you can sub in an equal amount of melted butter for the oil. It will be delicious, but it changes the texture and makes it a sponge cake rather than chiffon.*

DIRECTIONS:

1. Preheat the oven to 325°F. Grease or line cupcake tins or mamon molds.

2. Combine the dry ingredients (flour, sugar, baking powder, and salt) and sift three times into a bowl.

3. In a separate large bowl, combine the egg yolks, oil, and water Using a whisk or hand mixer, mix until well blended

4. Slowly add the dry ingredients to the wet ingredients, continuously mixing. Once all the dry ingredients have been added to the wet, continue mixing for a couple of minutes until everything is well combined, scraping the bottom and sides of the bowl as needed. Set aside.

5. Add the egg whites and cream of tartar to the bowl of a stand mixer with a wire whisk attachment (or a large clean, dry bowl and clean, dry hand mixer). Beat on high until the egg whites double in volume.

6. With the mixer still at high speed, slowly add the ½ cup granulated sugar. Continue mixing at high speed until the meringue reaches medium peaks (they don't deflate immediately, but they don't stand perfectly straight when you pull the whisk out).

7. Using a rubber spatula, carefully fold about one-third of the meringue into the egg yolk mixture. Continue adding meringue and gently folding it into the egg yolk mixture in 2 to 3 increments until all the meringue is added and the batter is evenly mixed (a few streaks

of meringue here and there is fine). Do this carefully since you want to maintain the air you whipped into the meringue to prevent it from collapsing while baking.

8. Using a ⅓-cup dry measuring cup, scoop the batter into your prepared molds.

9. Bake in a 325°F oven for 15 to 20 minutes until a thin knife inserted in the middle comes out clean. Remove from the oven, let cool slightly, and remove from the tins. If using toppings, add while mamon is still warm.

10. Enjoy! A delicious addition to breakfast and meryenda.

Lila's Malunggay Basque Cheesecake

Malunggay, also known as moringa, is a superfood that gives this delicious creamy cheesecake notes of matcha and white chocolate. An excellent party dish, but easy enough to make for any occasion!

YIELD: MAKES ONE 10-INCH ROUND CHEESECAKE

Ingredients:

4 (8-ounce) packages of plain cream cheese, room
temperature
2 cups granulated sugar

1 to 2 tablespoons malunggay (moringa) powder

7 eggs, room temperature

1 cup heavy cream

2 teaspoons vanilla bean paste or good quality vanilla extract

2 tablespoons flour

DIRECTIONS:

1. Preheat oven to 410°F. Line a 10-inch springform pan with parchment paper (NOT wax paper!) or aluminum foil. Place the springform pan on a sheet pan or cookie sheet. Set aside.

2. Using a mixer or sturdy whisk, beat together the cream cheese, sugar, and malunggay powder.

3. When the mixture is smooth and a uniform green color, beat in the eggs one at a time, then add the cream and vanilla extract, and whisk until everything is smooth.

4. Sprinkle the flour on top and mix until combined.

5. Pour the batter into the lined springform pan and place the pan (still on the tray) into the oven.

6. Bake for about 40 minutes. You want the center to have a bit of a wobble, but not slosh around. The top will be brown and slightly burnt-looking. If the top isn't browned to your liking, you can stick it under the broiler for a couple minutes, but watch it closely! You want it slightly burnt, not charred.

7. Remove from the oven and let the cheesecake cool on the counter or a wire rack for at least an hour. Once cool, put the cheesecake in the fridge for a few hours (preferably overnight).

8. Cut into slices and serve as is or sprinkled with powdered sugar and/or with berries (strawberries are a particularly good match).

9. Enjoy!

Elena's Red Chile Honey

Chile-infused honey is easy, delicious, and versatile, and Elena's version is sure to pack a punch! If you want a milder version, seek out mild dried chiles and/or shorten the steeping time. Great for both sweet and savory options (hot honey fried chicken, anyone?) as well as gifting!

YIELD: ROUGHLY 8 OUNCES

Ingredients:

5 dried Chile de árbol*
2 dried Guajillo chiles*
1 cup honey
Pinch of salt
2 dried Chile de árbol, optional (to garnish)

*Using dried chiles instead of fresh means the honey keeps for a long time since you're not introducing moisture. You can sub in whatever dried chiles you prefer (dried chipotle adds a lovely smoky flavor, for example) if you can't find/don't like the ones listed above.

If you don't want to mess with whole dried chiles, you can sub in 2 to 3 tablespoons of red pepper flakes/crushed red pepper. I like using Chile Quebrado, which is Mexican crushed pepper.

DIRECTIONS:

1. Crush the dried chiles (minus the optional garnish) in a food processor or mortar and pestle.

2. Add the crushed chiles, honey, and salt to a medium saucepan.

3. Cook over low heat, stirring occasionally, for about 15 minutes. Don't allow it to boil!

4. Turn off the heat and let the mixture steep for an hour

5. If using the optional garnish (unnecessary, but it makes the jar look pretty), add the whole dried chiles to a clean glass jar. Strain the honey into the jar and let cool before sealing.

6. Enjoy!

Keep reading for a special preview of

Guilt and Ginataan

*The next Tita Rosie's Kitchen Mystery
from Mia P. Manansala*

"Welcome to the thirty-fifth annual Shady Palms Corn Festival!"

Mayor Gunderson raised the corn cob scepter in his right hand as he looked over the crowd at the opening ceremony of the town's beloved Corn Festival. His wife stood to the side and slightly behind him, dressed in a complementary costume as the town's reigning Corn Queen: a long yellow dress with a lavish green cape about her shoulders and a crown whose points resembled ears of corn atop her head.

I enjoyed a good spectacle as much as the next person, but considering how much the mayor loved the sound of his own voice, I tuned out the rest of his speech as I finished preparing the Brew-ha Cafe booth. My best friend and business partner, Adeena Awan, was still setting up the drinks station where she'd be serving her usual house blend coffee, as well as the atole, sweet corn latte, and oksusu cha that she'd added to the special festival menu. Elena Torres, our other business partner and Adeena's girlfriend, was filling the compostable tea bags with the roasted corn we used for the oksusu cha and arranging the corn husk crafts that she and her mother had prepared.

My boyfriend, Dr. Jae Park, was joining the Brew-ha crew for the weekend as our resident grill master. Elena came up with the idea of a fusion elote, taking her beloved Mexican street corn and adding Pakistani and Filipino twists, to match with Adeena's and my respective backgrounds. Not only did Jae give us his mother's recipe for the Korean corn tea, but he'd also volunteered to handle all elote duties: slathering the corn with thick, creamy coconut milk before rolling it in a fragrant spice mix that included amchur powder and red chili powder, grilling it, then squeezing calamansi over the corn before sprinkling it with your choice of kesong puti or cotija cheese. It was a simple yet laborious task, but he seemed to enjoy himself (I wasn't one for gender stereotypes, but what was with guys and grills?) and I'd caught him sneaking more than one smoky, salty treat as he worked. The benefit of being the cook.

Meanwhile, I arranged the sweet offerings I'd prepared: mais ube sandwich cookies, mais kon keso bars, and mais kon yelo ice candy. Corn as a dessert ingredient may seem strange to some people, but Filipinos absolutely loved and embraced corn in all its salty-sweet possibilities. My first offering sandwiched ube buttercream between corn cookies, the purple yam's subtle vanilla-like sweetness pairing well with the salty-sweet corn. Cheese and corn are a popular savory pairing, but guess what? It makes one of my absolute favorite Filipino ice cream flavors as well, and I channeled that classic combo into a cheesecake bar with a corn cookie crust.

Mais kon yelo, literally corn with ice, was a Filipino dessert consisting of shaved ice with corn, sugar, and milk. My take on the simple, refreshing snack utilized those same flavors in a portable, easy-to-eat ice pop bag. However, if you wanted to try the traditional version, you could just pop down a few booths to Tita Rosie's Kitchen, the restaurant run by my paternal aunt and grandmother. While my aunt, Tita Rosie, handled the savory side of the menu, offering small cups of corn soup and paper cones full of cornick, or corn nuts flavored with salt and garlic, my grandmother, Lola Flor, reigned over the sweets. Ginataang mais, maja blanca, and the aforementioned mais kon yelo were the desserts on offer, a gluten-free sweet tooth's paradise.

They also had an extra helper at their booth, Jae's older brother Jonathan (or Detective Park as I still called him, despite him no longer being with the Shady Palms police department), who happened to be my aunt's boyfriend. He was handling all the customer-facing tasks since Tita Rosie's love of cooking and feeding people did not extend to the more business side of the restaurant, a fact that nearly cost her the restaurant last year. Luckily, my quarter-life crisis happened to coincide with this family emergency, and I had stepped in and set up a simple system for her and my grandmother to follow. After a few months and a couple of tweaks, business was booming.

I put the finishing touches on the Brew-ha Cafe booth just as Mayor Gunderson's speech drew to a close with "And please join me in a warm Shady Palms welcome as Shelbyville's Mayor Reyes says a few words to kick off the celebration!"

There was a bit of rustling in the crowd as Mayor Judy Reyes stepped up to the mic. This year, in an absolutely brilliant move by Beth Thompson and her former sister-in-law, Valerie Thompson (both heads of the town's most successful company and illustrious family, as well as the chamber of commerce), the Corn Festival was put on in partnership with the neighboring town of Shelbyville. Not only would this expand the reach of our festival, but our town wouldn't have to bear the brunt of the expenses. There was a catch, though.

Shelbyville was bigger, had way more money, and was home to the only community college in the area (you had to travel about forty miles before you got anywhere near a university, so higher learning opportunities were few and far between). As such, there was a fierce rivalry between the towns since the people of Shelbyville tended to look down on our town and most Shady Palms citizens felt we had something to prove. Our town's chamber of commerce had been hard at work trying to increase tourism and commerce in the area, so they decided to take advantage of Shady Palms's natural resources and charm, as well as Shelbyville's larger size and greater access to hotels and B&Bs. Mayor Reyes readily agreed, but left all the details to her assistant, who used the opportunity to go on a bit of a power trip. According to Beth, who loved dropping hot goss in our WOC entrepreneur group chat, the assistant provided a ridiculous list of demands that rivaled any celebrity green room horror story, including a stipulation that Mayor Reyes officially opened and closed the festival during the ceremonies on both weekends. That last bit was almost the dealbreaker for the self-important Mayor Gunderson, and it took weeks of negotiating and soothing to get him to agree.

Mayor Gunderson stood on stage, glaring daggers at Mayor Reyes who blithely continued with her warm, funny, and, most importantly, concise welcome speech. "I hope you all take advantage of the many wonderful things that Shady Palms and Shelbyville have to offer. Now if you'll excuse me, I saw a booth selling corn cookies that I'm dying to try. Remember to be kind and support local businesses!"

With that, Mayor Reyes exited the stage with her wife and headed straight for the Brew-ha Cafe booth, followed closely by her assistant. As they drew closer, Elena, our secret weapon when it came to sales (and just about everything else), greeted them cheerfully.

"Well, hello there, Mayor Reyes! Welcome to the Brew-ha Cafe. I'm guessing it was our corn cookies that you just referenced on stage? Thanks for that, by the way."

Mayor Reyes smiled. "Yes, I noticed your booth when you were setting up earlier. Your menu sounded so delicious and different from what most of the booths here are doing, so I knew you had to be my first stop."

The mayor's wife sniffed. "You are far too gracious, Judy. Though I suppose you're right that this booth is the only interesting one I've seen so far."

The mayor's smile grew strained, and her assistant, likely noticing this, stepped in. "Yvonne, didn't you say you were dying for a cup of coffee? I've heard it on good authority that this cafe has the best coffee in the entire county."

Yvonne smirked. "I hope your coffee is as bold as that statement."

Elena met her eyes in a challenge. "I guarantee that my girlfriend's drinks are the best in the county. And when you agree, I hope the good mayor uses us to cater some of her events."

Mayor Reyes laughed. "Considering you're brave enough to take on my wife, I'd be happy to. She'll take the biggest coffee you've got and I'd love some of your atole. It's been forever since I've had any!"

Adeena got to work preparing the drinks while the mayor's assistant studied our menu. "So oksusu cha is Korean corn tea? What does that taste like?"

"It's a bit of an acquired taste," I said. "It has a toasted nutty flavor, similar to barley tea or genmaicha green tea. A little bit savory, a little bit sweet. I'd be happy to give you a sample if you'd like."

He accepted the sample cup and took a few sips. He tried to hide his grimace, but failed, and Jae and I both burst out laughing.

"Don't force yourself if you don't like it," Jae said, holding his hand out for the cup to throw in the trash. "Like Lila said, it's an acquired taste. I used to hate it as a kid, but eventually became addicted to the iced version my mom makes. It's really refreshing in the summer."

The mayor's assistant handed it over. "Sorry! I try not to be picky, but you're right. It's somehow both savory and sweet, and I think I'm just not used to savory drinks. It's not bad, but it's like my brain and tongue don't know how to react."

Mayor Reyes handed a steaming cup of atole to her assistant. "Here you go, Zack. Atole is a corn drink you'll love, I'm sure of it. This is even better than my mom's, though don't let me catch you saying that to her."

"The coffee's really good, too," her wife muttered. "I think it might be even better than that new cafe that opened up near the boutique."

"Didn't I tell you that Shady Palms had the best coffee in the county?" Mayor Gunderson said, strolling up to join us. He was still wearing his Corn King costume and used his ridiculous scepter to point at Adeena. "Adeena! Coffee for both me and the missus."

I hadn't even noticed his wife joining us, but there she was, looking over our offerings while checking out Jae at the corner of her eye. She flushed when she saw that I noticed and tried to cover it up by ordering one of everything.

"Oh, and Dr. Jae, would it be possible to have the corn in a cup so I can eat it with a spoon? It's just so messy on the cob."

Jae smiled at her. "The mess is part of the fun! But sure, Mrs. Gunderson. Happy to accommodate you."

"Thanks for the recommendation, Mayor Gunderson," Mayor Reyes said, smiling over her cup of atole. "I have to stop by Shady Palms more often. You're so lucky to have such a wonderful business nearby. Maybe you can open a branch in Shelbyville."

She winked at us, clearly joking, but Mayor Gunderson's response was a little too strained to match the playful tone he was going for.

"Now now, Judy, are you trying to poach businesses from my town? That's not really in the spirit of our collaboration, is it?"

Yvonne rolled her eyes. "She was just joking, you humorless—"

"Yvonne," Mayor Reyes said sharply.

"You don't have to kowtow to him, you know. You're supposed to be equals in this collaboration. But whatever. Just continue grinning and bearing it, as always." Yvonne finished her coffee and tossed it in the trash. "I'm going to look around. Catch up with me when you're ready."

Mrs. Gunderson reached out to Yvonne as she passed, perhaps to play nice and convince her to stay, but a cutting glance from Yvonne was enough for her to snatch her hand back as if she'd been burned.

Mayor Reyes's assistant (I think they called him Zack?) rushed forward. "Mrs. Gunderson, you've lived in Shady Palms your whole life, right? Would you mind keeping me company as I wander around the festival? I'd love to learn more about the town from someone who's such a valued member of the community."

Mrs. Gunderson was a bit of a wallflower, always keeping to the background and letting her husband take the lead. But under Zack's attention and kind words, a smile unfurled across her face and she seemed to blossom.

"I'd love to! I'm on the historical committee, you know, so if you have any questions about our town's history, feel free to ask."

She fell in step beside Zack and started chattering away, and Mayor Reyes joined them, saying she'd love a guided tour of the festival from Mrs. Gunderson.

Mayor Gunderson glared at the trio as they moved away from him, but instead of following, he turned on his heel and headed in the opposite direction.

Once they were all finally gone, I turned around and noticed Adeena and Elena looking like the Jessica Fletcher-eating-popcorn gif as they shared a bucket of popcorn while enjoying the drama.

"OK, I get that we're at a corn festival, but how did you get the popcorn so fast? Do you travel with props for moments like this?"

Adeena winked. "You know how dedicated I am when it comes to a bit. But no, your sweet boyfriend left when things started getting heated and returned with snacks for us."

Jae turned red as he held out a cone full of Cornick from my aunt, a disk of corn tempura from our friend Yuki's booth, and other yummy corn-related snacks. "It was getting uncomfortable, and I figured I might as well make myself useful. I know what happens when you all get hungry, so I figured I'd grab food for you before it gets too crowded."

"He's a keeper all right," Elena said, grinning at him as she dipped the corn tempura disk into the accompanying sauce.

I helped myself to some tempura as well, and as I enjoyed my deliciously crisp, salty-sweet treat, I prayed that the argument we just witnessed would be the worst thing to happen at the festival and that it'd be smooth sailing from here on out.

I raised my sweet corn latte in a toast. "Here's to a successful, drama-free festival!"

Adeena, Elena, Jae, and I all clinked cups, though I was sure they were thinking the same thing I was:

When has Shady Palms ever been drama-free?

Thank you so much! If you stop by early tomorrow, we'll have plenty more stock available. And I'll make sure to plan better for next weekend."

I handed the takeout bag and drink holder to our final customer, who'd cleaned us out of what little we still had at our booth. It was early afternoon and we'd run out of stock much earlier than planned. I didn't know if it was Mayor Reyes's endorsement or just general word of mouth, but we'd had an endless stream of customers pretty much since we'd opened.

"You're closing already? Now where am I supposed to get a decent cup of coffee?" Yvonne, the Shelbyville mayor's wife, had stopped by several times that morning to grab more cookies and caffeine and verbally spar with Elena. She strolled up with our reusable travel cup in hand and a pout on her face.

"Sorry, but we're out. We'll make sure to stock up extra for tomorrow. Let us know if there's anything you'd like us to set aside for you," Elena said.

Yvonne studied her. "Will you be working the booth tomorrow as well?"

After Elena replied in the affirmative, Yvonne said, "Good. I trust you to surprise me then. See you all then."

"What is her deal?" I asked, watching her walk away.

Adeena gave me a look. "She's clearly flirting with Elena."

"That's flirting?" Jae asked.

Elena shrugged. "The combative types really seem to like me. Arguing with me is like their version of courtship."

"It's because you're so chill," Adeena pointed out. "They think it's a fun challenge to get you to break. They don't know that your weak point is—"

"You better watch yourself, love," Elena said, her tone playful but her eyes carrying a warning. "I know your weakness as well."

"And that's why we work so well together. The threat of mutual destruction powers our relationship." Adeena slung her arm around her girlfriend's shoulders and gave her a firm kiss on the cheek. "So, what do we do now with all this unplanned free time?"

"I wanted to check out the arts and crafts area," Elena said.

"And I've been wanting to hit up all the food booths since I haven't had a proper meal yet," I said.

"Ugh, typical. I really wanted to play some games." Adeena frowned at the two of us before turning to Jae. "How about you?"

Jae's eyes wandered around the large space, likely trying to find a compromise for all of us. "How about a round of Bags? Loser buys us all lunch and then we can check out the arts and crafts area together."

We agreed that was a great plan and headed to the area where various boards with holes were set up alongside containers of beanbags. Because this was the Corn Festival, the staffers were calling the game

"Cornhole," but we all knew it was really Bags. To save time, we decided to play in teams, so Jae and I lined up at one board, Adeena and Elena at the other. Jae used to play basketball and I played Bags all the time in college, so you'd think it'd be a quick game, but Adeena was the most competitive person in the world and Elena was somehow good at everything, so it was a fairly close game.

In the end, Jae and I prevailed, and Adeena and Elena bought us all hush puppies, fried corn, and cornmeal-crusted catfish from our friends George and Nettie Bishop at Big Bishop's BBQ. After our feast, we followed Elena to the arts and crafts section where we got our faces painted and Adeena, Elena, and I all splurged on some gorgeous beaded jewelry from a local Potawatomi artist. The sun was starting to dip by the time we were done with everything, but it was still too early to call it a day.

"How about one more competition?" Adeena asked. "Let's see who can get through the corn maze the fastest. Winner gets to choose all the activities for tomorrow."

The Shady Palms Corn Festival boasted the second-largest corn maze in the state. It was actually four separate mazes that could be completed individually, though if you wanted a challenge, there were checkpoints that connected the labyrinth so you could experience the full eight-mile mega maze. The Corn Festival was actually held over two consecutive weekends, with the first weekend celebrating the opening of the corn maze and more family-friendly activities, and the closing weekend focusing on musical acts and the beer garden run by Shady Palms Winery (which my cousin co-owned). The festival grounds would still be open during the week, but on a lesser scale and with fewer booths and events and prizes. While you could technically enjoy it at any time during the festival, the corn maze on opening day was something special.

Jae groaned. "That sounds like so much fun, but I promised my dad I'd hang out with him at home while Jonathan shows my mom around the festival. His health hasn't been great lately, so it's up to me to make sure he doesn't sneak any junk food while Mom's out."

"Oh, I think Jonathan mentioned that earlier. Make sure to stop by Tita Rosie's booth, I think she made something for you and your dad. Something healthy and delicious," I said, grinning. I knew his dad didn't think those two words went together, but I trusted Tita Rosie to prove him wrong.

"Will do." With a quick kiss and wave at the other two, he started walking off. "Enjoy your girls' night! And stay out of trouble!"

Adeena, Elena, and I headed in the other direction, the two women holding hands as I trailed closely behind them.

"Why does he say that every time he leaves the three of us alone? What does he think we get up to?" Adeena asked.

Elena and I both looked at her, eyebrows raised, and she laughed and raised her hands. "OK, fair. But we're just doing a corn maze at a Midwestern corn festival. Doesn't get much more wholesome than that, does it?"

Exactly. How much trouble could we get into in a corn maze? We were about to find out.

Photo by Jamilla Yip Photography

Mia P. Manansala (she/her) is an award-winning writer and book coach from Chicago who loves books, baking, and badass women. She uses humor (and murder) to explore aspects of the Filipino diaspora, queerness, and her millennial love for pop culture. A lover of all things geeky, Mia spends her days procrastibaking, playing JRPGs and dating sims, reading cozy mysteries and diverse romance, and cuddling her dogs, Gumiho and Max Power.

VISIT MIA P. MANANSALA ONLINE

MiaPManansala.com
 MPMtheWriter
 MPMtheWriter
 MPMtheWriter

Ready to find
your next great read?

Let us help.

Visit prh.com/nextread

Penguin
Random
House